To Catch a Raven

"I'm enjoying your company," he told her. "We aren't clashing."

"The day isn't over."

He chuckled. "There's that mouth again."

"The mouth you wish to tame."

"Very much so."

The familiar warmth rose, spread, and tempted. "Suppose I said go ahead and try."

"Then I'd say I need you to be clear. Is this a supposition or a challenge?"

What are you doing! She ignored the inner voice. "A challenge."

He reached out and ran a slow finger over her bottom lip, and the intensity that flowed from it made her eyes slide closed. "Are you sure?"

"Yes."

He leaned closer, and the heat of his nearness set off tiny flares even before he placed his lips against hers. Her body drank in the alluring sensations like a drought welcoming rain.

Something inside knew this man was going to change her life whether she wanted it or not.

Also by Beverly Jenkins

BEVERLY JENKINS

TO CATCH A RAVEN

—❧ WOMEN WHO DARE ❧—

AVONBOOKS

An Imprint of HarperCollinsPublishers

First Avon Books mass market printing: August 2022
First Avon Books hardcover printing: August 2022

Print Edition ISBN: 978-0-06-286174-0
Digital Edition ISBN: 978-0-06-286175-7

Cover design by Amy Halperin
Cover illustration by Anna Kmet
Cover image © Avalon.red/Alamy Stock Photo; © Shutterstock

FIRST EDITION

22 23 24 25 26   BVGM   10 9 8 7 6 5 4 3 2 1

TO CATCH A RAVEN

Prologue

San Francisco
May 1878

San Francisco jeweler Oswald Gant looked around his shop to make sure everything was ready for the imminent arrival of the princess and her entourage. He'd never met royalty before, and the anticipation left him elated and more than a bit nervous. Two members of her military guard had come in that morning to make arrangements for her purchase. They informed him that to ensure the princess's security, no one else was allowed on the premises during the transaction. With that in mind, Oswald had politely shown the last customers the door an hour ago. In the time since, he'd made sure no fingerprints marred the gleaming glass of his display cases and swept the floor to rid it of any dirt the day's customers might have tracked in. He'd also lowered the window shades to thwart gawkers passing by on the walk and placed the CLOSED sign on the front door. He wanted no one wandering in and ruining things. Pulling out his handkerchief, he mopped at the perspiration beading his receding hairline, and drew in a deep breath. After adjusting his tie and the cuffs of his suit coat, he was no less nervous, but he was ready.

The bell above the door sounded and the two escorts he'd met that morning entered first, resplendent in their blue military uniforms. They greeted him with a nod and took up positions at the door before announcing, "Her Royal Highness, Princess Nya of Kasia."

She entered in a faint cloud of perfume with her face masked by a thin veil. Its color and that of her rich gown and cape rivaled the brilliance of his most expensive sapphires. The kohl-lined eyes assessing him above the veil were dark and mysterious, and the skin beneath the arched brows glittered with the same shade as the gown. Her skin was brown, and that threw him. The escorts, one with blond hair and blue eyes, and the other with dark hair and eyes, appeared to be White men. Was she Colored? In the end, he was so mesmerized by her presence and how much profit he planned to make by overcharging her, he decided her race was of no consequence.

The princess spoke to the blond man in a language Oswald didn't understand.

"The princess doesn't speak American English," her man explained, "but she thanks you for accommodating her."

"Tell her I'm honored." Beaming, he directed the entourage over to the small table and chairs he'd set up by the case. "If Her Majesty would kindly be seated, I'll get the pieces you asked me to set aside."

The guard translated the request, and in a rustle of sapphire silk she crossed the room. The escorts took up positions flanking her, and Oswald hastened to the case. He returned with a small black velvet bag. While the princess sat silently, her jeweled reticule resting on her lap, he removed the contents inside the bag and gently placed them on a tray in front of her. Three rubies, two diamonds, two emeralds, and one perfect white pearl.

She nodded approvingly, and while the dark-eyed man counted out the money owed, she placed the stones back into the bag and into her reticule.

Oswald eyed the coins with confusion. "What kind of money is this?"

"French."

"San Francisco isn't in France. This is America. I take only American money."

The man countered calmly, "Francs are honored all over the world, Mr. Gant."

"American money or no sale."

The guard sighed and turned to the puzzled-looking princess. When he explained the situation, she erupted with verbal outrage. While the red-faced, tight-lipped Oswald silently stood his ground in response to her rising vocal anger, she withdrew the jeweler's bag from the reticule and all but threw it at him as she rose to her feet and stormed to the door. Oswald hefted the bag on his palm to make certain it wasn't empty, and before he could ask if she'd be returning, the princess swept out of the shop. Her escorts offered hasty assurances that they'd be back in the morning with American coin, then hurried off to catch up with the furious royal.

Later, after gathering himself, Oswald prepared to close for the day and head home, but first he opened the velvet bag to place the stones back inside the case. As he shook out the contents, his eyes widened and his breath caught at the sight of eight pebbles the same sizes and shapes as the stones and pearl that were supposed to be inside. Heart pounding, he almost fainted. When he recovered, he hurried to the nearest police station.

But by then, the blond-haired guard, Renay Deveraux, now wearing a traditional brown suit, was on a train bound for New York City with the diamonds. His similarly dressed, dark-eyed cousin, Emile, had an emerald and the pearl safely secured in his luggage on a steamer sailing to Mexico City. The weary Raven Moreau, having traded her princess finery for plainer attire, didn't mind riding Jim Crow by train back to her native New Orleans. Their gambit had been successful. She had her portion of the take, and was pleased knowing Oswald Gant, a member of a group of California business-men infamous for importing girls from China and selling them to bordellos up and down the coast, was now much poorer than he'd been at sunrise.

Chapter One

Boston
June 1878

Braxton Steele got off at the trolley stop closest to his father Harrison's Boston home and walked the rest of the way. They dined together once a week and always enjoyed each other's company. Harrison Steele was a well-known painter and illustrator. Between his work for a few of the local newspapers and the portraits commissioned by Boston's elite, both Black and White, he made enough to live a fairly comfortable life. Brax hadn't inherited his father's artistic talent, however. He made his living as a tailor and managed the estate left to him by his grandparents.

It was a lovely spring evening, and when Brax

arrived, Harrison was seated outside on the top step of his small home. "Greetings, son."

"How are you, Da?"

"Doing well for an old man. Come on inside."

His father was also a passable cook, and they sat down to a meal of roast chicken and root vegetables. The usually gregarious Harrison seemed subdued, however, and it gave Brax pause. "Is there something wrong?"

His father shrugged, saying quietly, "Maybe. Maybe not."

"Meaning?"

"When you have a past, sometimes it comes back to put its foot on your throat in ways you hadn't considered."

"That's certainly a definitive answer."

That earned him a rueful smile. Brax waited for more clues as to what this meant.

"Back before I married your mother, I was in love with a woman named Hazel Moreau. In those days I was an art forger, and she and her family were one of the best grifter operations in the South."

Brax paused with his fork on its way to his mouth. "An art forger?"

"Yes. I was exceptionally good at it, too."

Brax set his fork down and wiped his mouth on his napkin. "Why do I get the impression I'm going to need a drink for this conversation?"

His father's aging eyes twinkled. "You know

where the scotch is. Pour me one, too, if you would, please."

Brax returned to the table with glasses and the decanter. "In case I need more bracing," he explained, indicating the decanter.

His father nodded and after a sip asked, "Now where was I?"

"Hazel Moreau and art forgery."

"Yes." And for a moment no words followed. His father stared off into the distance as if memories of the past had returned. "She was the most beautiful woman I'd ever seen. Fiery, intelligent, driven. Her uncles and brothers were actors, swindlers, counterfeiters, and she, her siblings, and her cousins grew up in that life."

"How'd you meet her?"

"At a gambling house in New Orleans. I was working for the family as a counterfeiter. She was a bartender and an actress."

Braxton's curiosity was well piqued. "Why have I never heard about this before?"

"Because I left it all behind after I married your mother, or at least mostly."

"Mostly?"

"I dabbled here and there for a while, but once you were born I gave it up entirely."

Brax thought about his own past. "So, all those years I spent raising hell and sowing my wild oats was because it was in my blood?"

His father simply smiled.

Brax met the smile with one of his own. "I'll

take that as a yes. Go on with your story. What happened with Hazel?"

"Fell in love with her and she with me, but she had her cap set for a wealthy Mississippi Creole because he could secure her future in ways I could not. She was posing as a woman from an equally wealthy family and probably would have married the man had I not stood up during the wedding Mass and exposed her real identity."

"What!"

"I refused to let her marry someone else. All hell broke loose after that, of course. Arguments. Yelling. His mother fainted. The groom and his family demanded the truth. She denied everything at first, but as the uproar increased and fistfights broke out between the guests, she finally confessed her real identity and ran from the church. I went after her. Outside, she told me I'd ruined her life and the lives of any children she might have. Threatened to kill me if she ever saw me again, and that was that. Her brothers and uncles weren't happy with me, either. Promised me the same fate if I ever showed my face in New Orleans again. I moved to Boston and never returned."

"That's some story."

"All true." He stared off into the distance for a few more moments. "A lady Pinkerton came to visit me last week."

"A lady Pinkerton? What did she want?"

"To know if I knew of any Black people capable of pulling off sizable, well-planned swindles."

"Why would she come to you?"

"She said she got my name from one of my former associates but wouldn't reveal the name."

"So what did you tell her?"

"That I didn't know anyone with those skills. She refused to believe that. Threatened to send me to prison on fabricated charges if I didn't give her a name. So I gave her the only one I could think of—Hazel Moreau."

"And?"

"She visited me again this morning. Apparently, Hazel is still in the life and has a daughter named Raven. Someone has stolen one of the original copies of the Declaration of Independence."

"Was it Hazel?"

"No, but the Pinks have an idea who did. They want you and the daughter Raven to pose as man and wife and find it."

Brax stared at his father as if he'd been turned into an ear of corn. "I'm not getting involved in this."

"You don't have a choice."

"Of course I do, and I refuse."

"Then we both go to the penitentiary."

"But I'm not guilty of anything."

"They don't care. They'll manufacture something, and who do you think a judge will believe? Two Black men or a Pinkerton?"

Brax studied the grim set of his father's face and dropped his head. "Damn."

"Agreed. Pour yourself another drink, then pass me the decanter. We have much to discuss."

"Such as?"

"Traveling with the Pinkerton by train to New Orleans in two days to meet with the Moreaux."

Stunned, Brax passed him the decanter.

RAVEN HUNG THE last of the laundered sheets on the clotheslines strung between the pecan trees behind her employers' home and wiped away the perspiration on her brow. When she wasn't posing as royalty or some other fictional entity, she made her living as a domestic and she hated everything about washday: the burn of the lye on her hands, hauling the baskets of wet items across the yard and pinning them on the ropes so they'd dry. Such days began at dawn, and now, at midafternoon, she was as weary as the New Orleans air was humid.

Her employer, an older Creole woman named Antoinette Pollard, stepped out onto the second-floor verandah and called down, "Don't be dawdling out there, Raven. The mister will be home soon and he'll be wanting his supper. You need to get the cooking started so he won't have to wait."

Glad the old woman was too far away to see the loathing in her eyes, Raven replied, "Yes, ma'am."

Mrs. Pollard went back inside. Raven sighed and picked up the now empty basket. Although elaborate swindles like the one in San Francisco provided well for her sprawling family, they could only be done occasionally to avoid the scrutiny of the authorities. In between, she and her cousins Renay, Emile, and the others worked whatever jobs they could find in New Orleans to put food on the table and pay the bills.

"Hello, Raven."

Seeing eight-year-old Dorcas at her side, Raven smiled for the first time that day. Dorcas, an orphan added to the Moreau family the day after her birth, habitually appeared out of nowhere, but her presence at the Pollards' left Raven puzzled. "Why aren't you in school, Dorrie?"

"Mother Superior sent me home. She said I can't attend anymore."

"Why not?"

"I told Sister Mary Mathew her baby was going to be a boy and she fainted."

Raven hid her smile. Were she a nun, and an eight-year-old revealed her surely illicit pregnancy, she probably would've fainted, too. Dorrie possessed what the old people called Sight. She saw and knew things in uncanny and inexplicable ways.

"Does Mama Hazel know about this?"

"Yes. She's going to talk to the Mother, but she sent me to fetch you."

"Is something wrong? Is Mama ill?"

"No. She has visitors."

Raven looked over the Pollard house. "I have to make dinner for the Pollards or I'll lose this job."

"Mama Hazel said, 'Come now. You have a new job.'"

Raven's curiosity rose. Granted she didn't enjoy working for the Pollards. They were rude, miserly, and impossible to please. Having to endure the missus's complaints about everything from how the wash was pinned to the way the place was swept made her want to quit almost daily. To walk off now without notice meant there would be no reference for future employment, but if her mother needed her, Raven would worry about references later. The family always came first.

As if cued, Mrs. Pollard reappeared. "Raven, you know I don't allow visiting!"

"I do, but my mother needs me at home. I won't be returning."

"What!"

Raven set the basket down in the grass and took Dorrie's small brown hand. The air rang with Mrs. Pollard calling her name, but Raven kept walking to her mother's house a short distance away.

* * *

THE ABILITY TO quickly assess a situation was something Raven learned at an early age, so when she entered the parlor she took in the three strangers. Two Black men with brown skin and close-cropped beards stood together by the hearth. Although gray hair showed one man to be older, they resembled each other enough to suggest they were related. Both were stone-faced and tight-jawed, as if angered by something or someone. The third stranger, seated in one of the parlor chairs, was a plump, middle-aged White woman with graying brown hair and flint-colored eyes that assessed Raven's arrival with a cool distance. Raven's mother, Hazel, sat alone on the sofa, and although her mother's face gave nothing away, the muted, angry light in her green eyes, along with the hard faces of the men, let Raven know to proceed cautiously.

"Thank you for coming so quickly, Raven," her mother said. "Dorrie, can you go upstairs and keep Aunt Havana company?"

"Yes, ma'am." But before she exited, she paused before the woman and said, "You'll only be sick on the ship for a few days, then you'll feel better."

The woman stiffened and turned to Hazel for explanation.

"She's mistaken you for a woman at her school. It's nothing. Go on, Dorrie."

As Dorrie exited, Raven knew the explanation was a lie and wondered what the prediction meant, but before she could speculate further, Hazel introduced her to the strangers.

"Raven, these two gentlemen are the Steeles. Harrison and his son, Braxton." The sparks of lightning in her mother's eyes were now directed at the father, adding another layer to the mystery.

"Pleased to meet you, both," Raven said.

"Same here," the older Steele replied. The son, tall and clad in a well-made suit, was handsome enough to be one of her rakish cousins. The razor-cut mustache outlining his lips flowed neatly into the close-cut beard and enhanced his good looks. He appeared to be near her in age. His assessing onyx black eyes were hostile and cold. He offered her a stiff nod.

"And this is Miss Ruth Welch. She's a detective with the Pinkerton Agency."

Raven showed no reaction to the explosive surprise. "Pleased to meet you as well, Miss Welch."

"Likewise," Miss Welch said.

"Miss Welch wants our help with something we dare not refuse, or we go to prison," Hazel said.

Raven stiffened.

The Pinkerton swung angry eyes Hazel's way.

"Why are you so upset?" Hazel asked in response. "Was that supposed to be a secret? That is what you threatened us with, is it not? No sense in making a silk purse out of sow's ear. Am I right, Harrison?"

"Absolutely, love."

Love? Raven studied the two. Another surprise.

"I'm not your love," Hazel countered.

"At one time you were, and I was yours."

Hazel snarled a warning. "Harrison."

Raven found the exchange fascinating. She didn't remember her mother ever mentioning a man named Steele. She gave the son a quick glance, as if he might somehow hold a clue to the mystery of their parents' connected past, but saw only the hostile dark eyes of before.

Pinkerton Welch brought the conversation back around. "Let's get on with this, shall we?"

Hazel, simmering, settled back and crossed her arms.

Harrison viewed the detective with contempt.

Raven walked farther into the room and took up a position on the other side of the hearth. Her skirt and blouse were damp from doing the Pollards' wash and she needed to change into something dry. However, she wanted to get to the bottom of whatever this was first. There'd never been a Pinkerton in the house before.

"You Moreaux are a very interesting family," Welch began. "Grifters. Counterfeiters. Gamblers. Swindlers. Imposters. You name it, and there's a Moreau that fits the description. My agency has been receiving reports for years about some of the most well-planned and elaborate cases of theft we'd ever seen. The perpetrators have never left any evidence behind, but there was a common thread. Colored people were always involved. Many of our agents dismissed that factor because they refused to believe your race could be that clever. They insisted a White person had to be in charge of the ring. But during the war I worked with Miss Tubman and she was the most intelligent, cleverest, and most resourceful woman I'd ever met, so I wanted to investigate the crimes from that angle. I have to admit, though, had Mr. Steele not given me your name, the agency would still be chasing its tail."

Hazel spun to Harrison and snapped, "You betrayed my family again?"

"I had to give her a name, Hazel. She threatened our freedom. I was hoping you were no longer in the business or still living in New Orleans."

She appeared unmoved by the regret in his tone. The son's angry eyes were riveted on the Pinkerton.

Raven wondered what type of cooperation the detective was after. Threatening people's freedom was no way to initiate a partnership.

Welch reached into a black leather valise and withdrew a sheaf of papers. "After my talk with Mr. Steele, I spoke with the police here in New Orleans and a few other places, and found out you were sent to prison in Detroit ten years ago for the possession of counterfeit money, Miss Moreau."

When Raven didn't react, she continued. "So with that in mind, and going back through the cases, I've concluded that the Moreau family had to be the source of the crimes." She glanced down at her notes. "There was an incident in Philadelphia with a mulatto man posing as a priest who vanished with a very expensive jewel-encrusted broach. Then we have a young Colored singer claiming to be a queen from Africa, who promised nights of pleasure to men in New York, Miami, and Denver, only to disappear with the deposits the men laid down." She turned cold eyes on Raven. "I'm assuming that was you, and that you also pretended to be the princess who recently swindled a jeweler in San Francisco."

Raven held the accusing gaze easily and let the detective think what she wanted. In truth, the priest had been her cousin Renay, and the singer, her cousin Lacie. Like all the Moreaux, Raven knew better than to confess to any illegality real or imagined. "Why do you need the forced assistance of people you consider so disreputable?"

"To recover a stolen copy of the Declaration of Independence."

"From?"

"A state senator in Charleston, South Carolina." Welch reached into her valise again and withdrew a rolled-up parchment. Raven noted how fragile it appeared as Welch placed it on the small table beside her and unfurled it carefully. "This is a copy of the Declaration of Independence most Americans are familiar with."

Raven walked over to study it. The Steeles moved in for a closer look, too.

"Notice how on this version the signatures at the bottom are aligned by state. On the stolen one, states aren't listed, and the signatures are randomly placed, making it both rare and valuable."

Because she was from a family of grifters, Raven mulled over the possibility of making a counterfeit copy after finding it and holding on to the authentic version to sell off later. Would the Pinkerton be able to tell the difference? She'd discuss it later with her mother. "So how do you plan to retrieve it?"

"By sending you into his home."

"Alone?"

"No. Mr. Steele the younger will be going with you. He'll be posing as your husband."

Raven's mask dropped and her startled eyes flew to his. His eyes held both fury and a hint of amusement.

"You'll be the housekeeper. He'll be the valet and driver."

Raven questioned him, "Have you ever done anything like this before?"

"Of course not."

Lord. "Then why choose him instead of a male member of my family?" she asked Welch.

"Because I need someone who'll keep you on the straight and narrow, and another Moreau will not. Left to your own devices, who knows what the outcome may be."

Raven didn't care for this at all. "His father has betrayed my family twice now. How am I supposed to work with someone I can't trust?"

The son tossed back in a voice dripping with sarcasm, "This from a woman who swindles people for a living."

Raven raised her chin defiantly. Their gazes dueled.

Hazel spoke. "Why don't you have another way to achieve this?"

"We haven't found a way to get inside the house. The document is in the possession of Charlestonian Aubrey Stipe, a Democratic member of the South Carolina State Senate, as I noted a moment ago. He and his wife, Helen, were staunch supporters of the Confederacy, and their beliefs haven't changed. From the reports I've received, Mrs. Stipe will only allow Colored help in her home because it lets her believe she still owns slaves. Which is why we're sending you two."

Raven was finding this plan increasingly distasteful.

"How do you know he still has it?" Braxton Steele asked.

"Frankly, I don't. The original owner inherited the copy from her grandfather. Apparently the Declaration was printed and distributed to the public back in those days. Last year, the granddaughter saw Stipe's likeness in a newspaper and remembered him as one of the men in the reb unit that sacked her Richmond home and stole the parchment and other items during the war. She traveled to his office in Columbia to ask for its return. He laughed in her face. Told her it was a spoil of war and that he'd deny ever having the conversation with her about it. After the visit, she wrote to Mr. Pinkerton and proposed donating the document to the country if it could be retrieved. One of our agents met with Stipe, but he denied any knowledge of the theft."

"Yet you didn't threaten his freedom," Raven pointed out.

Welch bristled. "He's an elected official."

"And not subject to petty blackmail like us poor Blacks."

Welch's eyes turned hard. Raven showed no remorse.

"I can have you jailed again, Miss Moreau."

"Then do so, and good luck finding someone else to do the job." After the awful experience in a Detroit jail, Raven had sworn to never be jailed again. But the Pinkerton's hypocrisy needed to be addressed, jail or no jail. "I'd probably be more cooperative had you simply asked for our assistance and not threatened our freedom just because you believe you have the authority to do so." Did Welch know or care about the violence presently sweeping South Carolina? The racial killings had become so entrenched that one of President Grant's last official acts had been to send in federal troops to combat the terror.

Welch's lips thinned and she assessed Raven in a way that seemed to show the detective hadn't considered asking for assistance but chose to exercise her power instead. And if Raven didn't trust her before, she trusted her even less now.

"Let's get back to the issue at hand, shall we?"

Raven gestured for her to continue.

"You and Mr. Steele will be Millers. Lovey and Evan."

Raven glanced Steele's way. He showed no reaction. She kept her simmering temper hidden beneath her mask.

"The current housekeeper and driver are a married couple. A few days ago, the husband received a letter purportedly from his Texas family, but sent by my office, with word that his mother is on her deathbed. He and his wife are preparing to leave, if they haven't done so already. There's a Pinkerton operative in Charleston who's been there for the past six months working on another investigation and has ingratiated herself into the circle of Helen Stipe's friends. She's going to suggest you as replacements and claim you worked for me, her sister in Virginia. She'll tell Mrs. Stipe you plan to relocate to Charleston and are in need of employment. You'll come highly recommended."

Raven thought that a simple enough explanation but wondered what the other detective had been looking into. "Why doesn't Mrs. Stipe hire someone local to replace the people you sent the letter to about their dying mother?"

"She has a well-known reputation for being cheap. It's said the only reason the other couple continue to work for her is because she owned them before the war."

The Steele son asked, "How much interaction will we have with this other agent?"

"Minimal. Her mission there is winding down and she'll be supposedly leaving Charleston to visit family in Wales. As her sister, I'll be joining her in Wales eventually but will be accompanying you to Charleston to make sure you arrive safely and to tie up loose ends with the sale of her home."

Raven didn't like hearing that she'd be traveling with them, mainly because she didn't like this woman at all. "How big is the house, and is it located in Charleston proper or outside of the city?"

"In Charleston proper. It has two stories, and the servant quarters are behind the residence."

Raven filed that information away. "Do the Stipes have children?"

"No."

Braxton Steele asked, "Is our marriage a love match or arranged?"

Considering that to be an odd question, Raven asked him, "And that matters why?"

"Because our circumstances may determine how we respond to each other."

"A love match," Welch responded.

Her smug face made Raven want to toss her into a bayou filled with gators. *Love match, my arse!* "I can be whoever the role needs me to be, Mr. Steele." She assumed women flocked to his bearded handsomeness like butterflies to honeysuckle. She hoped he'd not be expecting Mrs. Lovey Miller to do the same when they were alone.

"I'm sure you'll do fine," he said.

"Of course she will," Welch added. "She just bragged about her family's skills. Did you not?"

Raven turned a withering eye on Welch, who met the look by continuing to appear pleased. "When do we leave for Charleston, and how are we traveling?"

"By train, as soon as my office wires me the funds for the tickets, which could be as early as this evening, so use your time until then to get acquainted with Mr. Steele."

Seemingly confident that she'd gotten the last

word, Welch rerolled the parchment, tucked it away, and rose to her feet.

Raven asked, "Is there a time frame for the operation?"

"I'll expect results as soon as possible, especially since you're so skilled, Miss Moreau. Don't forget your freedom and the freedom of everyone in this room is tied to your success."

Raven made the decision then and there to somehow make Welch pay for her high-handed arrogance. She didn't know what form it might take, or when it would come to pass, but come it would.

"It's been a pleasure meeting you all," Welch stated, not caring that everyone knew that to be a lie. "I'll show myself out."

Raven followed her and watched from the door as Welch entered a waiting hack and was driven away.

Upon Raven's return to the parlor Hazel asked, "Is she gone?"

"Yes."

"Harrison, do you still draw?"

"I do."

"How long will it take you to do a few likenesses of her?"

"If I have your keen eye to help me with the finer details, an hour maybe."

"Flattery will get you nowhere. I'm still furious at you, remember."

"I do. Looking forward to soothing that temper though. Why do you want her drawn?"

"So my people can show her face around the city. I want to know everything about her. Where she's staying, who she sees, where and what she eats. Everything. That she'd come here and threaten us this way . . ."

"I have my kit. I just need a place to work."

Hazel stood. "Okay, come with me. Raven, you and Braxton get acquainted. Your roles are key. I'll send out word for the family members I think will be helpful to meet here later. Once this gambit is over, Welch will regret ever hearing the name Moreau."

Hazel and Harrison exited, leaving Raven to deal with the man she'd soon be calling her husband.

Chapter Two

*B*raxton noted the hostility in the eyes of Raven Moreau. She was as beautiful as she was fiery, and he'd be drawn to her like a moth to a flame were she not a thief. That she'd not backed down or shown fear even in the face of Welch's threats was impressive. His anger at Welch's dastardly assignment equaled hers, but their families needed them to work together to get this mess resolved. Being civil was a good place to start.

"So, Lovey. How do we go about learning about each other?"

"First of all, I'd prefer not to be addressed by that name until we reach Charleston and the game begins. Secondly, I've been doing wash all day. My clothes are wet and I need to change. We can address our so-called marriage when I return."

Without waiting for a response, she left the parlor.

He watched her exit. So much for civility. This game, as she termed it, seemed destined to challenge not only his personal freedom, but, due to her tartness, his temper as well. He took a seat on the sofa and thought back on Welch's revelations about his soon-to-be pretend wife. Had she really enticed men with promises of her charms only to abscond with their money? What kind of family raised their daughters to play such a role? Now he'd be temporarily attached to this family of schemers, and he wasn't sure how he could overlook their attraction to crime. He'd lived within the law his entire life. That his father had once been in the confidence game, too, was something else he was still trying to make peace with. His thoughts were interrupted by the entrance of the thin little brown-skinned girl he'd seen earlier with Raven. She walked over and looked him in the eyes for a silent moment before saying, "My name is Dorcas. Everyone calls me Dorrie." A blue ribbon tied around her short soft curls matched the blue dress that looked to be a school uniform.

"Hello, Dorrie. Pleased to meet you. My name is Braxton."

"Pleased to meet you, too, Mr. Braxton. When you make my dress for the wedding, please don't forget to put red roses around the middle."

"Wedding?"

"The wedding you and Raven are having."

Did she know about Welch's plan? "There isn't going to be a wedding."

"Yes, there is. I already told Mama Hazel and the aunties, too, so please don't forget." She gave him a big smile and left the room.

Caught off guard, he wondered again if she was in on the plan. Would the Moreaux give a small child a role in this? He set his confusion and questions aside as Raven returned, wearing a simple black skirt and a short-sleeved oyster gray blouse. The collar and edges of the blouse's sleeves were frayed from wear, as was the hem of the skirt. She certainly didn't dress like a wealthy schemer, which gave rise to more questions. "Is the little girl Dorrie going to be involved with our trip to Charleston?"

"What do you mean?"

"She just told me not to forget to add roses to the middle of the dress I'll be making her for the wedding."

"What wedding?"

"My question exactly. She said you and I will be getting married."

Raven went still, then slowly drew her hands down her face and whispered, "Mary, Mother of Jesus."

"Problem?"

"No. It's nothing."

He was certain there was more to this than she was admitting, but he didn't know how to get at the truth. Further speculation was overridden by the entrance of two older women whose bright gold skin and green eyes bore a strong resemblance to Hazel Moreau. One was seated in a cane chair that moved on wheels, and the other woman pushed the chair from behind. Dorrie was with them.

Raven did the introductions. "Mr. Steele, these are my mother's sisters. My aunts Eden and Havana. We call her Vana for short. Aunts, this is Braxton Steele."

"Good afternoon, ladies."

From her chair, Havana said, "Hello. Lord Jesus, you're as handsome as your daddy was at your age."

"Vana," Raven said warningly.

"Hush. He is, isn't he, Eden?"

Eden responded. "Yes. He looks just like Harrison. Good thing Hazel decided she wanted that little Creole beignet from Mississippi instead of Harrison, otherwise Braxton would be your brother instead of your husband, Raven. We Moreaux don't marry kin."

"He isn't going to be my husband," she gritted out.

A Creole beignet? Brax was even more confused.

The aunts paid no attention to their niece's protestations. "Hazel told us a bit about what's happening with the Pinkerton. Once this is over, that woman needs to be taught a lesson."

Havana added, "And we celebrate. Been a long time since we've had a wedding. Raven, what kind of wedding cake would you like. Raven?"

"There won't be a need for a cake."

Havana countered, "You can't get married without cake."

"I'm not getting married."

"Dorrie says you are, and we all know she's never wrong."

He watched Raven drop her head and emit a soft, frustrated snarl.

Braxton was intrigued. "Never?"

"Please, stay out of this," Raven advised.

He countered, "I'm a tailor. If I'm to be married, I need the details so I can sew up a suit." Not that he believed a word of the girl's prediction.

"And my dress," Dorrie chimed in happily.

Raven's head dropped again.

Braxton felt as if he'd accidentally stumbled into the cast of a stage play. He didn't know what roles they were all playing, but Raven didn't appear to be enjoying her part at all. He found the whole thing fascinating.

Raven addressed her aunts. "Mr. Steele and I have things to discuss. We can talk about this cake some other time."

"We'll just proceed with the wedding plans without your assistance," Eden stated.

Havana added, "Braxton, she's been hard-headed all her life. Keep that in mind in your dealings with her."

"Yes, ma'am."

Raven shot him a glare hot enough to fry trout, but he shrugged it off. "After you, Miss Moreau."

She turned and he followed.

UPSTAIRS, AFTER SETTING aside Dorrie's shocking prediction that Raven would be marrying Braxton, Hazel watched Harrison glance around the room she'd converted into a library. "Is there enough light in here?" she asked.

He nodded and set his satchel on the table nearest the windows. For a moment, they simply stared at each other, and although Hazel had no idea what he was thinking, being with him after all the decades apart made the memories rise of her youth and her feelings for him.

"Been a long time," he said quietly.

"Yes, it has been."

"How are you, besides still wanting my head?"

She allowed a small smile to show. "I'm well. And you?"

"I've had a good life."

"Married?"

"Widower. Lost Jane when the boy was an adolescent. Been just he and I since. Did you marry the Creole?"

She scoffed. "After the madness at the church that morning? No."

"I suppose I should say I'm sorry, but even now I won't apologize for the feelings I had for you back then, Jade."

He called her Jade because of the color of her eyes, and hearing the nickname again hit her straight in the heart.

"You're as beautiful now as you were then."

More memories rose: the late night dinners after the bar closed, the walks in the moonlight, the love they'd made. To escape them and the feelings they spawned, she turned to the window and looked out over the overgrown acreage surrounding her home. "You haven't lost your gift of gab. Does your son have it, too?"

"Pretty sure he does. Was quite the cock of the walk in his younger days." He paused. "I'm having trouble believing he and your Raven will really marry though."

"Dorrie's never wrong, so it's going to be interesting to see the outcome. Raven's tough, focused, and has had her heart broken. She's determined, too. At the age of nine, she took it upon herself to get a job to help me put food on the table. Every time I made her employer let her go because I wanted her to attend school, she'd find a new one. A cock of the walk isn't going to impress her."

"There isn't a man alive who doesn't enjoy a challenging woman, even if it takes him a while to figure it out. If a marriage between them is meant to be, she'll be good for him. With all the wealth on my wife's side of the family, he's wanted for nothing in life, and women have always come easily for him."

Hazel looked back over her shoulder at him. "Your wife was wealthy?"

"Very. Her father owned a small fleet of merchant ships. Brax is the only grandchild, so he's inherited it all after Jane's death."

"He had the life privileges I wanted my children to have." She left unsaid that he'd been the reason that hadn't come to pass, but she didn't need to remind him of that. She could tell by the tender regret in his eyes that he knew. "Did you love your wife?"

"It was an arranged marriage. Her father was a tyrant. She couldn't abide the man he'd handpicked for her to marry, so she offered me a business proposal that allowed her to escape her father's clutches and me a life away from the docks so I could pursue my drawings. I admired her, respected her, and never brought her shame. But I never loved her. Not the way I loved you."

That went straight to her heart, too. "Let's get started on the portrait," she urged softly.

He nodded.

THE MOMENT BRAXTON stepped outside with Raven, he was assaulted by the late afternoon's thick heat and humidity, and was soon perspiring like he'd just waded out of the Mississippi River. The narrow dirt path she was leading him down cut through an area thick with towering trees and raised roots that made him watch his step. There was also an abundance of overgrown shrubbery that snagged his trousers, while other tall, spindly foliage had to be pushed aside to keep him from losing an eye. As she walked, skirt swaying, she offered no clues as to their destination.

"Where are you from?" she asked without looking back.

He pulled his attention away from the distracting rhythm of her skirt. "Boston."

"It doesn't get this warm, I take it."

"No. There's heat during the summer months, but nothing like this." He slapped at a mosquito feasting on his cheek. During the war he'd been stationed in South Carolina with the Massachusetts Fifty-Fourth. The biting insects had been unbearable. New Orleans seemed nearly as bad.

In a small clearing up ahead, he spotted a vine-shrouded gazebo. The weathered wood and stone structure showed its age. Two battered wooden steps led them up and inside, where a pair of stone benches green with moss and mold offered seating. He chose to remain standing.

She finally turned to face him. Arms folded across her chest, she assessed him silently. He assumed she was weighing how to approach this. She'd voiced her misgivings about partnering with him. However, the Pinkerton hadn't left them a choice. They were in this madness together.

"So," he said. "Here we are."

"I'd rather be elsewhere, or at least tied to someone who isn't a novice at this. So many things could go wrong."

"If we're being honest, I'd rather be elsewhere as well, or at least with someone who lives within the law."

"Have you expressed that opinion to your father, seeing as how he lived a similar life?"

"Touché. Do you always give as good as you get?"

"I don't suffer fools."

"Just the ones you cheat?"

"Are you always so judgmental?"

"Generally, no. I save that for the quality of the fabrics I choose and the patterns I make."

"Lord," she whispered.

"Now that we've broken the ice, what do you need to know about me?"

"Are you married?"

"No. You?"

She shook her head. "No. Age?"

"Thirty-eight. You?"

"Thirty-two."

"Lovers?"

"And you need to know this why?"

"In case someone who has your heart takes issue with this so-called marriage before we leave for South Carolina."

"You don't have to worry. It isn't as if we'll be alerting the newspapers."

He noted she hadn't answered his question. A woman with her beauty should have legions of men at her feet. "I'll take you at your word."

"I'm so relieved."

Her sarcasm rivaled her beauty. The unblemished bronze skin and the coppery curls rising above the red-patterned headdress like a crown reminded him of a Boston autumn. The season's brilliantly colored leaves and crisp cool air was always his favorite time of the year. "Is there a story behind why you were named Raven?"

"My grandmother Fanny named me. She said there were ravens in the trees during my birth. She took it as a sign. Why do you ask?"

"Because you don't look like a Raven."

"What do I look like?"

"Autumn."

"The season?"

"Your coloring reminds me of the changing trees."

She went silent for a moment, and he noted

her skepticism before she asked, "Is this called flattery in Boston?"

"Consider it a simple observation."

"The name's Raven."

"Understood." In spite of the tension between them, he was, for unknown reasons, enjoying the verbal fencing. "How often does Dorrie predict the future?"

"Not often. Have you ever been to Charleston?"

He knew a redirection when he heard one. "Yes. I was stationed in South Carolina during the war. Few of my memories from the time are fond." He'd enlisted in the Massachusetts Fifty-Fourth as a naïve young man intent upon freeing the enslaved and showing the doubting country that Colored men were as brave and stalwart as anyone else. After mustering out in April 1865, he'd returned home jaded, cynical, and angry at the bigotry his regiment had endured. The nightmares brought on by the deaths and horrors he'd witnessed haunted him for months.

Whether his being a veteran altered her perceptions of him was impossible to tell because her expression hadn't changed. He vowed never to play poker with her. "Have you ever been to Charleston?"

"Enough times to know my way around the city."

He wondered if those past visits were tied to swindling. "Do you have family there?"

"Yes. It's a small branch so we'll have assistance should a need arise."

"Good to know. I wonder if Pinkerton Welch is aware of that?"

"I've no idea how deeply she's been digging. However, I've learned to never underestimate an opponent or take anything for granted."

"I wonder if there are other detectives in the city for her support."

"Ones who don't believe the race is clever enough to do what we Moreaux do. That gives us a small advantage in the scheme of things."

"Why do I get the impression that there may be more afoot here than finding the document and turning it over?"

"Because when my family encounters someone as arrogant and high-handed as Detective Welch, there always is. We're like a nest of cottonmouths. Poke us and we strike."

He understood the desire to get back at the Pinkerton, but he wanted no part in their revenge. Returning home was his main mission—that and not going to prison. The detective had mentioned Raven's prison stint and he wanted to ask about it, but he doubted she'd be forthcoming about the details, so he set the questions aside. "So do you have a plan in mind?"

"Other than searching the house from top to

bottom, no. We may come up with something more detailed when we get there and size things up. I assume if Welch had a plan she would've shared it. Then again, maybe not."

"She seemed very focused on you."

"She didn't like my calling out her hypocrisy. People like her rarely do."

"Okay, what about the little things?"

"Such as?"

"Your favorite dessert. A husband should know that about his wife."

She paused as if thinking. "Pecan pie. Yours?"

"Apple crumble. Your favorite pastime?" he asked.

"Fishing."

"Really?" That surprised him.

"Do people not fish in Boston?"

"Men do, but not many women in my circle do."

"Moreaux love to fish. It's fun and you get something to eat out of it as well."

He found her accent enchanting. It wasn't so much a drawl as a musically toned mix of the different nationalities of the city.

"What do you like to do?" she asked.

"Designing the patterns I make for my tailoring business because I enjoy the mathematics tied to it. I also like good books. During the winter months, it's a good way to pass the time. Do you have a favorite book?"

She shook her head, looking as if she were uncomfortable, and wouldn't meet his eyes. In that moment he sensed a vulnerability in her that caught him off guard. Admittedly, they'd met only a short while ago, so he knew next to nothing about her, but the question seemed to have touched something that lay hidden beneath the tart-tongued warrior queen persona. To his surprise, a part of him wanted to seek it out so he could soothe it. He decided to change the subject. "Have you lived in New Orleans your entire life?"

"Yes. My family goes back many generations."

"Were your people slave or free before the war?"

"Both. My great-great-grandmother was enslaved by Spanish settlers. Some of her sons were freed, but her daughters weren't. By the time one of her daughters, my grandmother Fanny, was freed at age fifteen, there were free Moreaux and enslaved Moreaux. Some owned slaves that were family members but freed them, until that became illegal. Others put profits above bloodline and sold their cousins like the other masters in their class. Louisiana is a complicated place when it comes to the race. I'm assuming your family was free?"

"On my mother's side, yes. Her father, my grandfather, served with the English navy and settled in Boston after the Revolutionary War. My father, Harrison, was enslaved in Texas before escaping and making his way here. He met my mother while working on the Boston docks." He didn't know how she'd react so he didn't share that his grandfather owned a fleet of merchant ships or that because of his family's wealth, he'd grown up never knowing hunger or hard times. "Thank you for letting me know a bit more about you."

"Same here, but let me state this now so there will be no misunderstandings later. I'll be your wife in name only."

"Meaning?"

"We're both adults here, Steele."

"True, so I need to know exactly what that means."

"No intimacy of any kind."

"No pretend kisses?"

"No."

"Even if necessary?"

"I doubt that will be a requirement for our employment."

"And if it is?"

Her eyes narrowed. "I'm sure women come easily to you, but a kiss from you, pretend or otherwise, will not make me one of them. You're not my type."

"Because I don't make my living bilking people?"

"Because you think living within the law somehow makes you better than people like me."

"I never said that."

"Not in so many words, but you stink with it, frankly." She looked him up and down. "That appears to be a very expensive suit you're wearing, which makes me think you have some wealth, so save your charms and flattery for the sweet innocents you know back home, with their costly gowns and soft-soled slippers. I'll not be craving you or your cock."

He hadn't noticed someone else joining them until a woman behind him said, "I see this is going well."

"As well as could be expected," Raven replied, eyes blazing.

The ferocious setdown would have shriveled the pride of some men. Brax wasn't bothered. The tart-tongued warrior queen had returned. Her description of the ladies back home had been accurate, but none ever uttered the word *cock*, at least not within his hearing. That she'd voiced it so easily made his own tighten and gave rise to erotic thoughts he did his best to ignore.

"Mr. Steele, this is my cousin Lacie Deveraux. Lace, meet Braxton Steele."

She stepped into view. Her skin tone and hair were the color of a Spanish doubloon. Her eyes were green and her face was as beautiful as the rest of the Moreau women he'd encountered so far. "Pleased to meet you," he said.

Lacie eyed him. "Same here. Mama was right about his handsomeness."

"That's not helpful," Raven told her.

"Just stating fact. I was sent to get you two, so sheathe your swords and come on."

Raven shot him one last disapproving glance before they followed the cousin back the way they'd come.

Chapter Three

*A*s they set out, Raven heard the far-off laughter of children. The sound meant family had begun arriving as they did most days, and that softened her mood. She always enjoyed their presence no matter the reason. "Is Renay home yet?"

"Not yet. Supposedly later today."

Renay was Lacie's older brother. He'd gone to Chicago to handle a job involving a copy of Gainsborough's *Blue Boy*. The purloined painting would be passed on to the Moreau relatives in Havana, who'd send it on to their connections in Spain where it would be sold.

Raven was about to ask Lacie about her youngest brother, Antoine, when they were startled by Dorrie and a small group of young cousins bursting out of the trees. One of the boys hit Raven on the arm and yelled, "Cousin Raven's it!" And they ran off.

Raven and Lacie shared a grin. She noticed

Steele's smile and noted he had something inside besides judgment. He met her gaze but didn't say anything. Their walk resumed.

When they reached the house, she spied a crew of adolescent family members cleaning out the grills and smokers in the outdoor kitchen under the watchful eyes of Vana. The family came together on Sundays for dinner, and their work was part of the preparation. Due to Welch's assignment, Raven would probably be on the way to Charleston and miss the upcoming gathering. She added one more sin to Welch's slate.

The sight of the work on the grills brought up an old memory. "Lace, remember the time we bought the potion from that old conjure woman on Ramparts Street that was supposed to make us invisible so we wouldn't have to help in the kitchen?"

Lacie laughed. "We were invisible all right. Spent the entire day throwing up in the privy."

"How old were you?" Steele asked.

Raven thought back. "Nine? Ten, maybe?"

Lacie nodded. "We never bought anything from her ever again."

"Why would you waste money on something that couldn't possibly do such a thing?"

"We were children," Raven replied defensively.

"And," Lacie added, "if Aunt Vana was working you from no light to no light, you'd be looking for potions, too." She studied him for a moment before asking Raven, "Is he always so judgmental?"

"Apparently."

"That's too bad. What a waste of handsomeness."

From the storm clouds that formed in his dark eyes, Raven assumed he hadn't appreciated the assessment and she chuckled to herself. *Judge not lest you be judged* came to mind.

The interior of the house was filled with cousins of all ages, colors, and genders, representing the nine wings of the immediate family. Some were in the indoor kitchen assisting Aunt Eden with more preparation duties; others were standing, sitting, laughing, and talking, while a small group played cards on a table set up by the parlor's windows. The younger ones often gathered at Hazel's home after school to await being taken home by their parents once the workday ended. Some were old enough to have jobs and children of their own, and had stopped by for the camaraderie. As always, the noise level was high, but it fueled Raven's spirit like manna.

Over the din, Lacie said, "Aunt Hazel said for the three of us to meet her upstairs."

On the way, Raven stopped a moment to share hugs with those she hadn't seen in a while, kiss the soft fat cheeks of some of the babies, and look over shoulders at the cards a cousin held. Steele was silently assessing all the goings-on.

She knew that some people were overwhelmed by the size of her family, and she wondered if he was one of them.

They joined Hazel and Harrison Steele in the small library. As Raven met the question in her mother's eyes, silently asking how she'd gotten along with Braxton, Raven gave a tiny shrug. She'd share details later when they were alone.

"Come look at the sketch and see what you think," Hazel said.

They walked over and studied the pen-and-ink sketch. Raven was impressed. He'd captured the detective's face well: from the soft fleshiness of the aging chin and jaw, to the unsmiling sternness in her face and eyes. "This is very good."

"Excellent job, Da," his son said. "Excellent job."

"Thank you." Harrison looked between Raven and his son as if seeking answers, too, but Raven offered nothing. She'd let Braxton tell him his side of things.

Lacie said, "I'd like a duplicate to show around. Do you have more?"

"We wanted to get Raven and Brax's opinion first," Harrison replied. "How many more do you think you'll need, Hazel?"

"Can you make me five before nightfall? That way Lacie can show it around her gambling house when she leaves here."

Raven saw Braxton stiffen. "Yes, Mr. Judgmental, my cousin owns a gambling house, a very successful one, I might add."

"I didn't say anything, Miss Moreau."

"You didn't have to."

Lacie echoed Raven's misgivings. "Are we sure he's cut out for this Pinkerton game?"

"No," Raven replied tersely. "But we have no choice."

"And neither do I, Lovey," he replied.

"Don't start, Evan!" she tossed back.

"Stop fighting," Hazel warned quietly.

"He's going to get us thrown in jail."

Hazel shot her a quelling look.

Raven knew clashing with her mother wouldn't help matters but she wanted to whine and stamp her foot like a petulant child. The smug and stuffy Braxton Steele was going to be as useful as a hog with a fishing pole. Instead of pointing that out, she lowered the flame fueling her temper and focused on the situation at hand.

BRAXTON WAS UNACCUSTOMED to having himself disparaged so routinely. He might not know the ins and outs of bilking people, but back home he had a reputation for being both honest and fair in his personal and business dealings, not that Raven Moreau seemed to care. She'd accused him of being judgmental, and it was the pot calling the kettle black, because her perception of him was just as flawed.

Hazel's voice brought him back to the conversation. "Harrison and I will arrive in Charleston probably a few days after you do. I'll be sending a wire to the family there to let them know we're coming. Raven, if you could somehow get me the address of where Welch will be staying while we're there, that might prove helpful. I want to keep an eye on her."

Before Raven could respond, a tall man with blond hair and sky blue eyes entered the room. Brax watched her face brighten in a manner she'd yet to direct his way. "Renay, welcome home," she said.

The man gave her a kiss on the cheek and offered the same affectionate greeting to Lacie and Hazel. "Thanks. Got in a little while ago."

He turned his attention to Brax and Harrison. "Renay Deveraux," he said, introducing himself and extending his hand.

The Steeles introduced themselves.

"Pleased to meet you," Renay said.

Lacie asked, "How'd things go?"

"Went well. The prize is on its way." He looked around. "So, what have I missed?"

Hazel offered him a condensed version of the Pinkerton mission. When she relayed the part about the pretend marriage, the blue eyes shifted to Brax's and held there a long assessing moment before seeking out Raven's, who didn't mask her displeasure.

"Interesting," was his response. He studied Braxton once more before resettling his attention on Hazel. "Does the Pinkerton know how dangerous the Moreaux can be?"

"I doubt she does," Raven responded.

"Then we need to teach her."

"Agreed," Lacie said.

Hazel said, "Let's take care of family business first. After Raven and Brax find the document, we can discuss holding the detective's feet to the fire."

Renay asked, "Will you need my assistance in Charleston? I've nothing else planned at the moment."

Raven paused as if considering the request. "Since Mama and the Charleston family will be close by, I don't think I'll need much assistance, but just in case, it might be good to have you in the background, Renay."

"What about me?" Lacie asked. "I can help, too, if you need me. I'm supposed to be going to handle that Pennsylvania job but I can postpone it."

Raven shook her head. "Keep your date in Pennsylvania. Steele and I should be okay with the players we already have on the board."

Brax glanced over at his father's grimly set face. The seriousness of this affair wasn't lost on either of them, or so it seemed. The continuing conversation about taking revenge on the detective remained a concern. He wouldn't know his father's feelings on that until they conversed privately, but Brax already knew where he stood. He wanted this business to be over as quickly as possible so he could return to his quiet, uneventful existence in Boston. He knew a lot depended on whether he and the prickly Raven could work together; with the clashes they'd been having, that was another concern.

On the heels of that thought, three more people arrived. A man with ivory skin and jet black hair and eyes was introduced to the Steeles as Emile Moreau. With him was a thin, elfish young woman with sand brown skin and bourbon-colored eyes. Her hair was hidden beneath a green head wrap stylishly accented with gold beads and cowrie shells. Her name was Alma, and when she was introduced to him, her poker face reminded him of Raven's. The third person, Bethany Moreau, was a woman of towering height and build. She appeared to be about Raven's and Lacie's age. Wearing a gold head wrap and a flowing black caftan shot through with threads of gold and red, she had the presence of an ebony-skinned African deity. Her beauty was blinding.

"Pleased to meet you," he said, finally finding his voice.

"Same here," she replied, assessing him coolly. Hazel offered them the same information she'd given Renay about the unwanted partnership with Welch, and the new arrivals eyed Brax speculatively, especially upon hearing about the pretend marriage and his gambit inexperience. He braced himself for more derision but it never materialized. Instead, a discussion followed centering on items like travel logistics to Charleston, the size of the house, its possible layout, and the places his father's drawn portraits might be shown to ferret out information on Detective Welch's current presence in the city. Most of the talk was led by Raven. Answering questions, proposing scenarios, and deferring to those with a better idea, she had all the competence of a general preparing subordinates for battle, and he found her impressive. He wondered how long she'd held the role, and from whom she'd learned. Being inexperienced in such a situation, and thus unable to contribute anything of value to the conversation, Brax remained silent, watched, and listened.

A short while later, Hazel proposed they meet again the following day. "Before Raven and I leave for Charleston, I need to know what games you're running and where you'll be, so I can tell Vana and Eden."

After that, the gathering came to a close. He met Raven's eyes across the room but she held his only long enough to turn her attention back to her conversation with Alma. He and his father had yet to secure a place to sleep for the night, and he needed to get together with him so they could discuss lodging. He thought now might be a good time since he was tired from the day, and neither of them had eaten since arriving on the train from Boston with Welch. Before he could move, however, a voice stopped him.

"Mr. Steele, Emile and I would like to speak with you for a moment, if we may."

He turned to face Renay and Emile, and wondered what this might be about. "Of course."

"Let's step out onto the verandah."

Brax followed them outdoors and heard children's laughter from somewhere below. "What do you wish to discuss?"

Renay took the lead. "Raven."

"What about her?"

Emile asked, "You will keep her safe?"

He glanced between the two and noted their concern. "To the best of my ability, I will not let her come to harm."

"As her male cousins, it's our duty to ensure she's protected."

"Understood."

Renay added, "You will not harm her personally."

He knew what that meant. "She and I have discussed the boundaries of this pretend marriage. I'm a man of honor. I've never forced myself on a woman and don't plan to do so with her. You have my word."

They seemed satisfied with his pledge. Brax didn't take offense at their questioning. He was a stranger to the family, after all, so he understood their need for reassurance. "Were I in your position, I'd be asking the same."

The dark-haired Emile appeared impressed. "I appreciate that."

"As do I," Renay added.

The cousins each held out a hand, and Brax shook each in response. Their trust seemed genuine, and he felt as though a portion of the wall dividing him and the family had been partially dismantled.

"Are you three out here planning my demise?" Raven asked, stepping out to join them.

The smiling Renay and Emile turned her way and replied in unison, "Yes."

Braxton remained silent. By the affection in her voice and manner, it was obvious the two men held a special place in her heart. He, she undoubtedly wished elsewhere, and as illogical as he knew the question to be, he wondered what it might be like to have that affection for himself.

Giving Brax a cursory glance, she asked her cousins, "Did he pass muster?"

The men looked his way and again replied as one. "Yes."

"Since we all lie for a living, I'll take you at

your word." Addressing Brax, she added, "Just be careful, Steele. If they corrupt you, you'll never forgive yourself."

That said, she went back inside.

Brax sighed. "Is she always so tough?"

"Not always. This Pinkerton problem is resting on her shoulders and she's not happy being manipulated."

"I'm only asking because Dorrie has predicted a true marriage between us, so I'd like to know what I'll be getting myself into once we become man and wife."

Emile cocked his head. "Dorrie said what?"

Brax explained about the dress, adding, "Of course, I'm just pulling your leg. I don't actually believe her."

Renay and Emile shared a speaking look and again in unison laughed so loud and long, Brax swore they were heard in Boston.

"Does Raven know?" a wide-eyed Renay asked when he seemed able to speak again.

"Yes."

And another round of laughter shook them so forcefully, Brax thought they might fall over the railing to the ground below. The hilarity was contagious and he smiled in response. "Why is this so funny?"

"No offense, but Raven marrying someone as staid and proper as you appear to be? How mad is she?"

"She and I have been at odds over everything since we met, so I'm not sure about this in particular. You don't really believe Dorrie's prediction, do you?"

The still chuckling Renay said, "Dorrie is never wrong. Ever."

Emile added, "If she's predicting a wedding and knows what she'll be wearing, the deal is pretty much sealed."

Brax refused to take them seriously.

"Has anyone told you about our Dorrie?"

"No."

The humor on Emile's face was replaced by a solemnness that gave Brax pause.

"Her mother died giving her birth. The midwife declared Dorrie stillborn, but a minute later, she drew her first breath. She was named Dorcas after the woman in the Bible who came back from the dead."

A chill ran up his spine.

"She has what the elders call Sight," Renay added. "She sees and knows things a child her age shouldn't. Most times, she's just a little girl who likes to skip rope, play jacks, and sometimes get in trouble as most children do, but there's a side of her that predicted our grandmother's death, knows when bad storms are on the way, and what the sex of an unborn baby will be—among other things."

Emile further explained, "She doesn't offer

predictions often, but she's always accurate, so we've learned not to be dismissive."

"But not everything she tells us is something earthshaking," Renay said with a fond smile. "A couple of months back, I misplaced my favorite pair of driving gloves. She had no way of knowing they were missing or that I'd searched my apartment frontwards and backwards. She approached me during a Sunday family dinner and told me where to find them. Damned if she wasn't correct."

Brax didn't know what to think. He was from practical, ship-faring, god-fearing Boston. No one talked about people with Sight, at least as far as he knew. "No one can predict the future."

"Ignore Dorrie's gift at your own peril," Renay warned.

Emile smiled and playfully slapped him on the back. "You'll enjoy being a Moreau. Promise."

"And we could use a good tailor in the family," Renay told him.

Brax glanced to see Raven standing in the doorway. He wondered how much she'd heard. By the way she met his eyes and swiftly turned on her heel and disappeared, he guessed more than enough.

"Is it too early for cognac?" Raven asked after leaving the verandah and reentering the library.

She walked over to the small cabinet where her mother's liquor was kept and withdrew a bottle and a number of glasses before glancing around the room at her seated female cousins. "Anyone want to join me?"

Her mother and Harrison had retired to the study to work on the extra sketches, so only Alma, Beth, and Lacie remained. No one declined, so Raven poured a few fingers in each glass and passed them around. She raised hers in a toast. "To my sanity."

Smiles filled the room.

Bethany asked, "Does this have to do with the pretend marriage to the very handsome Steele the younger?"

Raven snarled and sat on the sofa beside Lacie.

Lacie grinned. "I think you have your answer."

"Dorrie says I'm going to marry him."

After those words, you could hear a pin drop.

Alma, the family's lock-picking expert, asked, "Marry? As in St. Louis Cathedral, before a priest, marry?"

Raven replied by taking a large swallow.

"Oh my word!" Beth responded, looking shocked. "Raven?"

"Not happy. Someone write that down so there will be an official record of my response."

Lacie chuckled. "Have to admit, he's not bad

on the eyes, but the stick up his arse will make for an awkward wedding night."

"Add that to the official response, too."

Giggles followed.

Raven placed her glass on the table beside her and dropped her head into her hands. "He's judgmental, smug, and on such a high horse it's a wonder he can see us humble folks down here on the ground." She added, "And after my debacle with Tobias, I'm not in the market for a husband of any kind, not even a pretend one."

"Not all men are bastards like Tobias, Raven," Alma pointed out.

"I know, but he was more than enough of one to make me want to swear off men for the rest of my life. I ended up in the penitentiary, for heaven's sake. Moreau women are queens of the game; we're not supposed to be left with egg on our faces."

"You need to stop being so hard on yourself," Beth said kindly. "Sometimes when we believe we're in love, our good sense goes on holiday."

"And mine went all the way to the moon. I'm never giving my heart to another man. Ever."

"Then marrying Steele should be right up your alley," Lacie said. "Your heart won't be involved."

"But who wants to be tied to a man you don't care about?" Raven asked her.

"There is that."

Alma said, "Maybe you will end up falling in love with him."

"Bite your tongue."

Beth said, "Either way, I want a front row seat because this sounds like it's going to be fun. Dorrie's always right."

"This time, she's going to be wrong."

"I want a good seat, too," Lacie said, and then asked, "I wonder if Dorrie's seen someone for me. Lord knows it would be nice to settle down and enjoy the love of a good man."

"You can have Steele."

As if cued, he and her male cousins entered from the verandah, and all conversation stopped.

Emile said, "Awfully quiet in here."

"We weren't talking about you, if that's your concern." Her eyes locked with Steele's, and rather than turning away like a shy virgin, she met his gaze straight on.

"Can we have dinner together this evening? Just the two of us?" he requested quietly as if they were alone. She was thrown not only by the way the intimate-sounding tone resonated through her, but also by the realization that the request left her no room to deny him lest she come off as the petulant child she'd compared herself to earlier. She was trapped, and everyone in the room knew it.

Hazel's entrance interrupted their silent battle. "Lacie, here's your duplicate of the portrait."

Lacie stood. "Good. Raven and Braxton are going to have dinner, so I'll take this and leave them to it. If the portrait draws any nibbles, I'll let you know." Portrait in hand, she flashed Raven a wink and exited.

Renay said, "You two enjoy your dinner. Aunt Hazel, the rest of us will be waiting downstairs."

As the cousins trooped out, they gave Raven knowing smiles, and she wanted to stake each and every one of them to an anthill for finding her dealings with Steele so amusing.

Her mother said, "Having dinner together is a good idea. Braxton, your father said you two came straight here from the train and haven't had a chance to search out a boardinghouse. We've plenty of extra room, so I've invited him to stay here. He's agreed, so of course you're welcome here as well."

"Thank you. I'll accept your kind offer."

She then spoke to Raven. "Vana has a pot of gumbo going. You two are welcome to use the verandah here for your meal if you like. I'll send someone up with the food and make sure you aren't disturbed."

Having no other choice, Raven offered her thanks.

Hazel departed, and Raven and Brax were alone. He asked, "What's gumbo?"

"A kind of soup. Everyone in Louisiana enjoys it."

"Then I'll look forward to tasting it. Can you show me where I can wash my hands?"

She nodded tightly. "This way."

Chapter Four

Her aunt Eden arrived with the food a short while later. Along with bowls and tableware, she'd included a still warm baguette, and a pitcher of water and glasses. After her exit, Raven ladled the steaming gumbo into a bowl and topped it with a helping of rice.

Watching her, Brax asked, "You don't eat the rice separately?"

"I suppose you could, but this is the traditional way."

"Okay." Mimicking her actions, he filled his bowl with both gumbo and rice, and followed her outdoors. There was a small wrought-iron table at the far end of the verandah, shaded by the branches of a large tree. She walked back inside to get the water and glasses. When she returned he was standing by her chair.

"A gentleman always assists a lady with her seating," he explained.

Rather than argue, she allowed it. As she sat,

the feel of his presence behind her gave way to a rising awareness she was determined to ignore. No man had the right to affect her this way after meeting him only hours ago.

Once he took his seat, she closed her eyes for a moment to say grace. When she opened them, his were on hers. His expression was hard to discern. "What?"

"Nothing," he said. "I don't want to be accused of being judgmental again."

"Say what you were going to say." No man had the right to be so exasperating, either.

"Just noting that you say grace and yet you steal from people."

"Sinners are supposed to pray. Pass me the baguette, please."

He complied.

Annoyed, she broke off a section of the bread and placed it on the charger beneath her bowl before dipping her spoon into the savory goodness that was gumbo. As she took her first taste, she noted his tentative movements, but she kept her comments to herself and waited for his reaction to the food.

It didn't take long. "This is very good."

"Aunt Vana's one of the best cooks in the city."

"It's spicier than it looks though. Especially this sausage. Is that what this meat is?"

"It's andouille. The Germans make it. I suppose in other places it would be called sausage but here, it's simply andouille."

They ate silently. He poured himself water from the pitcher. "Would you like some?"

"Yes, please." Once her glass was filled she said, "Thank you."

"You're welcome."

Their attention lingered on each other. Raven broke the contact. "So, what kind of food do you eat in Boston?"

"Nothing like this."

To her surprise, she enjoyed the easy smile he showed. It softened the harsh set planes of his face beneath the black close-cropped beard and eased a bit of the tension. He was definitely a feast for the female eye. Not that she cared.

He continued, "Back home, we eat hens, beef, root vegetables. Lots of beans and fish, and lots of soups to get us through the cold months."

"Sounds a bit boring."

"Compared to this, very much so."

"Glad you like it."

"I do."

They were staring at each other again. Raven swore she wasn't attracted to this man, nor did she want to be, yet something unexplainable was taking root in spite of that and infusing her with a different type of annoyance.

"Tell me about your family, if that's not too much to ask," he said.

"What do you wish to know?"

"Are you related to all those people I saw downstairs?"

"Yes. My grandmother Fanny had nine children. Six boys and three girls. Most of the people you saw are my cousins."

"So how are the people who were up here with us related?"

"Lacie and Renay are brother and sister. Aunt Eden is their mother. Aunt Vana is the mother of Emile and Alma. Beth is the daughter of one of my uncles."

"Do you have siblings?"

"A younger sister. Avery. She and her husband and their two daughters are living in California." And Raven missed them every moment of the day. "They moved there two years ago. What about you? Any siblings?"

"No. I'm an only child and my mother was an only child. My grandfather had family he left behind in England. I was very young the last time they visited, and with him and my grandmother and mother all deceased, I've no idea how to get in touch with them. My father had family, but they were all sold away during slavery, and he's never been able to locate them."

"That has to be difficult for him. So many people are still looking for family members." She felt lucky in the sense that the Moreaux knew the whereabouts of most of their living relatives and the burial places of the ones who'd passed on. "What's it like being an only child? I couldn't imagine growing up without a house full of cousins to play with, fish with, or fight over silly things with."

"It's much quieter."

She chuckled. "Moreaux and the word *quiet* are never spoken in the same sentence. Were you lonely growing up?"

For a moment he didn't respond, and she thought she saw sadness touch his eyes before it quickly vanished. "I suppose I was when looking at it from your point of view, but I had my books, my parents, grandparents, and a small group of friends, plus I had the pleasure of sailing all over the world."

"What do you mean?"

"My grandfather owned a small fleet of merchant ships and fishing boats. I made my first voyage as his cabin boy at the age of eight. I've visited a good portion of the world."

"Really?"

He nodded.

"So me calling you wealthy earlier was correct?"

He stilled and assessed her as if trying to decide how to respond.

"Sorry. That was a rude question even for me. I'm just trying to figure out who you are up there on your high horse."

Another small smile curved his lips. "Understood. I suppose my family would be considered that. My parents and grandparents owned nice homes. I grew up with tutors, servants, and have never gone without. My mother didn't have to work so she spent most of her days helping those in need, but we never flaunted our status. She called it quiet wealth."

"I've never heard that phrase before. How old were you when she passed away?"

"Fifteen."

"My condolences."

"Thank you. What about your father?"

"He died of yellow fever when I was four and Avery was two. He and my mother never married though." Yet another sin for him to judge her by, she supposed. "He was a Haitian seaman." None of the Moreaux sisters had had permanent men in their lives. However, each had known love and been fiercely loved in return. "My mother's never mentioned your father."

"I knew nothing about their past, either, until Detective Welch showed up. Apparently he loved your mother very much."

Raven was still wondering about their relationship, and hoped she'd have the chance to discuss it with her mother soon.

"Have you ever been in love?" he asked.

The question was unexpected, but she supposed it was a natural one considering the track of their conversation. In response, she thought back on her relationship with Tobias Kenny and its disastrous ending. "I thought I was, but it turned out badly, so . . ." Her words trailed off as if no others were needed. "How about you?"

He shook his head. "No, but I do plan to marry."

"It won't be with me," she said, toasting the statement with the glass of water in her hand. "Regardless of Dorrie's prediction."

He toasted her in response. "I agree."

They were again focused on each other, and she wasn't sure if learning more about him had aided or undermined her desire to keep him at arm's length. "Are you pursuing a love match?"

"No. I believe as long as the two people involved are evenly yoked, share similar values and outlooks on life, love isn't a requirement."

"I see. Well, you don't have to worry about me being a candidate. We aren't equally yoked at all. You have wealth. I cook and clean for others because I have none. You have strict boundaries on how life should be led, I don't."

"True, but if swindling is your way of life, why are you doing domestic work?"

"You haven't earned the right to know the answer to that question." And probably wouldn't in the short time they'd be together. The details of what had come to be called Fanny's Plan were for family only.

"I apologize for sticking my nose in places it doesn't belong."

She inclined her head in acceptance of the apology but felt no need to offer him one in return. What the family did with their money was none of his business.

They returned to their food.

After a few moments of silent eating, he wiped his mouth on his napkin and asked, "Is there a recipe for gumbo?"

"I suppose, but each person makes it their own way. Why?"

"I'd like to take it back to Boston so I can enjoy it as often as I like."

"You cook?"

"No. I employ one though."

"You have a cook."

He chuckled at the wonder she supposed her face was showing. "Yes, I do. Her name is Kate. I inherited her when I inherited my grandparents' home."

Other than the moneyed Black Creoles of New Orleans, Raven rarely came in contact with wealthy members of the race. "The gumbo won't taste the same without andouille."

"There's a German community with butchers back home. I'll see if they have any."

"And if not?"

He shrugged his impeccably suited shoulders. "I'll have it shipped north. As my grandfather often said: Anything can be had if you have enough coin."

"And I take it you have enough?"

"Honestly? I do. When my grandparents died, they left me everything—the house, the ships, the servants."

She noted how comfortable he seemed with his status. His manner lacked the braggadocio and arrogance often associated with the rich, even if he did sit on a high horse. "The unmarried young ladies and their mamas must be lined up at your door every morning."

"Most mornings, yes."

"Have you settled on the prizewinner?"

"Unofficially, I believe so. Her name is Charlotte Franklin. Lottie for short. Educated, pretty, impeccable manners, and a good conversationalist. Our mothers were good friends."

"But you don't love her?"

He shook his head. "She'll make a good wife though, and she wants to have children, which is fine with me as well."

"Sounds like a union made in heaven with a paragon of virtue."

"Your sarcasm is showing."

"My apologies." His amusement showed he wasn't perpetually pompous, and that also softened the air between them. Somewhat. She asked herself what it might be like to be with a man who owned ships, who had servants and seemingly ample wealth. Many women would be envious of the impeccable Lottie Franklin. In a way, Raven counted herself as one, if only because his wife wouldn't be bone-weary day in and day out from hiring herself out to wash clothes and mop floors. "So, you and your prized Lottie are evenly yoked."

"As much as is needed, yes."

"Then hopefully we can get this Pinkerton job done quickly and you can return home."

"That's my hope, too."

His eyes had turned serious, so she guessed there might be more he wished to say or ask. "Is there something else?"

"Yes. How can I get you to meet me halfway on this adventure, so we can get it done?"

"I think we've pretty much accomplished that by being out here. No?" she said.

"It has helped, but I'm not going to be as useless as you believe I'll be."

"Saints, I hope not."

He dropped his head, but not before she saw his amusement. When he raised his gaze to hers, he asked, "Are you always so sarcastic and direct?"

"People won't know where you stand if you take the long way around. I prefer to get to the heart of the matter. It saves time and there's less confusion."

He peered at her over his steepled fingers. "If I rein in my judgmental ways, will you do the same with your doubts about my ability to help?"

"To get you back to Boston as swiftly as possible, I will put a damper on whatever is necessary."

"You want me out of your hair."

"Just as quickly as you want me out of yours.

On that we are evenly yoked." Finished with her meal, she set aside her empty bowl.

As he did the same, he said, "The women back home rarely speak so boldly."

"That's unfortunate. Their mothers should raise them better. Bland food. Meek women. Sounds fairly boring where you're from, Steele. Hopefully, the men are good in bed, at least."

"Find us a bed and I'll give you dessert."

Her heart stopped.

Eyes blazing intensely, he added, "I can't speak for other men, but you'll remember my pleasuring you for the rest of your life."

And as she stared agape, he pushed back his chair and rose smoothly to his feet. "Thank you for dinner, Miss Moreau. I'll await your invitation for dessert."

Gathering his dishes, he walked away, re-entered the house, and left her sitting there, stunned and with lust pulsing between her thighs.

Dear Lord!

Chapter Five

*B*rax made his way back downstairs. The crowd of family had thinned somewhat, but there were still loud conversations and laughter. Searching for a familiar face, he found the aunts Eden and Havana in the kitchen. "I can wash up my dishes if you show me where."

"Just set them on the counter there," Eden told him. "I'll add them to the rest."

"Are you sure? You fed me; the least I can do is clean up after myself."

"I'm sure."

"Did you enjoy the gumbo?" Vana asked.

"I did. Thank you very much. I'd like the recipe to take home if there is one."

"There's no formal recipe but I'll write down how I make it."

"That would be appreciated." He placed the dishes where she wanted them, then asked after the whereabouts of his father.

"He and Hazel are having dinner out back," she informed him.

"I don't want to intrude on them while they're eating, but do you know which room we've been given for the night?"

Eden, slicing a large pound cake and placing the pieces on small plates, said, "Yes. Give me a second and I'll show you. Are you and Raven doing better?"

"I think so." He smiled inwardly and wondered if Raven had picked her sassy little self up off the floor of the verandah yet.

When the cake slicing was done, he thanked Havana again for the gumbo and followed Eden to a large bedroom at the back of the house. Inside its aging green plaster walls were two beds, an old upholstered chair, and a large, dark wood armoire that gleamed from loving care. He spotted his carpetbag and his father's travel items on the floor beside it. "Has the family always lived in this house?"

"Yes. My mother won the deed for it in a card game back when my siblings and I were small. We all grew up here, as did our children. This was once my brother Abram's room."

"Does he still live in New Orleans?"

"No. He moved to Cuba about a decade ago. A branch of the family is there."

"I see." But he didn't really. *Cuba? How many more Moreaux were there?*

"There's a washroom through that door there,

and clean towels and extra bed linens in the wardrobe. There will be breakfast in the morning, so come to the table when you're ready."

"How much should I pay for taking such good care of us?"

She shook her head. "You're our guest. Once you and Raven marry though, things will be different."

He gave her an eye roll.

"Scoff if you want, but don't say you weren't warned. Is there anything I can get for you before I leave?"

"No, ma'am. You've been truly kind."

"Okay. If I don't see you again this evening, sleep well."

"You, too. Thank you."

She departed, and Brax glanced around again. It was a simple room, lacking the carpets, nightstands, and other appointments of his bedroom back home, but it was clean, the beds appeared comfortable, and after the long day, he was looking forward to a good long night of uninterrupted sleep. He spent a few minutes unpacking what he needed for the evening and hung a clean set of clothes for the next day in the armoire. Once that was accomplished, he stepped out onto the covered, screened-in porch attached to the room and savored the descending dusk and the much cooler evening air. A battered settee and a wooden bench offered seating. He chose the settee and in the silence exhaled. *What a day!* From their arrival, to the multitudes of Moreaux, to a little girl everyone believed predicted the future, to dinner with the sassy and prickly Raven. He chuckled inwardly remembering the shock on her face when he left her on the verandah. Tossing out the dessert challenge hadn't been intentional, but more of a response to her cocky dismissiveness. He assumed by the aspersions she'd cast on the carnal abilities of Boston's men, she was no novice, making him want to learn firsthand if she was as spirited and uninhibited with a lover as she was in life, but wanting and actually doing were two different things. A dalliance with her was illogical at best, considering what they'd been paired to do, and their clashing personalities, no matter Dorrie's prediction, was another matter. He wasn't Raven's type and she certainly wasn't his. She'd say he was back to being judgmental, and she'd be correct because it was impossible not to be.

He thought back on her response to him questioning why she was a hired domestic. *You haven't earned the right to know the answer to that question.* Were the family's ill-gotten gains tied to some sort of secret? Could they be funneling the profits elsewhere because they weren't the ones controlling the strings, and were only being paid a small cut for their participation? He had many questions and no way of knowing if they'd ever be answered.

Hearing footsteps in the room, he stood just as his father appeared. "Ah, there you are. How was your dinner with Raven?"

"Interesting. How are you?"

His father sat on the bench. "Fingers a bit sore from all the sketching, but other than that I've no complaints. I didn't realize how much I've missed New Orleans though. Been away far too long."

"What have you missed?"

"The food, the atmosphere, the way the people move through life. There's a joy here you don't find in other places."

"Had my first taste of gumbo earlier, and I have to agree with you about the food. There's certainly nothing like it in Massachusetts."

His father nodded and smiled. "You and Hazel's daughter getting along better?"

He shrugged. "I suppose you can call it that. We've agreed to set aside our differences to get the job done, but she's quite a handful."

"So was her mother. Still is."

"Have you two reconciled?"

"No. Not sure we will, but she's worth the chase."

"A chase that ends where?"

"I'm hoping she'll allow me back into her life."

Brax wasn't surprised by that. He'd seen the light in his father's eyes when the two were together. "And if she does?"

"Then I'd move here, more than likely. There's no way she'd consider leaving New Orleans, especially not for Boston, of all places."

"You'd abandon your son for a pretty face?"

"The second she agrees."

They laughed. Brax didn't begrudge his father's pursuit. His parents' marriage had been arranged but they'd gotten along well, and he knew his da had been lonely since his mother's death. As his son, Brax of course had concerns about the Moreaux, but his father didn't need or want advice, so he remained silent on that, and hoped the quest for a second chance at happiness would be successful. "I have a question about something that's been bothering me."

"What is it?"

"Why is Raven working as a domestic if the family is so good at what they do? No one here looks like they're living lavishly."

"The money isn't spent on luxuries."

"What's it spent on?"

"Lifting the family out of poverty."

That was confusing. "Explain that."

"It's something they call Fanny's Plan. Fanny was Hazel's mother. Her plan was to use whatever methods she could to give the younger generation the means to start businesses and schooling, which in turn would guarantee they and their children would never face the challenges Fanny and her children faced growing up. And she didn't care if she had to beg, borrow, or steal to accomplish that. Hazel marrying into the family of that rich Creole had been part of that plan. All the money made off the swindling, the gambling, and the other enterprises are ensuring the young have a future."

"Welch accused the family of masquerading as priests and royalty and other things. That has to take skill. Did Fanny teach them, and if so, who'd she learn from? Or was she clever enough to learn the skills on her own?"

"According to Hazel, Fanny was owned by a family of actors and musicians who traveled all over the South. They played at fairs, revivals, theaters, but the shows were a cover for the cons and swindles they pulled off in the places where they performed. Fanny grew up helping maintain the costumes, mixing and applying the face paints, and anything else that needed doing. She was taught to read and play the piano—also had a nice singing voice so they sometimes gave her small roles. Hazel said they called Fanny the Singing Pickaninny. At some point they freed her, and she took all she'd learned, and her two oldest boys fathered by one of the owner's sons, and started a family troupe of her own. When the boys grew older, she used the connections she'd made through her owners to have them apprentice with some of the best counterfeiters, forgers, and con men around. They in turn passed that knowledge to their siblings and then down to their children."

Braxton was impressed. Life had to have been incredibly difficult for her and her children. In truth, things hadn't changed very much. The percentage of the race possessing enough wealth and prestige to deem themselves comfortable was small. In some parts of the country, the numbers were rising but certainly not with anything akin to speed.

His father continued. "You have to tip your hat to Miss Fanny for setting her mind on success in the face of the bigotry, barriers, and injustice the race has to fight just to breathe sometimes."

"And you derailed her plan for Hazel by your actions on Hazel's wedding day."

"Yes."

"Did you know about the plan back then?"

"I did, but my love for her and hers for me mattered more in my mind."

"But not in Hazel's mind?"

"No. She was willing to marry anyone to give her children a future and I understood her decision, I just didn't agree. I'd grown up enslaved, barefoot, and hungry. For many years, running away only changed the enslaved parts of my life. However, I was convinced that given the chance, I'd be able to provide for her, but the Creole had what she needed at the time—wealth, a good name, a home, access to education for her future children."

"No wonder her menfolk ran you out of town."

"I was just grateful they let me leave with my life. The Moreau family was furious with me, especially her mother." He added, "Hazel wasn't supposed to tell me about the plan, so don't let on that I told you."

Brax nodded and mulled over his father's story. It provided some answers to his questions, but there was still more to unravel. How long would the plan continue? Were Raven and the cousins being forced to participate, or were they willingly contributing? "The family is talking about taking revenge on the Pinkerton. Do you agree with them?"

"As a churchgoing man, no. But as a formerly enslaved Black man whose freedom may be taken away by Welch's lying, I hope they send her to hell."

Brax understood his father's stance and admitted he agreed. "And for her to send us into South Carolina, of all places. Is she aware of what's happening there?"

"Why should she care?" his father asked. "It's not as if the supremacists are killing her kind."

Dusk had given way to night, and the moon and stars were out.

His father stood. "It's late and been an awfully long day. I'm going to bed."

Brax understood. "Good night, Da. I'll be in shortly."

His father went inside and Brax sat in the darkness thinking about all he'd heard, and about Raven Moreau. He thought he better understood the source of her challenging personality. She and her family hadn't been handed the soft, uneventful life his family had provided him. There'd been no servants, balls, or tutors, just a day-to-day struggle to carve out a place in a world designed to ensure they failed. Yet Miss Fanny had waded into the mire and brought into being a plan that circumvented that design. Although he and Raven were unevenly yoked and probably would never see each other again after this was all over, his fascination with her continued to grow.

UPSTAIRS IN HAZEL'S bedroom, Raven sat in one of the chairs while her mother sat on the bench of her mirrored vanity table and prepared her hair for sleeping. As she brushed and braided the oiled strands, the sight brought back to Raven memories of her and her sister, Avery, watching their mother going through the same ritual when they were small. Her mother had been younger back then, and in Raven's eyes the most beautiful woman in the world. She remembered how they'd used the time together to talk about their day, share laughter and family gossip. There'd been life lessons, too, and her mother's dreams for their future. In those days, Raven had no idea that future would include Welch or the Steele men. She wanted to ask about her mother's relationship with Harrison Steele, but didn't want to be chastised for sticking her nose in her mother's business, so she waited for a way to start the conversation.

"So did all the extra drawings of Detective Welch go out?" Raven asked.

"Yes. Hopefully, it won't take long for one of them to bear fruit. I sent one along to my web as well."

Her web, formed before and after the war, consisted of women from all walks of life who'd met each other via churches, hairdressers, and other places women gathered, such as business associations and the various markets in the city. They secretly passed vital information, both political and personal, impacting the well-being of the communities of color. Some were prominent women, while others operated in New Orleans's shadowy underworld. "Do you think that copy of the Declaration would be worth something if we could duplicate it and arrange a sale?"

"I'm not sure, but it is something I'm wondering about also. We do know a couple of excellent forgers. I'm not sure how long making a copy of it might take though, or how long we'd have to turn the original over to Welch. Let's wait until we see how this unfolds first. So, how did the dinner go with Braxton?"

"Let's call it interesting." It would be some time before she got over the dessert comment, and the lust she'd been left with. Thinking back on the moment made the heat rise all over again. "He's quite different from the men I know. He has servants and owns ships."

Her mother eyed her in the mirror. "Harrison said his wife had wealthy parents."

"And they left everything to his son."

"I suppose you want to know about me and Harrison?"

Her mother had always been able to read the minds of her children. "I do, but I didn't want to get smacked for being nosy."

That earned her a smile. "Okay, this is what happened." And she told Raven the story.

When she finished, Raven asked, "How angry were you?"

"Angry enough to want him tossed into the Mississippi with boulders tied to his ankles. He messed up everything. I don't ever remember Mama being so upset." She paused for a moment, as if thinking back. "I did love him though. So much. But love won't pay the grocer, or help establish a business, or put a family member who's passing through Harvard Medical School."

Raven agreed. Fanny's Plan had provided so much for Moreaux on both sides of the color divide, and the sacrifices had been many. Her mother and Harrison were just one example.

And Lacie and Renay's youngest sibling, Antoine, was another example. Fair enough to pass as White, he was currently a student at Harvard Medical School, and on a path to success that would probably have him marrying outside the race in order to keep the ruse going. In doing so, he might never be able to interact publicly with his family again. His mother, Eden, while bereft at the idea of possibly losing her son, had come to grips with that reality, and as Antoine pointed out through his tears on the morning he left New Orleans for Cambridge last year, no matter whom he married, his children and their children would always carry the Moreau blood in their veins.

"And now?" Raven asked. "How do you feel about him?"

"At first, seeing him after all these years made me angry all over again, but obviously things happen the way they were supposed to. Had I married that day, I wouldn't have met the man responsible for the most precious gifts life's ever given me—you and Avery."

That filled Raven's heart.

Her mother finished her hair and tied it up in the dark blue bandana. She turned on the bench and faced Raven. "Deep down inside, I still love Harrison. Probably always have and always will. I apparently never get over the men I've truly loved."

"Does that apply to my father, too?"

"Yes. I was beside myself when he died. I will always, always miss Josiah and the love we had." She quieted for a moment before continuing. "In truth, I should be apologizing to Harrison for breaking his heart. I wanted us to be together so much, but he was as poor as the family was back then. Mama said she understood how I felt about him, but she couldn't give me her blessings because he couldn't lift my future."

Raven could imagine how sad her mother must have been.

"Harrison didn't care about Mama's plan though, and stood up in that church and exposed me, and honestly, deep down inside, beneath my anger, I loved him all the more. After word got around about the wedding debacle, there wasn't a Creole family from here to Haiti that didn't know my true identity, so there was no way I could pass myself off as someone else. In the end, I wound up still poor anyway, so I may as well have defied Mama and chosen Harrison instead."

And in the years before the plan began paying off, Raven remembered just how poor they'd been. Even though her aunts and uncles were doing whatever they had to do to lift their circumstances, Raven left school at age nine, over her mother's objections, to begin doing laundry to help put food on the table. Dorrie's generation would never know the hunger and poverty Raven, Avery, and their cousins Renay and Lacie endured growing up, and in Raven's mind, the sacrifices they'd all made during those lean years had been well worth it to spare them such misery.

Hazel said, "And now because Mama's plan did work, we can retire the games if we want."

Surprised, Raven stared.

"There's been enough money invested both legitimately and otherwise for us to slow down and savor the fact that there are now young Moreaux sprinkled in places north, south, east, and west. And that most are thriving, whether they've opened a small cigar company, in medical school, wearing the robes of a judge, or driving their own hack. I'm sure Mama's up in heaven very pleased."

Raven knew things were going well economically when there'd been enough funds to send Antoine to Harvard, but she'd no idea just how well. "Do the rest of the cousins know?"

She nodded. "I told my sisters to let them know, so I'm assuming they've been told by now."

"So what do you plan to do now?" she asked her mother.

"Rest. Maybe put Harrison out of his misery and agree to spend these last good years with him so we can enjoy loving each other the way we wanted to when we were young. Or watch you find your place in life. You've given the family your entire being," her mother said softly.

Emotion filled Raven's throat.

"When Mama was on her deathbed, she said she'd put money away for you and Avery, Renay, Emile, and the cousins your age, so you'd be able to build your lives once the games were done. I had our banker check, and the account's grown substantially since the war, especially the investments my brothers put into silver. Your portion won't be enough for you to spend your days shopping, sipping *café*, and eating beignets, but it will allow you to find a small place of your own, and not have to hire yourself out for the rest of your life."

Tears stung Raven's eyes. This was so unexpected, she didn't know what to do or to say.

"So, once we get this last thing done for the Pinkerton, I turn over the funds and you can decide what you want to do with them." Her mother added, "And maybe find a man who'll stand up for you the way Harrison stood for me. If that's what you want."

"Tobias left me gun-shy."

"I know. He was a snake. It would be something if Dorrie's prediction came true and you ended up as Braxton's wife."

"It isn't going to happen, and please don't say Dorrie's never wrong. If I had a dime for every time I heard that today, I could spend the rest of my life shopping and sipping *café*."

"Okay. He is handsome though."

"So are lemons until you bite into one."

Her mother laughed.

Raven stood. "Thank you, Mama."

"You've earned the right to have your own life, so think about who you wish to be. It's never too late."

Raven wiped away her tears and held the green eyes of the woman who'd always wanted more for her daughters, and whom her daughters had always wanted more for, just as much. There were tears in her eyes, too. Walking over, Raven let herself be enfolded by the arms that had held her this way for as long as she could remember. As the hug tightened, Raven placed a kiss against her soft cheek. "I love you so much. Sleep well."

"You, too, love. I'll see you in the morning."

BUOYED BY HER mother's love and the surprising news about the plan, Raven left her mother and went across the hall to the bedroom she shared with Dorrie whenever Raven spent the night away from her employer. She tiptoed in so as not to disturb the little girl's sleep, only to find Dorrie awake and drawing on white butcher paper by the light of the turned down lamp beside her bed.

"What are you doing awake, Dorrie?"

"I have a question."

Raven crossed the short distance to the bed. Although Dorrie loved to draw, she wasn't very good and it was always difficult to figure out just what the picture was supposed to be. Raven sat down on the mattress edge. "Is that a horse?"

Dorrie shook her head. Her hair was tied up in a red bandana and her sleeveless green nightgown was faded from many washings. "It's a dog."

"Oh, I see that now."

"Cousin Vanita just got a puppy so I drew her a picture of it."

"I see." Raven wondered if the question Dorrie intended to ask was tied to getting a pup, too. Hazel was allergic to dogs, so Raven and Avery had never been allowed one.

Dorrie continued drawing, adding what Raven supposed passed as fur on the horse-looking dog. "Ask me your question and then we both need to get to sleep, sweetie."

Dorrie paused and said, "Do you think I can ask Mr. Brax about something the next time I see him?"

Raven assessed her silently. "Is it about the wedding?"

"No, something in my dream that I don't understand. He was in the dream with me."

"I see," Raven replied, even though she didn't. "Then I suppose it will be okay."

Dorrie gave her a smile. "And you shouldn't worry. They aren't going to find her."

"Find who?"

"The lady on the boat."

She remembered Dorrie mentioning a boat to Welch. Was this prediction tied to that? "Who's looking for her?"

"A man sitting behind a very tall table and another man standing next to a short one."

"Standing next to a short man?"

"No. A short table."

Raven had no idea what this meant. That she and the missing Welch were somehow involved piqued her curiosity. Aunt Vana believed that when Dorrie came back to life after the stillbirth, she'd returned as an oracle from the pantheon of Haitian and African deities. After living with the exceptional child for the past eight years, Raven was inclined to believe anything, except that she and Steele were to marry. His handsome face slowly rose in her mind and she mentally pushed it away. "You should put your pup away for now. Time for sleep."

Dorrie nodded her understanding and set the drawing and pencil on the nightstand. Raven stood, tucked her in, and gave her a soft kiss on her cheek. "Sweet dreams, my love."

"You, too, Cousin Raven."

Raven lowered the lamp to just a whisper, and while Dorrie snuggled under the thin sheet, she changed into her nightgown. Once that was accomplished, she doused the light completely and climbed into the small bed next to Dorrie's.

It didn't take long for Dorrie's soft snoring

to be heard, and as Raven lay in the dark, she thought back on her mother's revelation about the plan. Now that it was done, her life could become her own, but what did that mean? All of her skills were tied to the game, or her work as a domestic, so she had no idea if she possessed others. Knowing that sometime in the near future the only house she might have to clean would be the one she owned, pleased her. First though, the Pinkerton matter had to be taken care of, which shifted her thoughts to her pretend husband. He'd certainly surprised her at dinner with his sensual boasting. Just thinking about it left her breathless all over again. There was apparently much more to him than judging people and owning ships, and she'd found their talk at the table more enjoyable than she'd imagined she would. She also hadn't imagined wanting to learn if he was skilled in bed as he'd claimed. Unsure what that meant about herself and her future dealings with him, she decided not to think about it and drifted into sleep.

RUTH WELCH SET her carpetbag on the floor beside the bed of her rented room and dropped down tiredly into the lone chair. She was not as young as she once was, and the long train travel from Boston to New Orleans had taken its toll. She was pleased the operation was under way, however. In a few weeks' time, she'd hopefully be in a position to turn the stolen Declaration of Independence over to her superiors, hand the Moreau clan over to the local police, and receive the accolades and promotion she deserved. The Pinkerton Agency didn't employ many lady detectives, but all were measured against the great Kate Warne, the company's first. Warne's guarding of Abraham Lincoln was the stuff of legend. Ruth was determined to be legendary as well and had been chasing that goal since the war's end. Only one of her cases had caused enough of a stir to get her noticed by her supervisors, and ironically enough it had occurred in New Orleans, six years ago. The case involved a gang of supremacists and a hunt for their death books listing names of prominent Colored officials and political leaders targeted for assassination. In order to break the case, she'd had to betray one of Harriet Tubman's best operatives, a regrettable yet necessary decision. The operative, Zahra Layette, had married into one of New Orleans' most influential families of color, the LeVeqs. Were they to learn the woman they'd known then as Wilma Gray had returned, they might seek revenge. To keep her presence unknown, Welch planned to stick to the shadows. It was the reason she'd chosen a boardinghouse on the city's outskirts. The location reduced the chances of her being seen and unmasked, or having her whereabouts ferreted out by the Moreaux, who were undoubtedly interested in her comings and goings.

But for the moment, she just wanted to forget about everything and sleep. Changing into her nightclothes, she took a moment to secure the deadbolt on the door and poured herself a small portion of her favorite brandy to help her sleep. With that done, she doused the lamp, made herself comfortable against the bed's clean sheets, and closed her eyes.

Chapter Six

*A*n hour or so before dawn, Raven was gently shaken awake by her mother's hand. "Wake up, love. We know where Welch is staying."

Struggling to make sense of the words, Raven sat up in the dark and dragged her hands over her bleary eyes. "Where is she?"

Her mother answered, and added, "I want Miss Ezra to take her breakfast. Vana is cooking it now."

Still half asleep, Raven nodded. "Okay. I'll get her ready."

"Mr. Winslow will drive."

After her mother's departure, Raven left the bed to wash up and get Miss Ezra ready.

GRAY-HAIRED MR. WINSLOW stopped his wagon in front of the boardinghouse on the outskirts of the city, and set the brake. In the early morning silence punctuated by distant birdcalls, he climbed down to help his passenger. Miss Ezra was an old woman, dressed in a well-worn skirt and blouse and with an old green tignon covering her gray hair. Due to her age and the pains in her legs, her descent was difficult, so he let her take her time. Welch's breakfast of grits, ham, biscuits, and cooked sweetened peaches was on a covered tin plate kept warm by the heat of a small brazier in the wagon's bed. He wrapped the plate in hand towels to keep Miss Ezra from burning herself and passed it her way.

"I'll be back directly," she assured him.

He nodded and watched her slowly make her way to the door.

A middle-aged White woman with dyed red hair answered the bell, and upon seeing Miss Ezra, smiled kindly. "Good morning, Auntie. May I help you?"

"I brought breakfast for the Yankee woman that rented the room from you yesterday."

Confusion came over the landlady's face.

Miss Ezra explained, "The lady had supper at my daughter's shop yesterday and asked if we could bring her breakfast. Said she wasn't sure if you served meals or not."

"Ah. Come on in."

Miss Ezra stepped into the aging parlor. "Did she have breakfast already? Don't like to waste food."

"No, she hasn't. She's in the second room on

the left. I don't know if she's awake yet. You go on and knock. I need to check on something in the kitchen."

"Thank you kindly."

The landlady hurried away and Miss Ezra knocked on the designated door. It was answered promptly and opened. "Yes?" Welch snapped impatiently.

"Your breakfast, ma'am."

Welch took the plate without a word and closed the door in the old woman's face.

"You're welcome," Miss Ezra snarled under her breath in response to the bad manners, and trudged back out to the wagon.

Once she was aboard, Mr. Winslow drove them away. When he was certain they were far enough from the house not to be seen, he removed his gray wig. "Damned thing is hot."

Raven, taking off her shoes to remove the pebbles that hobbled the way she walked, said to Renay from beneath Miss Ezra's stage paint, "Rude woman didn't even say thank you. Hope she enjoys spending all day in the privy."

He looked over. "Chapter one in the book called *Never Poke the Moreaux*."

Raven smiled, wiggled her bare toes, and settled in for the ride home.

RENAY DROPPED RAVEN off at the front of her mother's house and drove back to his apartment in the Quarter. Carrying her shoes, Raven went inside. Her mother and the Steeles were seated at the dining table having breakfast.

"It went well?" her mother asked.

Raven nodded. "Yes."

Harrison Steele's eyes went wide. "Raven?" His son's face showed the same surprise.

She smiled. "Morning."

"My goodness. I didn't know that was you."

"Meet Miss Ezra," she said, moving her attention to his son and wondering what he was thinking. Like his father, he was staring mouth agape.

"I saved you some breakfast. Sit and eat," her mother invited.

"Let me remove this paint first and I'll be right back."

"I'll come with you, I need to speak with you a minute." Hazel rose to her feet. "Excuse me, gentlemen. I'll be right back."

Still holding her shoes, Raven unconsciously sought Brax's gaze again before she exited with her mother.

In her bedroom, Raven asked her mother, "What did you want to speak to me about?"

"A note I received this morning after you left. I need to read it to you."

Embarrassment crept over Raven. She'd quit school at the age of nine and was not a proficient reader. As a consequence, she avoided the written word whenever possible. Her mother knew her child and said, "You know you can go back to school."

Raven sighed. They'd had this conversation more than a few times. "I'm too old to be in a schoolroom with little children reading out of a primer. Please, just read what you wanted to share with me."

Hazel's lips thinned but she didn't push.

Raven took a seat at the vanity to remove the face paint, and Hazel read:

Dear H,

The woman in the portrait bears a strong resemblance to a person my family knew six years ago as Wilma Gray. If this is indeed she, do not trust her. Ever! HT has severed ties with her as have all other agents in my circle. Should the opportunity arise, I would very much like to speak with Gray as I owe her for nearly causing the death of one of my beloved daughters-in-law.

If my House can be of any assistance in your dealings with this Judas, please let me know.

Sincerely yours,
J. LV-V

Raven stopped and met her mother's eyes in the mirror. She knew the name behind the initials. They belonged to Julianna LeVeq-Vincent, who in her own quiet way was one of the most influential and wealthiest women of color in the city. Her sons and their wives were also highly regarded for their political and charitable efforts on behalf of the race. Raven had no idea her mother knew the famous family but supposed she shouldn't be surprised. Hazel Moreau was equally as influential.

"So, if Welch is really this Wilma Gray, my gut feeling about not trusting her was correct." Raven thought this revelation to be quite the turn of events.

"Yes, so we need to be even more wary. I've no idea what the detective did to draw the ire of the LeVeqs but it must have been serious. So once this mission is over, we'll do our best to put Welch within reach of Miss Julianna's revenge."

"I wholeheartedly agree." Pleased with the plan, Raven went back to removing the paint.

Her mother said quietly, "I know I'm beating a dead horse, but think about school, love. There are evening classes for adults. Or better yet, let me help you with your reading."

"I'll think about it."

Hazel shook her head and smiled. "You know it's a sin to lie to your mama."

"But I love you. Does that count?"

Hazel squeezed Raven's shoulder affectionately. "I love you, too. I'll see you back at the table."

After removing the last vestiges of Miss Ezra from her face, Raven joined the others in the dining room. Feeling Steele's eyes on her, she helped herself to the food and tried to deny being affected by his presence. She added a bit of butter to her grits and seasoned them with salt and pepper. Then she took two biscuits from the clay warmer, added them to her plate along with a slice of ham, and began to eat.

Harrison asked Hazel, "Do you think the Pinkerton will come today and let us know when she's ready to leave for Charleston?"

Raven shared a look with her mother. Keeping her face free of reaction, Raven drank a swallow of water and let her mother reply to his question.

"I doubt we'll see Welch today," she told him. "The detective's probably not feeling well."

Raven glanced up to find Brax watching her. She knew he might be many things, but a mind reader he was not, so she wasn't worried about him figuring out what her mother meant. She took a small bite out of a biscuit.

Harrison cocked his head. "You've spoken with her?"

"No."

"Then how can you be sure?"

"Let's call it women's intuition."

He studied her and then Raven before asking, "Why do I get the feeling that there's something here you aren't telling me?"

"Because there is." She directed her attention Brax's way. "Braxton, do you have any less tailored or older clothing with you?"

"What do you mean?"

"If you're going to be playing the part of a houseman, you should dress like one, not like the house's owner."

He nodded and gave her a smile. "I understand, but no, I don't."

"I'll have Raven take you to a shop where you can purchase some things more fitting for your station. The supremacists have been attacking our well-dressed men. I don't want you to become a target."

"Neither do I."

"Raven, will you take him to see Etta?"

She dearly wanted to say no, but she knew better. Spending the morning with him hadn't been on her list of things to do for the day. "Yes, ma'am. Is there anything else you want me to do for you while I'm out?"

"No. Getting him appropriately outfitted is enough for now. I have some things I need to put in place before we leave for Charleston. I'll swing by Etta's place and let her know you're coming so she can have some things picked out for him. Harrison, if you'd like to come along, you're welcome."

His face brightened at the invitation. "I'd like that."

"Raven, if you see anything you need for the journey while you're there, have Etta add it to my account."

"Okay." Etta, short for Henrietta, was among her mother's many first cousins and owned a small cluttered shop that sold secondhand clothing and other goods. She was a tiny woman whose outrageous personality had always been a familial source of legend, laughter, and joy.

Hazel pushed back from the table. "Then Harrison and I will leave after I get these dishes cleared up."

Raven countered, "Don't worry about that, Mama. I can take care of them. You and Harrison go on." Any delay she could find to put off her time with Braxton Steele was one to grab.

"I'll be glad to assist," Braxton added.

Raven studied him. He'd grown up with servants and probably knew next to nothing about the chore. "Thanks for the offer, but I should be fine alone."

"Many hands, quicker work, no?"

He had her, and she sighed. "I suppose."

Her mother looked on approvingly. "Harrison, let's go get the carriage. Raven, I'll leave you the wagon. Eden should be here shortly to keep Vana company."

"Okay. Where's Dorrie? She said yesterday the Mother Superior isn't allowing her to return to school." Raven remembered that Dorrie also had a question for Steele.

Hazel was plainly displeased by the decision. "I'll be having a word with the Mother soon, but for now, Dorrie's out back with Vana and Drina. Drina's going to tutor her until we get this resolved."

Drina was one of Emile's younger sisters. She was studying to become a teacher, which made her an ideal substitute for the nuns. In a perfect world Raven would have a tutor, too, to make up for her truncated education, but at her age, she doubted her desire to read better or learn about the things that piqued her curiosity was realistic.

Hazel and Harrison made their exit, leaving Raven to finish her breakfast while Brax drank his coffee.

When she was done, they gathered up the dishes and he followed her into the kitchen. She poured hot water from the stove's reservoir into the two large wash pans in the sink. After adding soap flakes to one, she placed the first batch of the dirty dishes inside. "Do you know how to dry?"

He smiled. "Yes, ma'am, I do. Why would I not?"

"Servants," she said, washing up a few plates before sticking them in the clean water to rinse.

"Ah." Using the dish towel she'd given him, he began drying. "There are no servants on sea voyages. Dish cleanup was one of my many duties."

She'd forgotten about his cabin boy story. Glad to know he would be helpful and not just in the way, she kept washing.

"Have I earned the right to ask about your Miss Ezra?"

She washed the bowl her mother had placed the scrambled eggs in. "Depends on what you want to know." She put it in the rinse pan.

"Do you pretend to be her often?"

"Your definition of *often* and mine may differ, so let's say she comes out to play when needed."

"And she was needed this morning?"

"Yes." She paused and assessed him. The reason behind the morning visit affected him as much as it did her, so she debated whether to share the whys. She thought back on her pledge to meet him halfway and decided to act on that and throw him a bone. "We didn't want Welch to show up without warning today and demand we go to the train station, because we aren't ready. So Miss Ezra paid her a call and brought her breakfast."

Puzzlement filled his tone. "How would breakfast delay our leaving?"

"If it's mixed with a purgative it will."

His eyes went as wide as the plate in his hand.

Raven washed a coffee mug. "She'll be spending her day running back and forth to the privy. She'll not have time to pay us a visit."

"Ah. That's what your mother meant?"

Raven nodded.

He studied her, and she saw the many questions he was struggling to form.

"And you just waltzed in and gave her the food?"

"I did. Sometimes things don't line up perfectly but in this case they did."

She explained what took place.

"But what if she'd been at the landlady's table already?"

"I would've told the landlady I was looking for someone else and had the wrong address and left. Welch wouldn't have recognized Miss Ezra, so there was no chance of her realizing it was me. And if she had shown up today, I suppose we'd be on our way to Charleston."

"That's a pretty novel solution."

Raven shrugged. "True, plus she needs to be taught a lesson for her being so insulting and insufferable. I know people who'd've slipped a poison in the food and been done with her altogether. At least she's still alive."

The level of intrigue made his head spin. "How and when did you find out where she was staying?"

"One of my cousins who owns a hack showed the sketch around to some of the other drivers and found the one who'd brought the three of you here yesterday. He was the same driver who waited outside and dropped her off at the boardinghouse. My cousin stopped by early this morning to let Mama know what he'd learned."

"I'm impressed."

"I'm impressed you know how to dry dishes."

"We really must do something about that sassy mouth of yours."

"You think so?"

"Yes."

She admittedly enjoyed challenging him. "Many have tried. Few have succeeded."

"They've obviously been going about it in the wrong way."

"And you'd correct that how?"

"By spending a few quiet moments kissing you until that mouth is soft and kiss-swollen. Maybe bite that bottom lip gently enough for you to moan for more."

Raven swallowed with a suddenly dry throat.

"Has anyone tried that?"

She cleared her throat so she could respond. "No." The sensual moment spread through her blood like warmed cognac. Shaken, she forced her attention back to the sink. "Let's finish up these dishes."

"Sure."

His amused, knowing tone and gaze made her want to sock him in his handsome nose. Fuming silently and still tingling, she noted that this was the second time he'd left her at sixes and sevens. If it happened again, she'd be calling his bluff.

* * *

AFTER THE LAST dish was put away and the dishpans emptied, Brax went to the room he'd shared with his father for his shoulder harness and pistol, and the money needed to pay for his purchases. With the harness concealed beneath his suit coat, he left to join Raven at the wagon. On his way, he heard Dorrie call his name. Stopping, he smiled as she ran to his side.

"Good morning, Dorrie."

"Good morning, Mr. Brax. Will the knives cut my feet?"

"Knives?"

"Yes. You and I will be wearing knives to walk on a mirror."

Thinking this was the oddest little girl he'd probably ever meet, he studied her for a moment and tried to make sense of what she might be alluding to. "I'm not sure what you're talking about, Dorrie. Can you tell me more?"

"It was really cold and I had on a lot of coats and I had knives on my feet. Will they cut me?"

"Were you bleeding?"

"No." There was such sincere concern on her small face, he felt compelled to figure this out for her. He mulled over the clues again. *Knives. Mirror. Cold.*

Then the answer came to him or at least he thought it might be an answer. "It sounds to me like we were ice skating, Dorrie."

She cocked her little head.

"Have you ever seen a pair of ice skates?"

"No."

"The things you called knives are the blades that you stand on that allow you to glide across ice. The blades are attached to a boot. The mirror is probably ice. Have you ever seen ice?"

She shook her head.

"Ice forms when it gets so cold water freezes. Where I live, ice skating is one of the things we enjoy doing during the winter months."

"Will you teach me to ice skate when I live with you?"

He blinked and stood speechless for a moment. Having no idea what she meant by living with him, he decided there was little harm in playing along. "Of course."

She smiled. "Thank you." And she ran off.

Still puzzled, he watched her disappear behind the house.

"You were very patient with her."

He spun around and found Raven behind him. From her words of praise, he wanted to conclude he'd impressed her, but her poker face made it difficult to tell. "It took me a few moments to figure out what she was referencing. She looked so concerned. Not sure what she meant by living with me though."

"Me, either. You ice skate?"

"Yes, my grandfather taught me when I was young."

"Is it fun?"

"Yes. You fall a lot when you first start out, and the ice is awfully hard, but once you learn to balance on the blades, it's fun. You can race, play tag."

"I see."

She appeared to be evaluating him in a new light. "She said she's never seen ice."

"It rarely gets that cold here."

"What about you?"

"Once, during a job in New York many years ago. The cold was so terrible, I haven't gone back since. I don't understand how people can live there."

"You'd adapt."

"No. I'll stay in New Orleans where I don't have to worry about walking on knives or it being so cold my bones ache. Are you ready to leave?"

"I am, if you are."

"I am."

SEATED BESIDE HER on the bench while she drove the horse-drawn wagon down the dusty road, Brax thought back on their conversation in the kitchen. "Should I apologize?"

She looked his way. "For?"

"My description of how I'd handle your mouth."

She turned her attention back to the road. "I asked a question. You answered. No apology needed. It's not as if you kissing me will actually happen."

For most of his adult life, women had fallen over themselves to prove how amenable they could be in his presence, and he'd arrogantly accepted that as a normal female response. Raven was setting his normal on fire, and the flames had him enthralled. As he'd told her cousins, he'd never forced himself on a woman, so unless she changed her mind, he'd have to content himself with enjoying her fierceness, mesmerizing beauty, and captivating speech like a child looking longingly through the window of a candy shop.

Traffic had been sparse on the narrow road that led away from her home, but she'd made a turn a few yards back that put their wagon, pulled by a big mare, on a wider road with much more activity. "How far are we from the Quarter?"

"Another half an hour or so."

He noted how competently she managed the reins. "When did you first learn to drive?"

"When I was eleven or twelve, I guess. I prefer horseback though."

"You drive well."

"Thank you."

They were now in a slow-moving caravan of wagons, carriages, and small buggies. To their left were vehicles going in the opposite direction. On the edges of both sides were people walking. There were men, young and old, burdened down with bales of cotton in bulging burlap sacks tied to their backs; women balancing baskets on their heads filled with everything from vegetables to laundry, and elders of both genders shepherding small children. Most of those walking were Black. Seeing them reminded him how surprised he'd been when he first came south during the war. Having been born and raised in Boston, he'd never seen so many of his own kind in one place. That same feeling returned yesterday when he exited the train and viewed the people at the station.

When they finally entered New Orleans proper he wasn't prepared for the masses of people of all colors filling the street. The walks fronting the business and buildings were teeming with people dressed in everything from business suits, to homespun, to rags. Traffic was moving at a snail's pace due to the vast numbers of vehicles pulled by horses, mules, and even a few cows. Vendors hawked sweet potatoes, freshly caught fish, and potions of all kinds. There were ragpickers, free-running dogs, and to his further surprise, a group of Black nuns. "There are Black nuns here?"

Seeing the wonder on his face, she laughed softly. "Yes, Steele. They're the Sisters of the Holy Family. They've been here since before I was born. The Oblate Sisters of Providence in Maryland are also Black, and their order is much older."

That amazed him, and he wondered how many other people knew nothing about the two convents of Black women of the Catholic church.

The traffic came to a stop, and puzzlement filled her face.

"What's wrong?"

"Not sure why we aren't moving. Maybe there's a funeral procession or a trolley accident up ahead." She stood and peered down the street to try and determine why they weren't moving. Off in the distance came the sound of horns. He knew from talking to his father that New Orleans celebrated funeral with horns. "Is it a funeral?"

"No."

Her face was now etched with concern. She looked around, and then behind her. "We need to get over to the side."

Other vehicles were doing the same. She reined the mare to the right while trying to avoid crashing into the wagons and buggies nearby. People on the walks had come to a stop as well. Vendors on the street corners were hastily moving their stands. The horns sounded closer. "What's this mean?"

"Supremacists are marching."

He froze.

She explained while she jockeyed for a space, "Now that the Democrats control the state government again and the soldiers are gone, they're bold enough to do what they want, when they want." She finally managed to get them to a spot away from the middle of the road and set the brake. Moments later, the men marched silently into view. They were in columns of five across. Brax estimated there were one hundred in the procession. All wore white cotton robes with a white flower on the chest.

"Because Congress banned the Klan back in '71, the supremacists now call themselves rifle groups," she explained with disgust. "This one is known as the New Knights of the White Camelia."

The participants' faces were hidden inside burlap hoods with holes cut out for their eyes. In their hands were rifles, clubs, coils of thick ropes, and bullwhips. It was a show of force meant to intimidate. As they moved into full view, the surrounding quiet was so heavy it was as if the world was holding its breath. A blast from their horns pierced the air and was greeted with a smattering of applause and a few hearty cheers from some of the observers, but the majority of those on the walks and in the jumble of vehicles simply watched. He glanced at Raven and noted her grimly set features and the rifle across her lap. That she was prepared to protect herself pleased the soldier in him.

"Do they do this often?"

"Often enough."

Northern newspapers, both Black and White, were filled with reports of the deteriorating situation in the South brought on by the withdrawal of the last federal soldiers in place since the surrender of the Confederacy. The newly instituted state constitutions cobbled together by Black majority conventions in places like Louisiana, Georgia, and South Carolina were being replaced by ones returning legislative control to those who'd initiated the war. The moves signaled the demise of Reconstruction, and newly freed Black citizens were paying the cost of the reversals with the erosion of their rights and with their lives.

After the supremacists moved on and out of view, traffic began untangling itself, and he and Raven were once again under way. Brax knew he'd always remember this.

The shop owned by Henrietta Moreau turned out to be more of a small warehouse than the traditional store he'd imagined it to be. They'd entered through a door in the back, and the dimly lit interior was so crammed with items it reminded him of his grandparents' attic. As he and Raven snaked their way down a narrow aisle in the middle of the chaos, he spotted picture frames, farm implements, cooper's barrels, and stacked wood. Tables laden with tarnished cook pots stood next to wooden crates filled with plates, teapots, and long-handled wooden spoons. They skirted horse collars, dress forms, stacks of bricks, fishing poles, books, and two rocking chairs. As they neared the front, the interior brightened to show racks of clothing, hobbyhorses, waders, sewing notions, and one wall of shelves holding folded bolts of cloth. In the midst of this were customers milling about. A man with a little girl were going through a table filled with shoes. Assisting them was a tiny birdlike woman wearing a gray dress and a matching tignon adorned with glass beads and feathers. The woman looked up and saw him and Raven, and a smile crossed her aged but unlined copper-skinned face. "Raven. How are you, darling?" The musical lilt in her speech was like Raven's.

A smiling Raven walked into the woman's open arms for a hug. "Hello, Etta. How are you?"

"Fine, dear, just fine."

Raven stepped out of the embrace and the woman looked at him. "Is this the intended groom I've been hearing so much about?"

Raven threw up her hands. "Does everyone in New Orleans know about this?"

"I think so, honey. Hazel stopped by earlier to let me know you two were coming and told me everything. I even met his handsome father. Maybe we'll have two weddings."

Raven sighed and introduced him. "This is Braxton Steele. Steele, this is my second cousin, Henrietta Moreau."

"Pleased to meet you, ma'am."

"Same here. Oh, Raven, you two are going to make such beautiful babies."

Raven growled. "We're not making babies."

"Sure you are. Dorrie's never wrong. Were I thirty years younger, you and I would be throwing dice for this handsome fella. Winner take all."

Raven dragged her hands down her face. Brax tried not to show his amusement. Raven might be in control of many things, but her family was not among them.

Etta glanced around as if not wanting to be overheard and asked, "Has he kissed you yet?"

"Etta!"

"The answer is no, then. Look at this man, girl. Stop walling yourself in. He's handsome, well-spoken, dresses well. And looks like he knows his way around a woman's pleasure. You could do a lot worse. Then again, making a man wait for it can pay off in very delicious ways, too."

As if expecting him to comment, Raven warned, "One word out of you and you'll walk home."

He chuckled and remained silent.

Raven sighed audibly and collected herself. "Etta, we're here to get him some used clothing."

"I have some things ready. Let me finish helping that man and his daughter find a pair of shoes, and I'll be right back."

She left them.

"Interesting lady, Miss Etta."

"Having a large family can be exhausting."

"You don't say."

"This isn't funny, Steele."

"I never said it was, and since I don't want you driving off without me, I'll go look at the fabrics on the shelves over there while she helps her customer."

"Good idea."

Not hiding his amusement, he walked away.

Chapter Seven

Raven loved her cousin Etta, but at the moment wanted her staked out on the anthill next to her other cousins for being so incorrigible. Beautiful babies, indeed. Were Etta thirty years younger, Raven would gladly toss Steele her way, no dice necessary. As for how Etta could determine Steele's prowess in bed was anyone's guess, but according to the stories told about Etta's past, she'd been well loved, too. She'd been a formidable jewel thief back then, one of the best around. In fact, the ruse in San Francisco with the pebbles was something she'd taught Raven.

Raven watched Etta finish helping the man and his daughter with the shoes. After their departure, Etta checked on her other customers before drifting over to where Steele stood in front of the shelves of fabrics. Raven couldn't hear what they were discussing, but the conversation seemed centered on a bolt of blue fabric he appeared interested in.

Something Etta said made him turn and look Raven's way, and his eyes captured hers. The intensity she saw in them made her remember his heated description of how he'd tame her mouth, and the resulting warmth brought on by his words. The memory rekindled her internal debate about whether to acknowledge an attraction to him or stick to the denial. No matter the outcome or how she felt about his personality and views, he was indeed a gorgeous man, from that rakish beard to his regal bearing. He would indeed sire beautiful children. Etta's predictions aside, they just wouldn't be with her, but with someone far more cultured and refined who hadn't sung on street corners for money at the age of five or begun cleaning houses a few years later. That person would also be able to name her favorite book and not feel shamed for never having read one in its entirety. She looked away, breaking the contact.

She wasn't ashamed of being nosy though, and so walked over to join them to see what they were about. She reached them as Etta said, "Okay, I'll ship this to your shop along with your note."

"Thank you."

Seeing her, Etta said, "You can bring him around anytime. I've been trying to sell this beautiful blue silk for months, but no one's been able to pay my asking price."

Raven eyed the midnight blue silk. "It's very beautiful."

He nodded in agreement. "I've never seen a blue this dark before."

"What will it become?"

"A gown more than likely. My seamstresses will undoubtedly duel at dawn for the chance to work with a silk this rich. The purchaser will be envied."

"Possibly your prizewinner?"

He stilled and took her in, in a way that made her so aware of him it was difficult to keep her breath even.

Eyes smoldering, he said quietly, "Maybe I'll make it for you to wear during dessert."

She almost fell over.

"No?" he asked, tone playful.

"No," she somehow managed to toss back.

The smiling Etta chuckled softly. "Yep. Beautiful babies. Let me take this to the counter so I can ready it for shipping, then we'll get the clothing you'll be needing for Charleston."

She left carrying the bolt of silk, while Raven, needing to distance herself from this decidedly seductive man and rein in her heightened senses, turned her attention to the other fabrics on the shelves. There were plain cottons, thin flannels, ticking, and less costly silks in a variety of shades. "What made you decide to become a tailor?"

"It started when I was my grandfather's cabin

boy. One of my duties was to help repair the sails. At first, I was terrible at it, but over time, I grew better. By my third voyage, the crew members were bringing me their shirts, trousers, and other garments to repair, and I found I enjoyed the stitching and making things whole again. I apprenticed for a few years with a tailor in Boston my mother knew, and when my grandfather passed away, I took some of the funds I inherited and opened my shop."

"One of my younger cousins is an apprentice here in the Quarter."

"If I can assist him in any way, let me know."

"You mean that?"

"Yes, Raven, I do. Why would I make the offer if I didn't?" he asked quietly.

She shrugged. "I don't know. I guess I don't see you as the helping sort."

He looked away, not bothering to hide a small bitter smile. He turned back. "I wish you'd take the time to know the real me. Let me see if Miss Etta's ready with the clothes." And he left her standing there.

She watched him stride off. Had she hurt his feelings? He'd spent all day yesterday being judgmental about everything under the sun; how was she supposed to know he had a soft spot? She was torn between wanting to apologize and annoyed at him for making her consider doing so.

She waited with Etta while he tried on the garments behind a screen set up for that purpose. When he was done, he handed Etta the ones he'd settled on. "How much do I owe you?"

"Nothing. After you purchased that silk, I can afford to give them to you at no cost."

"I'd prefer to pay for them."

"Are you not listening?"

Humor curved his mustache-framed lips. "Whatever you say."

"Thank you."

Etta put the clothing in a canvas sack and handed it to him. "You two take care of yourselves in Charleston. Raven, make sure you bring him back in one piece so I can dance with him at your wedding."

Raven knew it was useless to protest. "I'll do my best." She turned her attention to Steele. "Are you ready?"

He nodded.

Raven gave Etta a parting hug and a kiss on the cheek. That done, she and Steele stepped out into the sunshine.

They made the short walk back to the wagon and once aboard, she picked up the reins and asked, "Are you hungry?"

"I could eat something, yes."

"Fish okay? There's a place nearby that has great fried fish sandwiches."

"Sure."

She studied his face. "My apologies if I hurt your feelings back there."

"Thanks. I appreciate that. I'd like for us to get along."

"So do I." She'd replied without thought and realized she mostly meant it.

"Then let's put the incident behind us and try and enjoy the rest of the day."

"Let's do that."

PINKERTON DETECTIVE RUTH Welch was not enjoying her day. Lying across her bed, panting with distress, she prayed that whatever was ailing her had run its course. An hour or so after breakfast her stomach began roiling so violently that she'd eschewed the room's chamber pot and bolted to the boardinghouse's privy out back. Relief had been only temporary. So far, she'd made three more trips and doubted her body had anything left to give. A tap on her closed door drew her attention and she called weakly, "Yes?"

"It's Mrs. Abbott. May I come in?"

"Yes."

The door opened a fraction and the landlady stuck her head inside. "Just wanted to check on you. Are you all right?"

"No," Welch replied as angrily as her infirmity allowed. "My stomach is in distress from whatever you fed me for breakfast."

"I didn't feed you breakfast."

"Sure you did. You sent me a plate by the old Colored woman who works for you."

"That old woman didn't work for me. She arrived by wagon and said you made the arrangement to have the breakfast delivered."

Ruth sat up as best she could. "What?"

The landlady repeated herself.

"I never made any such arrangement."

"Well, she certainly doesn't work for me."

Ruth fell back on the bed. Who was the woman? Where had she come from? As she tried to make sense of it, a possible answer surfaced. *Moreau!* She'd bet a bottle of her favorite brandy that the woman had been sent by the Moreaux, or was maybe a member of the diabolical family itself, but before she could give the conundrum more attention, her stomach roiled. She struggled to her feet, forcefully pushed past the landlady, and made another dash to the privy.

RAVEN AND BRAX purchased their sandwiches and she drove to a forested bluff above the Mississippi. A short walk through the trees and untamed surroundings took them to a clearing that offered a place to sit. Below them was the port of New Orleans filled with ships and riverboats of all sizes and the workers loading and unloading the cargos.

"We can sit here," she told him.

"Let me take off my coat, so you can sit on it."

"Thank you, but it isn't necessary. The ground

isn't damp and this is an old skirt. A little dirt won't ruin it."

"Are you sure?"

"Certain." She'd never had a man make such an offer before, and she was touched by his show of concern.

He didn't appear convinced by her response but sat beside her and looked out at the activity below. "I never knew the New Orleans port was so busy."

"Louisiana exports a lot of sugar and timber, and New Orleans is one of the busiest ports in the country, I'm told. Before the war it was even busier, but it's been neglected for some time and silt is blocking the channel. Supposedly the people in charge are looking for a solution."

They began eating. She'd grabbed a canteen of water from the wagon so they'd have something to drink.

"How's your sandwich?" she asked.

"You were right. This fish is outstanding. Is all the food here so well seasoned?"

She smiled. "Yes, because if it isn't, we won't eat it."

"Boston could learn a thing or two from the cooks here."

She turned to him. "See how nicely we're getting along. We're making small talk and everything."

He laughed. "Yes, we are."

"And since I'm making nice, thanks again for being so kind to Dorrie this morning."

"You're welcome. Is she family? Your cousins told me the story of her birth."

She shook her head. "She isn't blood. When her mother passed away, the only other family she had was an elderly aunt. She didn't want Dorrie. Said her being dead and then alive meant the devil was in her, so the midwife brought her to Mama, and she's been with us ever since."

"It was kind of your mother to take her in."

"It's what she does. Her six brothers sired quite a number of children by their wives and mistresses. Mama has made it a point to bring the children together regularly so they'll know their cousins and half brothers and sisters, and that they're all family. Even though the mothers may not get along, the children do because of her."

"Where are you uncles now?"

"Uncle Abram is in Cuba. My uncles Saul and Tomas died of yellow fever in '67. Uncle Isaac was killed in '66 during the Mechanics Institute massacre when the New Orleans police, rebs, and supremacists joined forces to stop the new state constitution from being formed. It was a horrific day. Many people lost their lives."

"I'm sorry for your loss. I read about the killings in the newspaper. People up North were outraged."

She thought back on how the family grieved,

then turned her mind away to block out the memories of her mother's pain. "Uncle David was killed at the battle of Gettysburg, and Uncle Ezekial, the baby of the family, drowned on his fishing boat during a storm."

"Lots of tragedy," he said quietly.

"More than our share, I believe. My uncles were outrageous, bigger-than-life individuals. We miss them very much."

"My condolences."

"Thank you."

"And my apologies for making you sad."

"None needed. My guess is you were wondering why you hadn't seen many menfolk so far."

"Honestly, I was."

Raven looked out at the Mississippi stretching as far as the eye could see, and drew in its muddy, tangy scent. To her it was the scent of life. Death. Family. Home. Even with all the tragedy, she couldn't imagine living anywhere else.

"I'm enjoying your company," he told her. "We aren't clashing."

"The day isn't over."

He chuckled. "There's that mouth again."

"The mouth you wish to tame."

"Very much so."

The familiar warmth rose, spread, and tempted. "Suppose I said go ahead and try."

"Then I'd say I need you to be clear. Is this a supposition or a challenge?"

What are you doing! She ignored the inner voice. "A challenge."

He reached out and ran a slow finger over her bottom lip, and the intensity that flowed from it made her eyes slide closed. "Are you sure?"

"Yes."

He leaned closer, and the heat of his nearness set off tiny flares even before he placed his lips against hers.

He murmured, "I've been wanting to taste you since dinner yesterday." And taste her he did; tentatively at first, lulling her, inviting her mouth to open with gentle licks of his fire-tipped tongue. And when he bit her bottom lip softly, she moaned just as he'd predicted. She knew she should've listened to her inner voice's warning. Now it was too late. Her body drank in the alluring sensations like a drought welcoming rain.

He eased back, and she fought to catch her breath. He looked down at her with blazing eyes. "Would you like to hear what I'd do to you were we in my bedroom at home?"

His voice was mesmerizing and so seductive she could only reply, "Yes?"

He kissed her again. "Once this mouth is ripe enough for my liking, and yours, like now, I'd ask you to slowly undo the buttons on your blouse because nothing arouses me more than a woman willingly undressing, and if you agreed, I'd move my kisses down your throat."

Melting, she felt herself sway.

"I'd ask you to lower your shift and offer me first one breast to pleasure until your nipple is hard as a jewel, then the other."

Raven wondered how long she could live without breathing. This man was far more dangerous than she ever could have imagined.

"Then I'd ask if you wanted more . . . and if you said yes, I'd have you raise your skirts and touch yourself to let me know how wet you are. Are you wet, little corvus?"

The torrid power of him fueled a sweet ache of longing between her thighs. "Yes," she whispered to herself, brain turned to mush.

"Good."

Only then did she realize she'd replied aloud. Her eyes popped open in shock.

He simply smiled.

Appalled at how easily and totally he'd put her under his spell, she longed to toss back something pithy, but her ability to speak had gone missing. It took all she had to not ask him for more.

Leaning over, he gave her one last lingering kiss. "As I said yesterday, you'll remember my pleasuring you for the rest of your life. Are you ready to go back to your mother's place?"

Her mind was so muddled and dulled, she had trouble understanding what he'd asked. When she was finally able to shake free, she answered, "Yes."

He stood and offered his hand. She viewed the hand and then him. Something inside knew this man was going to change her life whether she wanted it or not. Accepting his assistance, she placed her hand in his warm, strong one and shakily got to her feet. "Do you do this often?"

"Do what?"

"Seduce women over fish sandwiches?"

"No. You're the first."

"Good to know." Glad her brain could form speech again, she picked up the canteen and the refuse from their meal. Together they made their way back to the wagon.

ON THE DRIVE back, Brax admitted he hadn't gotten nearly enough of her kisses. He wanted more; a full night of her being in his bed, more. She hadn't said a word since leaving the bank, and he wondered what she might be thinking. "You've been awfully quiet," he said.

"I'm not speaking to you."

"Why not?"

"Because you're way too good at this, and who knows what you'll have me saying or doing next."

"The possibilities are endless."

"Exactly, and I don't even like you, Steele."

He laughed.

"Stop laughing. This isn't funny."

"I'm sorry."

"Liar. And what the hell is a corvus?"

"It's the Latin word for raven."

"So you speak Latin, too? Jesus."

"Only a little. It was one of the subjects my tutors touched upon."

She shook her head and he found her reaction so incredibly endearing, he wanted to pull her onto his lap and pleasure her until the Mississippi froze over.

"We're going back to no more kisses. None," she stated firmly.

"Whatever you say."

Her look of annoyance made him smother the humor bubbling inside.

"I mean it."

"I'm sure you do, but you were the one who challenged me, remember?"

"I don't need reminding."

"Thought maybe you had forgotten, considering what transpired after."

"I'm not talking to you."

He couldn't remember ever having such an amusing conversation. Thinking back on her responses to his kisses and heated questions confirmed just how swept away they'd both been. And as then, he was hard as a ship's mast.

Shifting in his seat to accommodate his arousal, he decided it might be best to think about Boston in winter for the remainder of the drive rather than all the scandalous things he wanted to do with her to seek relief. It was damned difficult, however.

Chapter Eight

After a morning of sending wires to family in Charleston, paying a call on Julianna LeVeq-Vincent, and alerting Etta that Raven would be stopping by, Hazel and Harrison returned home and shared lunch on the study's verandah.

"You think you're ready for Charleston now?" Harrison asked, setting aside his now empty plate.

"As ready as I can be," Hazel said. "Welch will probably be here in the morning. I just wish we knew more about the targets. Usually we gather our own information before going in. This time, we're having to rely on someone who's proven she can't be trusted, and that's worrisome."

He nodded understandingly.

"But thankfully, Raven's resourceful and can think on her feet, so I'm certain she'll manage any surprises that might crop up. My main concern is the knife Welch will put in her back. I know it's coming, sooner or later. The mother in me wants to protect her from it, or come up with a way to prevent it."

Hazel set that aside for a moment and studied the man she'd wanted to marry all those years ago. Age had grayed his hair, and time had added weight to his once slender frame, just as it had to hers. She'd enjoyed his company as she handled the day's errands. They'd talked, laughed, reminisced. After the death of Josiah, the father of her girls, she hadn't taken any lovers because she didn't want stray men around them, and she was also focused on keeping a roof over their heads and food on the table. In those days, Fanny's Plan had been in its infancy and there wasn't a spare dime to be had. Being with Harrison now made her realize how much she'd missed companionship. "Even though Welch makes me see red, I'm glad she brought you back into my life."

He seemed surprised by her admission. "Really?"

She nodded. "I cursed you for years, and when you showed up yesterday, I cursed even more, but now . . . "

"Now what?" he asked softly.

"I can look back and see why you did what you did that day at the church."

"A purely selfish man moment. Purely selfish. If I couldn't have you, neither would he. I'm sorry for wrecking the dreams you had for your life."

"And I'm sorry for breaking your heart, and

what we might have had, had I chosen you. Chosen us."

"You weren't going to go against your mother."

"No, I wasn't," she admitted. She reached across the table and gently covered his hand with hers. "I want a second chance, Harrison."

Seemingly moved by what he read in her eyes, he laced his fingers with hers. "I didn't think I had the standing to ask that of you after all this time, but I want that chance, too."

"Then let's."

"You wouldn't tease an old man, would you?"

"No. Not about this. I'd like to spend however many years I have left with you."

"Okay then. Do you want marriage, or shall we do without the formalities?"

"What would you prefer?"

"A wedding. In front of a preacher, with you all dressed up, me in my best suit, and the world watching. And afterwards, a reception with cognac, music, dancing, and cake."

She laughed. "Then that's what we'll do."

He tugged gently on her hand and guided her over to his side of the table and onto his lap. She wrapped her arms around him, and he held her against his heart. For a moment they sat in afternoon silence, content. He gently raised her chin. Looking down at her, he ran a loving finger over her lips before kissing her with a passion that had lingered for decades.

"And after the reception," he whispered, "a lively wedding night."

Eyes sparkling, she replied, "A *very* lively wedding night."

THAT EVENING AFTER dinner, Raven was glad to see her cousins arriving for the meeting. Their presence would give her something to focus on besides Braxton Steele. Since returning home, everywhere she'd turned the memory of his potent words followed, whispering, seducing, reminding her of what she'd felt and how much more she wanted. He was standing on the far side of the room, arms crossed, watching her with veiled amusement, as if he knew the effect he'd had on her. That knowing gaze made her want to stuff him in a barrel and ship him back to Boston, Detective Welch's mission be damned, but only after more of his kisses.

Once everyone was seated, she took in the attendees. Renay and Lacie. Emile and Alma. Bethany. Her mother, Hazel, and Harrison. Eden and Vana. They'd all come together to let Eden and Vana know what games they were running and where they'd be because the aunts would be in charge of the family until Hazel returned from Charleston.

Emile spoke first. "Lacie and I are heading to Titusville, Pennsylvania, to sell stocks in a soon-to-be-built oil refinery." Titusville was the nation's oil boomtown. Much money was being made both legally and fraudulently.

Lacie said, "We're sure the town will have its share of con artists, but I doubt there will be an Italian count with an English duchess mistress looking for investors."

Emile put on his best Italian accent and said, "On behalf of the Italian government I will take all of their money."

And Lacie added in an English accent, "And of course, I'll be there dazzling them with my beauty and ladylike titters."

"Not to mention titties," Hazel pointed out, which drew laughs.

Lacie stood and performed an elaborate curtsy. "I'm a woman of many weapons. All dangerous in their own way."

Beth was on her way back to Atlanta to reprise her role as the great African queen Mela, whose ability to reach the dead through her seances had been filling the family coffers with funds from wealthy Whites in that city and other places around the country for the past two years.

Alma reported that she'd be leaving town the next day for Chicago. "Our faith healer cousin Cicero has been running a nationwide traveling revival, and Chicago is his next stop. I'm going to be one of the people in the crowd invited on stage to be healed and help out with anything else he may need. Etta may be joining us in about ten days when we play New York City. She says she misses shopping at Tiffany's."

Raven smiled and felt sorry for the fabled jeweler.

Once the reports were done, Raven took over. "As we discussed yesterday, Steele and I will be heading for Charleston more than likely tomorrow. My main concern," Raven admitted, "is that Welch will betray me."

She told them about Hazel's note from Julianna LeVeq-Vincent. When she finished, there was concern on everyone's faces—especially the Steeles. Raven realized she hadn't shared the information with them and should have. Braxton Steele's tight-set jaw reinforced that, and she made a mental vow to speak with him once the meeting ended. "I don't know when she'll strike, but I'm quite certain she will. My problem is not knowing when."

Emile asked, "I know Renay will be going with you, but are you sure you won't need more of us there to keep an eye on things?"

Renay said, "We should be fine. Family's there, too, remember."

Raven said, "I agree with Renay. My hope is that finding the document and giving it to her will be enough to send her back to wherever she came from and never see her again. Mama and I initially tossed around the idea of forging a duplicate and keeping the original, because frankly that is how we Moreaux conduct business, but we won't have the time. The copy Welch showed us yesterday is very detailed and intricate, not something that can be forged in a few hours, or even a few days. So Steele and I will concentrate on finding it, turning it over to her, and returning home as soon as possible."

She looked around the room. "Any questions or concerns?"

No one had any.

Hazel stood. "As you should know by now, we've come to the end of Fanny's Plan, so this will be my last gambit. And hopefully everyone else's as well. Admittedly it's been fun, but now we get to carve out boring, nonadventurous lives like the rest of humanity, and I can't wait."

Laughter and applause followed that.

"The money Fanny set aside for those of you here will be in your accounts in the next few days. Until then, happy hunting and bring yourselves home in one piece. Okay. Go home."

Once the others departed, Raven, Braxton, and their parents remained. "I'm glad you shared your concerns about Welch turning Judas," Hazel said.

"I wanted everyone prepared in case they did need to rally on our behalf, and my apologies to Harrison and Braxton for not sharing the note earlier," Raven said.

"I did tell Harrison," Hazel added.

Raven turned to his son. "Then my apology is for you. It totally slipped my mind."

And it had, thanks to being seduced over a fish sandwich.

"Understood. It's been a busy day."

Busier than she could have ever imagined.

Hazel added, "I spoke with Julianna this morning to find out if she had anything else about Welch she could share. All she had to add was that Welch claimed to be an Irishwoman from Boston, but in the aftermath of her last visit, neither Julianna nor Miss Tubman was able to corroborate the claim."

"So, she could be anyone from anywhere," Brax said. "Does she actually work for the Pinkertons?"

"Yes. That at least is true. Miss Tubman used her contacts to verify it. The Pinkertons know her as Welch. She's also known to be ambitious from what Julianna was told."

Raven found nothing wrong with an ambitious woman. However, threatening the freedom of others to advance your goals wasn't something to applaud.

"And so you'll know, Harrison and I have decided to marry," Hazel said.

The surprising news rendered Raven both shocked and speechless.

"At our age we can't afford to dither, so we're just going to do it."

Harrison looked between Raven and his son. "I hope we have your blessings."

"Not that it will matter," Hazel cracked, smiling.

"Of course you do," Raven replied sincerely.

"Mine as well," Braxton said.

Raven knew her mother still had feelings for Harrison, but hadn't expected this outcome. "Congratulations, Mama," she said, giving her a strong hug. Over the years, her mother had made so many personal sacrifices. She deserved happiness.

"We'll keep this a secret for now and celebrate once the Charleston job is done."

Raven agreed.

"We'll see you two in Charleston," Hazel said in parting.

They exited the library, and Raven was left alone with Steele.

"That was certainly unexpected."

"Very."

"So, are you speaking to me now?" he asked.

"I suppose I'll have to considering we'll be man and wife starting tomorrow, but I'm doing it under protest."

His smile replied and hers responded. He then asked seriously, "Are you worried about Charleston?"

She nodded. "I always worry when I start a new job. So much can go wrong, but I try not to let it overwhelm me. I usually don't get much sleep the night before though."

"I'd offer to help if I knew what you needed to make things less worrisome."

There was a sincerity in his tone and manner

she found touching. "There's really nothing for it," she replied, determined to not let him affect her any more than he already had. "I'll be better once it all begins."

"Then how about we sit somewhere and maybe just talk to take your mind off things?"

She'd never had anyone offer to shoulder her burden this way. Usually, she'd spend the night before a job lying in bed tossing and turning while wrestling with all the many ways she and her cousins could be exposed and arrested. This job for Welch would be their last, and she was glad because she was weary. "Sure, but you have to promise to keep your lips to yourself."

"Understood."

She didn't trust him for a minute. "Let's go sit outside."

It was a breezy night, and fast-moving clouds periodically raced across the moon. She hoped it didn't mean a storm was on the way. Train travel was always a challenge. Heavy rain would only make the journey to Charleston that much more arduous.

Braxton sat silent while she stood leaning on her elbows on the railing, looking out at the night. It never occurred to him that she'd be uneasy heading into a gambit. He just assumed she'd be brazen and cocky, but apparently he'd been wrong. Were her family members equally concerned about the outcomes? Did they have trouble sleeping, too?

She glanced back at him. "Tell me a cabin boy story."

It was a surprising topic of conversation. Rather than wonder why she'd chosen it, he honored the request. "My first voyage was a short trip to Baltimore, and I was seasick the entire time there and back."

She turned, startled.

"I was completely miserable, and being sick made the trip seem to last an eternity. Once I returned home, I had no interest in setting foot on a boat ever again, but my grandfather insisted the only way to cure me was to make me sail again."

"Did your parents agree?"

"They did, but if they hadn't, it wouldn't have made a difference. My grandfather ruled our lives, and if he said up was down, no one corrected him."

"Sounds like a nice man."

"He was hard, but mostly fair. I'd probably not be the man I am today without his stern guidance, although I rarely appreciated it growing up. The only time anyone defied him was when my mother married my father."

"He didn't like Harrison?"

"No. He supposedly hated the idea of his only daughter marrying a formerly enslaved dockworker."

"People and their prejudices."

"I know, but he forgave her after my birth. He

still didn't like my father any better but tolerated him for siring a grandson."

"How generous of him. How'd Harrison handle being looked down upon?"

"He said he'd married my mother, not her father, so my grandfather's opinion didn't much
matter."

"Good for him. Would your grandfather have
approved of your prizewinner? What's her name
again?"

"Charlotte Franklin, and yes, he would've approved."

"A woman like me would've probably given
him apoplexy."

"Undoubtedly," he replied, amused.

"I'm not the fashionable yoke-loving belle of
the ball."

No, she wasn't, but he found her fascinating
nonetheless. "You're your own woman."

"But not the kind men value. Too mouthy, too
straightforward, too everything a woman isn't
supposed to be."

"In polite society's eyes, yes."

"Good thing I don't put much stock in polite
society then. I happen to enjoy me."

"I've decided I do as well."

"Don't lie, Steele. I give you apoplexy, too."

He laughed. "You do, but I'm finding I enjoy
having to reassess things because of you."

"Things like what?"

"My own prejudices about women, for one.

I've never met one who challenges me the way you do. Honestly, those I know back home all but trip over themselves to seek my approval."

"That's tied to your wealth, and the fact that you don't favor an ogre."

"Thanks for the compliments but you don't care about my approval."

"No, I don't. It's sort of the way Harrison felt about your grandfather. Your approval doesn't matter because when this Welch job is done, you'll return to Boston and yoke your life to—what's her name again?"

He shook his head at how totally incorrigible she was. He wanted to put her across his lap, spank her audacious behind, then raise her skirts, slide two fingers into her warmth, and have her ride them until she orgasmed screaming his name. "Charlotte Franklin."

"Yes, Charlotte Franklin, and I'll be here in New Orleans going about my life."

"And giving some man apoplexy."

"If I find one worthy enough."

The idea of her being with an unknown someone who'd get to enjoy all she was didn't sit well, he realized. Not that he had any say in her future, but a small budding part of him wished he did. The unforeseen admission caught him so off guard, he had no idea what to do with it or about it. "What would make the man worthy?"

"If he accepts me as I am, rough edges and

all. He'd have a sense of humor and an appreciation of family."

"Anything else?"

"Love me like he loves breathing."

Brax felt his world shift on its axis.

"I believe in love and won't settle for less," she explained further. "You stated you don't need to be in love. To me, that's just one more example of why you and I are unevenly yoked."

The night's silence rose between them, before she added, "And I want him to be as passionate for me in bed as out."

"More straight talk."

"So there'll be no misunderstandings. I desire to be both mistress and wife."

Her bold statement took him aback.

"No man of mine will need to seek his pleasure elsewhere."

"You will be prized."

"As will he."

Brax had never had such a frank conversation before with a woman, but then he'd never met a woman like Raven Moreau before. From what he knew, married women didn't openly embrace the physical aspects of marriage; if anything, they viewed it as a duty. It never occurred to him that there might be women in the world who saw it differently. Yes, being around her was reshaping his thinking in many ways, and on many subjects. He envied the man she'd eventually choose, even though the thought of her being with someone else was again unsettling.

"Would you want your wife to be your mistress as well?" she asked.

"I doubt there's a man alive who'd say no, honestly, but I'm not sure the women of my class would embrace that as a goal. I could be wrong, however." He supposed this was a lead into how Charlotte might feel about it.

"I won't ask about your prizewinner's take on the matter because that's between the two of you."

"I appreciate that." The seed had been planted though, intentionally or not. How would Charlotte feel? He supposed a marriage built on companionship could be a passionate one, but he didn't see her desiring to be his mistress as well, at least not in the way he imagined Raven would be. And with that thought, he questioned something else. How could he return to Boston and pick up the reins of the staid, no-nonsense existence he'd planned to live out after having Raven blaze across his life like a comet? The answer had less to do with his expectations of Charlotte and more to do with his own expectations of what he wanted the decades of living ahead to hold. Yet would he completely change how he viewed the world based on a brief encounter with a woman who would probably not remember his name in a year's time? That she might look upon their being together as nothing more impactful than autumn leaves tumbling in the wind also left him unsettled.

"You give me apoplexy, too, Steele." She looked back at him seated in the shadows at the small table.

He wasn't sure what to make of her surprising statement. "Is that a good thing or a bad thing?"

"I'm still trying to decide. It's been a while since I've been with a man."

Raven didn't know why she'd just confessed what she had. It made more sense to thank him for distracting her, say good night, and go inside, but their encounter at lunch refused to let her be. She kept remembering, feeling, wanting. The embers left behind continued to glow.

"What are you saying?"

She got to the point. "That, Lord help me, I want more."

He responded in a voice as dark and velvety as the night. "Then come sit on my lap and let's discuss it."

Raven closed the short distance between them and settled herself atop his thighs. He was warm, solid. The nearness made the embers glow hotter, and when he lifted her chin to bring her eyes to his and placed his lips gently against her own, her need rose and spread its wings.

"What would you like, little corvus?"

"Kisses, touches."

He drew a brazen knuckle slowly across a hardening nipple. "Here?"

Desire clouded her vision. "Everywhere."

"Then undo your buttons for me."

Hands shaking, Raven complied with fumbling fingers. Once the blouse was opened, he lightly traced the hardened tips of her nipples through the tattered, washed-out length of indigo cotton binding her breasts. "Will you take this off for me?"

She untied the small knot in the center and slowly removed it. His watching her made the embers blaze to flames. She removed her blouse as well, leaving herself bare to the waist, to the moonlight and the night's breeze. He kissed his way down the edge of her throat, and she, remembering his words from that afternoon, filled her hands with her breasts and silently offered him first one and then the other. He feasted while she arched sensually, and her alto voice crooned softly with delight.

"Is this what you wanted?" he husked out as he bit her gently.

"Yes," she groaned.

"Where else do you want my touches? Do you want them between your thighs?"

The way his mouth kept capturing hers, and then lowering to seduce her nipples until they pleaded, made it difficult to think, let alone speak.

He whispered hotly against her ear, "I want

to watch you come, but I need your consent before I can give you my fingers to ride."

His scandalous words and expertise left her hovering on the edge of an orgasm. Needing no prompting, she raised the front of her skirt and opened her legs. "Please, yes."

"The next time we do this, it'll be my cock."

"Promises, promises."

"Sassy woman." He kissed her roughly and eased aside the split in her drawers to ply the small kernel of flesh whose only purpose was pleasure. As heat climbed and spread, he eased in two fingers imbued with so much erotic magic, she cried out as the orgasm shattered her a second later.

He said softly, "It has been a long time, hasn't it?"

Rattled by her body's response, sensation was all she was aware of. That and the soft touches he slid over her and in her while she tried to put body and mind back together. Once she could finally frame speech again, she said shakily, "Thank you," and kissed him deeply. Reaching between them, she ran a possessive hand over the rock-hard proof of his arousal, and holding his burning eyes, began undoing the closure of his trousers. His hand gently covered hers.

"That isn't necessary."

"Of course it is. You've given me pleasure and I want to repay you in kind."

"Raven—"

"Quiet, Steele."

Bare-breasted as an autumn-skinned goddess, she slid down his body to her knees, undid the front of his trousers, and exposed him. After a few well-placed, torrid licks, she closed that mouthy mouth around him and took him straight to heaven. "God, woman."

"See how you're rewarded when you do as I ask?"

The sultry, languid licks, sucks, and warmth of her talented attentions had him arching up out of the chair in ardent response. She tantalized him from tip to scrotum, and the orgasm gathered like a storm. "I'm going to come."

"Then do it and stop talking."

Chuckling, he expected her to pull back, but she continued to ply him so erotically, he came with a shout so loud, he slapped his hand over his mouth to keep it from reverberating to the Quarter, while she took all he had to give.

When he could move again, he reached down and guided her back onto his lap. He didn't expect her to cuddle close but she did. He draped his arms around her and kissed the top of her hair. As he wondered how in the world he was going to let her go when it became time to return to Boston, the silence was torn by another shout. He and Raven stared at each other.

"Since the only other man here is your father,

he and Mama must be practicing for their wedding night."

And the idea of that was so unexpected and outrageous, they covered their mouths and laughed uproariously.

Once the humor faded, their eyes met. "Thank you again," she voiced sincerely.

"I'm always at your service."

Suddenly shy, she glanced away. "This was a one-time thing, Steele."

"Whatever you say." And his smile appeared.

"Stop smiling," she fussed, unable to hide her own amusement.

"If I do, will I get another reward?"

She punched him playfully in the shoulder. "Don't make me hurt you."

He leaned down and kissed her into silence. "You can run me over with a wagon as long as I can kiss this mouthy mouth, and tease you here . . ." He ran a slow finger around her nipple, then slowly pushed up her skirt, and touched her still damp and pulsating warmth. "And here . . ."

Still greedy, she parted her legs to let him play. Heat began rising again.

"You should go inside, little corvus, before I lean you over this table and take you from behind until you scream my name."

"You are so scandalous," she whispered.

"I know. Isn't it glorious?" And the gloriousness continued as he dallied between her now wantonly parted thighs while she lay against him still bare-breasted, with her skirt hiked to her waist. "Come again for me . . ."

When he gave her his fingers to ride again, his free hand kept her nipples begging, and his mouth captured hers possessively. Increasing his thrusts, her hips rose and fell and she broke again on a strangled cry that she buried into his hard chest to keep from being heard.

"Good girl."

Moments later, when her world righted, Raven gave him a parting kiss and walked on drunken legs back inside.

Brax watched her go and was left seated in the darkness to ponder the problem she presented to the well-laid plans he thought he had in place for his future. He was no longer content to simply go through life with no thought to passion or adventure or thinking being evenly yoked was all he needed for his existence. He realized he needed more. Wanted more, and maybe with a woman he could love like he loved breathing.

Chapter Nine

$\mathcal{R}$aven awakened an hour before dawn to a morning of pouring rain. Thanks to Steele, she'd slept like a baby, and the memory of their time together made her smile, but the weather would further impact what would undoubtedly be a long day. Before bed, she'd packed what she'd be needing for the trip and was certain Steele had done the same. Detective Welch would probably arrive early in hopes of catching them off guard so she could exercise her authority by making them rush around to meet her departure timeline, but Raven had no intention of giving her that satisfaction. She desperately wished she could put off the trip. Knowing she had no choice, she left her bed, took care of her needs, and got dressed.

Steele was already at the table when she entered for breakfast, as were her mother and Harrison. Steele, giving no indication of how scandalous they'd been last night, nodded a greeting and she returned the same. Seeing her mother and Harrison made her smile inwardly as she remembered the shout she'd heard last evening, but she only offered them a simple good morning. She fixed herself a small plate of bacon and grits, added a cup of coffee, and took her seat.

Her mother asked, "How'd you sleep?"

"I slept well for once. How about you?"

Her mother shot Harrison a quick glance and smiled. "Slept well, too."

Raven raised her coffee cup, sipped, and let her amused eyes say to Steele what words could not. His responding gaze showed he understood.

The two couples spent the time discussing Charleston. Hazel talked about her plans for the job and the disguise she'd settled on. They'd just finished the meal when the door pull sounded.

"That's probably Welch," Hazel said. "I checked the schedule yesterday and the train is scheduled to depart at nine."

Raven looked up at the clock on the wall. It was now a bit past six-thirty. "I'll get the door."

It was Welch. Her olive-colored travel attire and matching hat showed signs of the rain still pouring down. "Good morning," Raven said.

"The train leaves at nine. I hope you're ready to depart."

"We're just finishing breakfast. If you haven't eaten, there's food left."

"Is that supposed to be funny?"

Raven feigned confusion. "I'm not sure what you mean."

"I should have you arrested for whatever you put in my food yesterday."

"What are you talking about?"

"Don't play innocent with me. You know good and well you or someone in your family laced my food with a purgative."

"I have no idea what you're talking about. None of us saw you yesterday or knew where you were staying. How could we have put something in your food? Have you made an enemy here in the city that might be responsible?"

Raven saw the wheels turning in the detective's head as she considered the question. She wondered if the LeVeq family came to the Pinkerton's mind.

"No," Welch lied.

"That's very curious, I must say, but the Moreaux had nothing to do with it. I hope you're feeling better today." The lingering effects of the purgative could be seen in her slightly sallow complexion and the dark circles under her eyes. But as Raven said to Steele, at least it had been a purgative and not poison. The detective could be lying in a pine box instead. "Mr. Steele and I are ready to leave. Just let me retrieve my carpetbag from my room."

"Do it quickly."

Veiling her reaction to the harshly spoken demand, Raven left Welch standing by the door.

Upon returning, she shared a farewell hug with her mother and Harrison. They'd see each other in Charleston, but no one shared that fact with Welch. After Steele finished his goodbyes, he and Raven, soon to be Lovey and Evan Miller, followed the detective out to the hack waiting in the rain.

At the train station, Raven wondered if she and Steele would be allowed to sit with the White passengers. With the rollback of progress tied to the demise of Reconstruction, some railroad companies were practicing segregation, and forcing members of the race to ride in the gambling cars and, in extreme cases, with the cattle and other livestock. To her relief, the conductor honored their tickets, so they settled into seats in a row behind the still sour-faced Welch.

The rain was falling even harder and Raven could barely make out the scenery through her window. As a result, the train's pace could be bested by someone walking. She prayed they wouldn't be delayed by washed-out tracks, a common hazard of travel during bad weather. Beside her, Steele fished around in his small travel case. "I have a few books," he said to her. "Would you like one to help pass the time?"

She shook her head. "No, you go ahead."

"Are you certain? I've a copy of *Alice's Adventures in Wonderland*."

She forced a smile. "No, but thank you for offering."

He studied her for a long moment. "Okay. Let me know if you change your mind."

She nodded and turned back to her rain-shrouded window.

Their journey proved more troublesome than she'd imagined. The storm followed them across the South, washing out tracks, decoupling cars, and causing delays. One incident in Mississippi, tied to floodwaters over the tracks, lasted more than twelve hours. Another delay, this time in Georgia, occurred when the conductor never arrived for his shift and the passengers spent the night sleeping on board while a replacement was found. Because there was no single railroad that handled the trip from New Orleans to Charleston, they also had to endure numerous changes en route via rail lines with names like Barnwell, Northern Mobile Girard, and others named Gulf, Macon and Augusta, and Montgomery Eufaula. Steele read most of the way. Raven looked out of the window, torn between focusing on the memories of Steele's masterful pleasuring and worries about the job ahead, while Welch kept a stern eye on them both.

On day four the weather finally broke. Their relief at finally crossing into South Carolina was muted as they dragged themselves to yet another connecting train. Welch handed them their tickets. As they waited to board, Raven noted all the people of color walking to the cars at the back of the train. She assumed she and Steele were going to be riding Jim Crow. Being separated from Welch suited her just fine as long as they weren't relegated to the stock car with the animals.

But Welch seemed not to have picked up on these subtle clues. As she boarded, the conductor eyed her and them.

"Coloreds in the back," he said gruffly.

Welch waved a dismissive hand. "That's okay, they're under my supervision. I'll vouch for them."

Raven sighed. Steele gave Raven a look and shook his head at Welch's apparent ignorance.

The conductor said to her, "Ma'am, I don't care whether you vouch for them or not. They ride in the gambling car. You can join them there if you want, or you can walk to the next stop and be told the same thing—Coloreds ride in the back."

"Surely an allowance can be made."

After all the delays they'd endured to reach this point in the trip, Raven had no intention of walking to the next stop, and Welch declaring them her charges as if she were some kind of plantation overseer only made Raven's temper rise. She handed the tight-lipped conductor her ticket and Steele did the same. That done, they headed to the back of the train.

AFTER BEING COOPED up for the past two days in a gambling car filled with cigar smoke and the sour smell of unwashed men, when Raven and Steele stepped off the train in Charleston, she savored the early afternoon's fresh air and the sunshine. "I'm so glad we're here," she said to Steele.

"I am as well. Hoping the journey back will be faster and less of a pain in the behind."

She agreed.

Welch walked up and said impatiently, "We're here. Let's find a hack to take us to the Stipes' residence."

Raven glanced at Steele and wondered if his thinking was aligned with hers. She was certain they'd face the same Jim Crow barriers hiring a hack as they had on the train, but she decided to let Welch find that out for herself. For a woman who claimed to have worked with Miss Tubman, the detective seemed ignorant of the way the world worked in the South for members of the race.

They followed her to the hacks lined up outside the depot and stood back as she approached one. Out of earshot, she struck up a conversation. The driver looked past her at them and shook his head.

Steele said, "You'd think she'd know something about this."

"Too busy being important in her own mind, I suppose."

"You're probably right."

"I can't wait until we can get rid of her."

"I agree."

When Welch was turned down for the third time, Steele looked around. "There are some of our drivers over there. Shall we?"

"Yes. We'll be here until Christmas waiting on her to figure things out."

They approached a hack with an older gentleman seated behind the reins. He greeted them with a nod and a kind smile. "Where can I take you?"

Raven, remembering her role as the wife, let Steele answer. "The Stipes' residence."

The driver studied them for a long moment. "Stipe the state legislator?"

"Yes."

"Why? If you don't mind an old man's nosiness."

"We're going to work in the household."

"Ah. He's not a friend of us Colored people. Just so you know."

"Name a Democrat who is, or at this point, name a Republican. What can you tell us about him?"

The old man said grimly, "One of the biggest supporters of what folks down here call the Mississippi Plan—organized terror and violence to keep us from voting, holding office, and having schools."

"Why did we fight the war?" Brax asked, knowing there was no answer.

"I agree. Name's Mason Golightly. Come on and get in."

"Thank you, sir."

Welch came hurrying over. "What are you doing?"

"Getting a ride to the Stipes' house. Have you hired a hack yet?"

"No one will take Coloreds."

Raven said, "Coloreds will. You're welcome to ride with us, or ride separately and meet us there."

She looked from Raven and Steele to Mr. Golightly. "Do you know where they live?"

"Yes, ma'am. Like the little lady said: You can ride with us if you've a mind to."

She was plainly frustrated. "Fine, I'll go with you."

She crawled into the backseat while they squeezed onto the bench with Mr. Golightly. Once everyone was settled, the big chestnut mare led the hack away.

Raven noted that the homes in Charleston lacked the grillwork and boxlike structure commonly seen in New Orleans, and that instead of the residences facing forward, they were set sideways on their lots to take advantage of the southern breeze off the waters of Charleston Harbor, an inlet of the Atlantic Ocean. The larger homes of the wealthy hid their slave quarters behind vegetation, rendering them virtually invisible from the street. Raven often wondered why but had no answer. One of the ways the city did resemble her hometown was the overwhelming presence of the race. During the ride to the Stipes' she saw dark faces everywhere: walking, driving wagons, working outside shops, and at construction sites. One of her relatives said that before freedom, members of the race outnumbered the Whites in both the city and the state nearly three to one, and from what she was viewing, the percentage hadn't changed much, if at all.

The Stipes lived in a large white house made of wood and brick, and it, too, sat sideways like the homes around it. Mr. Golightly stopped in front and they got out. Shrubs and trees accented the structure both front and back. After Welch paid the fare, Mr. Golightly drove away and the three of them walked to the door.

A very thin middle-aged White woman wearing an overabundance of face paint, a dated gown too large for her frame, and an awful light brown wig answered the door pull and viewed them with wariness. "May I help you?"

Welch introduced herself as Annabelle Clarkston, the sister of Adelaide Clarkston, and Raven and Braxton as the Millers.

"Oh, the couple Adelaide recommended I hire."

"Yes," Welch said, smiling.

"Please, come inside. I'm Helen Stipe."

They entered and Raven discreetly looked around. The interior was well furnished, and to her relief the dark wood floors, white walls, and upholstered furniture all appeared to be exceptionally clean. That meant she'd hopefully spend less time scrubbing and mopping, and more time searching for the purloined document.

Mrs. Stipe said, "I wasn't aware that you'd be accompanying the Millers."

"My sister wanted me to see to a few details tied to the selling of her home, so I decided to come along and to make sure they arrived safely. I'm glad you took her up on the recommendation. You couldn't ask for better employees."

Mrs. Stipe eyed them. "Good to know. Dahlia and Sylvester, my former help, will be hard to replace." She moved her attention back to Welch. "So, you'll be joining her in England?"

"Eventually."

"Well, let's hope you'll like it there. Frankly, your sister is one of the nosiest people I've ever met. When she wasn't asking questions about everything and everybody, she was spreading gossip."

Welch startled.

Raven wanted to guffaw, but instead said, "You have a nice place, Mrs. Stipe." She made a point of not speaking in her natural New Orleans–toned voice.

"Thank you. I purchased this house after the war. Our old place outside the city was much larger. It was commandeered by the Yankee invaders and turned into a field hospital."

"I see."

With so much paint on her face it was hard to determine her age, but her hands had the visible veins and spotted skin of a woman past her prime. Above the mantle hung a large portrait of a handsome younger man with dark hair and eyes, very much in his prime. Raven noted Welch staring at it. Mrs. Stipe apparently did, too. "That's Aubrey, my philandering, adulterous husband. Pretty, isn't he?" she asked bitterly.

Raven and Steele shared looks of surprise. Welch appeared taken aback as well.

"Mr. and Mrs. Miller, bring your bags and come with me. I'll show you your quarters."

They followed her silently.

The trek took them outside to an area behind a stand of trees. They passed a brick building with a line of windows across the top. Mrs. Stipe explained, "The former owner had quite a few slaves and they lived in this building. The kitchen's inside and so is the laundry. You can explore it later."

A short walk later, they passed another barrier of trees and shrubbery that led to a small one-story cottage. It was made of wood and painted white. On the porch was a rocker. Planters holding red and pink flowers flanked the blue painted door.

"This is where you'll be staying."

Raven found it way nicer than she'd expected.

"The former owner's mother lived here. I gave it to Dahlia and Sylvester because it didn't make sense to leave it empty, and it gave them some privacy."

Inside they found the interior small, but the front room had enough space for a sofa and a chair. There was a hearth and a small kitchen. Off the kitchen were a bedroom with a large bed and a connected washroom with a claw-foot tub.

"The pump's out back," she informed them.

Raven was extremely impressed.

Mrs. Stipe said pointedly, "Mrs. Miller, I'll expect you to prepare my meals, keep up the house, do the marketing and the laundry. Mr. Miller, you'll do the driving, chop any wood that's needed, and keep the trees and shrubs trimmed. Sylvester was also my husband's valet, but since being elected he spends most of his time in Columbia and is rarely here, so you'll drive me instead, especially on Wednesday afternoons when I visit my sister, Emaline. She lives on the other side of the city."

He nodded.

Raven hoped the document they were after was in the house and not in the husband's legislative office.

"Dahlia and Sylvester left on short notice, but the pantry is well stocked and I've had a friend provide me with meals since their departure. We'll go to the market tomorrow so you'll know where it is. I know you just got off the train but I'm paying you to work, so I'll be expecting supper by five. You can rest up after. If you're hungry now, get yourself something to eat. Here's the key to the building."

"Thank you."

"Any questions?"

Braxton spoke up. "How many days a week will we be expected to work and what are we to be paid?"

"You'll have Sundays off. As for pay, your kind worked for free in exchange for food and a place to live all my life. So forgive me if I forget that times have changed," she explained with a tone that didn't hold an ounce of remorse. She then quoted a compensation sum Raven deemed low, but not low enough to argue about because she didn't plan on being employed long enough for it to matter.

With that, Mrs. Stipe left them.

Detective Welch spoke first. "She was certainly interesting."

"Did you know the husband wouldn't be on the premises?"

"Him being a state senator, I assumed most of his time would be in Columbia."

"And if the document is there and not here?"

"Then I suppose I'll have to come up with another plan, won't I?"

Raven hated Welch's flippant attitude. Solid information was vital for an operation like this to be successful. If the document was indeed in his office, this trip would be a waste of everyone's time and energy. She also didn't like the possibility of being further tethered to Welch if a new plan became necessary, because who knew how long it might take for the detective to come up with one?

Welch asked, "Do you have any questions for me?"

"Where will you be staying in case we need to speak with you?"

Welch wrote down the address and handed it over. "As I said, the sooner you find the document, the better."

Steele nodded.

Raven offered nothing.

Welch gave Raven an icy look of disapproval and departed.

"Thank you, Jesus!" Raven declared once they were alone.

Steele chuckled.

"I really don't like that woman," she stated.

"Do tell."

Raven showed her smile.

"I must agree with you though. I don't like her at all."

"Plus I don't think she knows a gator from a butter churn. Another plan indeed."

"You don't have to hide your true voice when we're alone," he told her.

"I do. Going back and forth between them is

a good way to get tripped up. I don't want New Orleans accidentally slipping out and have to explain why my speech has changed."

"That makes sense, I suppose, but I've grown accustomed to your New Orleans speech, and find that I'm missing it."

Raven thought that was one of the sweetest things a man had ever said to her but wasn't sure she wanted to reveal that. He was already more than she could handle. "My true accent will return in time. Promise."

"I'm holding you to that."

His tone affected her senses like slow ripples across a pond. Needing to change the subject, she asked, "So, what are your impressions of our employer?"

"More astute than Welch relayed, and definitely not having an enjoyable time in her marriage."

"Philandering and adulterous. I got the sense that his sins aren't a secret."

"As did I."

"I do agree with Welch on one thing. I vote we find this document as quickly as possible so we can get the hell out of here."

"I vote the same."

She glanced around the cottage's interior. "Thanks to Welch's poor intelligence gathering, we don't know if it's tucked away or lying around in plain sight, but let's assume hidden for now. If you were him and wanted to hide something in an unlikely place, where would it be?"

"Do I get a reward if I give the right answer?"

She snorted. "Be serious."

"I am serious."

She rolled her eyes.

"Okay. Were I the adulterous and philandering legislator, I'd hide it in the slave sleeping quarters. Not this little place here, but in the building we passed on the way."

"Why?"

"It's not being used."

She'd thought the same and was impressed by his deduction. "You're good at this."

"I'm good at many things."

This was the first time they'd had any privacy since the night on the verandah. He was a beautiful, bearded god of a man who'd probably been tempting women since birth. "I'm not taking that bait."

"Are you certain?"

His small ghost of a knowing smile and vibrant dark eyes were two of the most potent weapons in his amorous arsenal. Both made her senses unfurl and open like petals of a bloom under the morning sun. He had no right to be able to affect her by simply standing across a room. "Put your magic away, conjure man. Let's go see what the kitchen has to offer to eat. I'm starving."

"As am I."

Determined to ignore the double meaning of those softly spoken three words and the way they made her nipples tighten and sensual warmth flow languidly through her thighs, she removed her bonnet and led him back outside.

Using the key, they entered the brick building and closed the door behind them. The air was stuffy and the interior silent as a tomb. Steele reopened the door again to let in what little breeze was to be had, and propped it open with two bricks that were on the ground beside it as if for that purpose.

A short hallway led into the kitchen.

"Larger than I expected," Raven said, looking around. "Plenty of counter space for preparing things. Modern stove looks fairly new."

"As does the cold box."

She eyed a table and the two chairs set against one wall. It was large enough to sit and dine and could be used for preparation if extra space was needed. At the far end of the room was a large two-sided stone sink. There was a door beside it.

He walked over and opened it. "Pump's right here."

She liked knowing there was easy access to water when it was needed. "Not too bad, so far. It's probably awful to cook in here during the summer months though."

"What do you mean?"

"No window."

He glanced around. "That makes no sense."

"It does if you aren't the person doing the cooking."

A pantry held items like coffee, sugar, flour, lard, spices, and rice, along with jars holding put-up fruit like peaches. Jars holding green beans, cabbage, and succotash stood beside them. In baskets beneath were sweet potatoes and a wilted bunch of carrots that had seen better days. She disposed of those. In the cold box she found the remnants of a ham. A quick smell let her know it wasn't rancid so she found a knife in one of the drawers and cut off a few pieces and laid them on a plate. There was a partial loaf of stale bread in the bread box. After checking it closely for mold, she made sandwiches. She planned to make a more substantial meal for dinner. If she didn't drop from weariness first.

They ate the sandwiches, washed them down with water from the pump, and then went to explore the rest of the building. The laundry was across from the kitchen, with clotheslines strung above their heads. No windows in there, either.

A short flight of stairs took them up to the second floor, where they discovered two rooms. Each held four wooden bedsteads built low to the ground. The floors were covered with dust. "Sleeping quarters," he said.

She nodded. The room had a lot of windows. "Do they open?"

He walked over. "They look painted shut."

She shook her head at the lack of comfort afforded the people who spent their captive lives making life easier for the people who owned them. She glanced around with an eye for a place to hide something. On the surface there was nothing. "Let me try something. I'll need you to be quiet for a moment."

He grinned but didn't ask about a reward, but she knew he was thinking it. She took a slow walk around the room and knocked on the plaster walls, listening for a change in the sound.

When that yielded nothing she examined the floorboards for colors in the wood that didn't match, then with her eyes closed ran her hands slowly over the walls again to feel for seams or repairs. Nothing. The second room turned up just as empty.

As they walked back down to the main floor, he said, "You're good at this."

Echoing him, she tossed back with a smile, "I'm good at many things."

Done with the searching for the moment, they washed up the lunch dishes and returned to the cottage.

Once inside, Raven dropped down tiredly onto the sofa. "I could sleep for a year."

"You should take a nap."

She shook her head. "I'll have to get up shortly in time to make her dinner. When I go to sleep tonight, I want it to be uninterrupted. It's been a long day."

"It has been. We've only the one bed, so you take it and I'll make do out here."

"Are you sure?"

"No, I'd much rather sleep with you, honestly, but I'm not going to impose myself. I'd rather be invited."

She wasn't touching that bait, either. "Then how about we switch off. I'll take the bed tonight. You sleep in it tomorrow night."

"That might be a good compromise."

"Then let's do that."

"Okay."

Raven found clean bed linens in a large chest in the room. After putting them on the bed and handing Steele some for the sofa, they unpacked their clothes and other belongings and stowed their travel valises and carpetbags in the room's small closet. She viewed the bed longingly. "I think I should go sit outside because if I stay in here any longer I'm going to crawl into bed and it'll take a cannon to wake me up."

Outside, she sat in the rocker and he took a seat on the lip of the porch. "Where'd you learn the wall-knocking technique and all the other things?"

"Family, of course. My uncle Saul. He was a master at finding hidden safes and the like."

"Is he the one who drowned at sea?"

She shook her head. "No, that was Ezekial. Saul died during the yellow fever outbreak in '67. Over three thousand people lost their lives that summer."

"Is it always that serious?"

"No, sometimes the numbers are much smaller. Each summer seems to be different. There's already been a few deaths this year so far. I just pray we don't have a repeat of '67."

WHEN IT CAME time for dinner, Raven began her preparations in the kitchen while Steele used the time to familiarize himself with the Stipe horses and carriage, and the tools he'd be using to maintain the landscaping.

When the food she prepared was ready to serve, Raven placed a clean tea towel over the plate and walked it the short distance to the house. Assuming the meal would be eaten in the dining room she'd seen earlier, she entered it and found their employer seated at the table.

"You're to be commended, Mrs. Miller. You're on time."

"You said five, ma'am, not ten minutes past, or a quarter past."

Raven set the plate down. "It was too late to start bread, but I will make some tomorrow."

"That will be fine."

Raven turned to go.

"No, stay. In the future you and your husband will eat in here with me."

"That isn't necessary."

"No, it isn't, but it is what I prefer. Dahlia and Sylvester always ate supper with me. Made us feel like family."

Raven didn't know how she felt about that but knew what she was supposed to say. "I'll let my husband know."

Stipe nodded. "Go fix yourself a plate and come back. I'd like to learn a bit about you. Bring your man."

"Yes, ma'am."

Raven left and returned with Steele. They sat and ate and gave their rehearsed answers to the questions she posed about where they'd met and how long they'd been married. "Mr. Miller, you sound like a true Yankee. What state?"

"I lived with my grandparents for a while growing up in Maine; that might be what you're hearing."

She studied him as if assessing his explanation. "Are you faithful to your wife, Mr. Miller?"

He didn't hesitate. "Until the day I die, ma'am."

"Is he?" she asked Raven.

"Yes, ma'am." Impressed by the lie he'd made up on the fly about Maine, Raven gave him a loving look, and he reached over and gently squeezed her hand in response.

Mrs. Stipe appeared pleased. "Good. This house doesn't need another adulterer. Aubrey sins enough for every man on the Carolina coast."

Raven heard the anger in her words and the pain beneath.

"I never should have married him," she said wistfully. "Especially knowing my only asset was my fortune and my slaves. I wasn't a beauty and ten years his senior, but I wanted a husband and he wanted to be something other than dirt poor."

Raven wasn't sure why she was telling them this, but it made for an uncomfortable moment. She glanced at Steele. Whatever he was thinking lay hidden behind the mask he was so good at donning.

Mrs. Stipe added, "I'm probably going to take an ax to him when it's all said and done, but it won't be today."

The hairs stood up on the back of Raven's neck. Steele's mask dropped for a second, revealing his shock.

"And you don't have to call me Mrs. Stipe. My slaves called me Miss Helen. I prefer that."

"Yes, ma'am."

"Were both of you free Coloreds?"

They nodded.

"Then pretend as if you weren't and we'll do just fine." She rose to her feet. "I won't need you anymore this evening. Get everything cleaned up and I'll see you in the morning. Breakfast is always at seven."

And she left the room.

Raven and Steele retrieved the dishes, and on the walk back to the kitchen, she said, "The sooner we leave here the better."

"Can it be tomorrow?"

"From your lips to the good Lord's ears."

AFTER THE KITCHEN was cleaned and the dishes done, they sat on the porch and watched the sunset. Raven thought their small cottage was the best thing about Charleston so far. She enjoyed the flowers on the porch, the rocker, and the coziness of the place. "Do you really think she'll take an ax to her husband? Or was she pulling our leg?"

"I've no idea, but if she does, I hope we'll be gone by then. I don't want us implicated in any way."

Raven agreed. "One moment she seems kind, the next she's talking about axes and wanting us to pretend we were enslaved."

"Interesting woman. Will you need my help with breakfast in the morning?"

His answer was the sound of her softly snoring. Chuckling and finding her endearing once again, he very carefully picked her up from the rocker, and carried her into the bedroom. He laid her down as if she were both fragile and precious before covering her with a light quilt. He doubted she wanted to sleep in her clothing, but he hadn't the right nor the permission to undress her, so he leaned down, pressed a kiss against her cheek, and tiptoed out of the room, closing the door behind him.

He was exhausted as well, and in spite of his chivalry wasn't looking forward to sleeping on the small sofa. He walked back outside instead and watched the dusk give way to night. In his perfect world, the stolen document would be found quickly. His attraction to Raven still needed closure but he was ready to return to Boston. He missed the city, his work at his tailor shop, and his role with the charity projects he sponsored and helped with as well. After his return from the war, he'd thrown himself into the good works championed by his mother and grandparents and began contributing not only his money but his time to those in need. It was as if bearing arms on behalf of the race and freedom had shown him his life's purpose.

Presently, however, his purpose was to find a purloined copy of one of the nation's founding articles. One that, when brought into existence, didn't consider men with skin like his even worthy of a mention. That this mission was in the hands of people of the race held its own irony. He pulled his thoughts away from that maddening subject and chose to muse upon Miss Raven Moreau instead, and thought back on the talents she'd displayed in her searching. It would never have occurred to him to knock on walls or study the way floorboards were laid as clues to hidden places. He'd been fascinated watching her use her fingertips to locate unseen seams in the plaster. If the object they were after was indeed on the property, she'd find it, and he had no doubts. Until then, he'd do his best to stay out of her way so she could do her job, support her in every way, keep her safe, and not do anything that might mess up her plans. Wanting to have her in his arms again and loving her slowly and fully wasn't supposed to be on the official list, but was on his personal one. The memories of their night together on the verandah were so vivid and potent, he'd take them to the grave, and he wanted very much to add more. Smiling at that, he stood, slapped at a mosquito searching for a nighttime meal, and went inside to sleep on the sofa.

Chapter Ten

*R*aven awakened before dawn to the ringing of an ax. Bleary and disoriented, it took a moment for her to recognize her surroundings. Once she did, she sat up slowly and ran her hands over her sleepy eyes. Surprised to find herself fully dressed, she tried to recall why. The last thing she remembered from the night before was being on the porch with Steele. She supposed she'd fallen asleep and he'd put her to bed. In spite of his outrageously scandalous nature, he'd proven his gentlemanly side again, and she was grateful for that. She hadn't brought many changes of clothing and what she had on now was wrinkled and damp from sleep, but he hadn't taken advantage of her by undressing her while she'd had no say.

The ax rang out again, and because it sounded close by, she assumed it might be him splitting wood. Leaving the bedroom, she walked to the back door. It was still dark out and he was half lit by the flames of two torches as he worked. His shirtless state allowed her to view his lean sculpted torso, shoulders, and arms, and even half asleep, she approved.

He brought the ax down again and in the short break of silence when he stopped to free the blade, she called out quietly, "Good morning."

He looked up, and the wavering flames illuminated his smile. "Morning." He set the ax aside and picked up his shirt from the grass. Pulling it on, he walked to where she stood.

"Did you sleep well?" he asked.

"I did. How about you?"

"Let's just say the floor turned out to be a better choice."

She felt guilty hearing the sofa had proven inadequate. They'd both been exhausted from the travel and he'd deserved a good night's sleep, too. "I'll take the sofa tonight. It will probably fit me better."

"I don't mind the floor."

He said it with such sincerity, she didn't know whether to believe him or not. "We can talk about it later."

"Okay. I'm almost done here. There's wood in the kitchen but I didn't think there was enough to last the day, and it'll be too hot to chop more later. Also pumped you some water. It's in a bucket in the washroom."

His kindness was moving. "You've been busy."

"It's what a faithful husband is supposed to do."

She knew he was teasing but there was a thin thread of something else that touched her feelings in a way she found difficult to name.

"I'll carry the wood to the kitchen. You go get washed up."

She nodded and added, "Thanks for putting me to bed last night and for pumping the water."

"You're welcome. Just one of many husbandly services I offer."

Amused, she shook her head and went back inside to begin her day.

AFTER BREAKFAST, MRS. Stipe gave Raven a tour of the house's upper floor. She was shown Mrs. Stipe's large, well-furnished bedroom with its hearth and heavy dark wood furniture, and told it was her job to make the bed daily and clean the washroom. She was also given a schedule as to when other tasks were to be completed, like putting fresh sheets on the bed, dusting, and mopping the floors. Having been a domestic most of her life, Raven had no problems with the assignments but during the tour she kept her eyes open for anything and any space that might serve as a hiding place for what she'd been sent to find.

"How often do you want the walls washed?"

"That's done twice a year. Right before Christmas and again before the Fourth of July."

Mrs. Stipe then led her down a short hallway.

She stopped near two closed doors. "This door leads to my late mother's room. She lived with us for a few years after the war."

She opened it. It was shadowy and hot. The shutters were closed. There was a bed, two wardrobes, a chest, and a vanity with a mirror attached. "Most of her things are still stored here. I should probably get rid of them but I just can't part with them yet."

"How long has she been gone?"

"A decade in November."

Raven wondered if the stolen document was somewhere inside. "And the room across the hall?"

"It belongs to Aubrey. I take pleasure in keeping it locked."

"You don't want me to clean it?"

"No. He wallows in adulterous filth. He deserves to wallow in the same when he's here."

Raven needed to get into that room. "When was the last time it was cleaned?"

Her response was a shrug. "I've no idea. A few months ago maybe. Dahlia handled the cleaning."

"I don't mean to be disrespectful but have you had it checked for vermin?"

Mrs. Stipe startled.

"If mice have somehow gotten in, keeping the room closed up gives them a nice place to stay and multiply. How long has it been since your husband used it?"

"Six or seven months. When he's in town he stops by just long enough to make sure I'm still alive to write the bank drafts that support him, but he sleeps elsewhere."

Raven glanced over at the locked door. "Just to be safe, I should go in and check for vermin. You don't want rats sharing this lovely house with you."

"I suppose you're right. We'll talk about it after the ball."

"Ball?"

"The one I throw every year to benefit Charleston's chapter of the Daughters of the Cause. We're raising money to put up statues of heroes like General Lee and the great Stonewall Jackson. Chapters all across the South are doing the same. It'll be our way of commemorating the bravery and sacrifices of the men who fought to preserve our way of life."

"And yours is held when and where?"

"It's held here, of course, in about three weeks."

"And what are my expected duties?"

"To make sure everything runs smoothly."

Another detail missing from Welch's intelligence gathering. "How many guests do you usually entertain?"

"Fifteen, maybe twenty. I only invite those wealthy enough to contribute."

"I see."

"Dahlia usually handled all the fine details

like bringing in extra servants and cooks. Since you have no roots here, I'll have my sister's housekeeper, Eula, lend a hand. She's been with our family all her life, and remained loyal after the surrender, unlike so many of the other ungrateful wretches who ran off and left us to fend for ourselves."

Raven detested the idea of her search being delayed so she could help raise funds for monuments to men who'd wanted to keep the race enslaved, but she kept the disdain from showing on her face. "I look forward to helping," she lied.

Mrs. Stipe smiled. "Good. It's always such an elegant affair. We bring out our hoop dresses and our best jewelry. It's an evening to celebrate what we lost when everyone knew their place."

"I'm sure it will be memorable, but you don't want it to be remembered for any mice that come uninvited, so you should let me clean your husband's room."

Mrs. Stipe sighed. "I suppose you're right. Constance Manning is always looking for ways to outdo me, and she'd never let anyone forget it if something like that happened. I'll get you the key later."

"Thank you." Raven didn't know who Constance Manning was nor did she care, but applauded the woman for being the means to an end. With any luck, the stolen item would be in the husband's room and Raven and Steele would be gone before the ball.

* * *

AFTER THE TOUR, they set out for the market. Mrs. Stipe directed the way from her seat in the back, while Steele drove with Raven seated beside him on the bench. Once they arrived, Mrs. Stipe remained in the carriage while Raven and Steele meandered their way through the maze of vendors and shoppers to purchase the staples the household needed. They bought sweet potatoes, rice, honey, candles, and yeast. She and Steele were new faces to the women selling the merchandise and were met with smiles and questions about who they were and who they worked for. Some of the women, most of whom were Black, offered the names and locations of their churches, the best doctor in the area, the best seamstress, and the maker of the best Sunday hats. A few of the women flirted outrageously with Steele in a good-natured way that left everyone within earshot laughing when a few told him to keep them in mind if his wife ever kicked him out.

As they continued on their way, Raven stopped for a moment at a stall selling scented soap. She picked up a bar, and it smelled like heaven. She asked the woman at the table, "What is this scent?"

The woman smiled. "Noisette roses."

"Thank you. It smells wonderful."

Steele asked, "Would you like it?"

Raven set the soap back in the basket. "I

would, but I don't have the coin and I don't think our employer wants me buying soap for myself with hers."

He picked up the bar and asked the lady, "How much, ma'am?"

She relayed the price. He counted out the amount and passed the paper-wrapped bar to Raven, who stared at the soap and then up at him in a mix of wonder and confusion.

"Another one of my husbandly duties," he explained.

"But—"

"What else is on Mrs. Stipe's list?"

"Well—" She stopped. Across the way, she spotted her mother seated at a stall selling eggs and hens. Beside her was Maisie, a Moreau cousin. "I need some eggs."

"You go ahead. I see some lamp oil I want to purchase."

Her mother's green eyes were hidden behind spectacles with blue-colored lenses. Her hair was beneath a gray wig and a white headscarf. The oversize black dress she wore was reminiscent of the dresses worn by most of the city's servant class, and a thin rubber mask overlaid with stage paint altered the shape and age of her face. She looked nothing like herself. "How much are your eggs, ma'am?"

A price was quoted in a voice that wasn't Hazel's. Raven took a casual look around the market to see if they were being observed, and there stood Welch a few tables away studying some baskets that were for sale. "I see the cat's here," she said only loud enough for her mother to hear, and nodded a greeting to Maisie.

"Been here most of the morning," her mother replied in an equally low tone.

Raven paid her for the eggs. Keeping an eye on Welch, she said, "I need some mice."

Hazel raised an eyebrow. "How many? Dead or alive?"

"Either. Two, maybe three." In a more conversational tone, Raven asked, "How fresh are these hens?"

"Killed this morning."

"I'll take two."

Cousin Maisie stood, and as she wrapped the hens and put the eggs in a small basket, she said, "It may take a day or two for the mice."

"As soon as you are able will be fine. I'll try and catch some on my own in the meantime." Raising her voice, she said, "Thank you very much for the hens."

"You're welcome," both women replied.

Raven walked over to Steele. "Do you need anything else?"

"No. Do you?"

She shook her head.

"Then let's go back to the carriage. Mrs. Stipe is probably melting in this heat." On the way, he asked, "Did you see Welch?"

"I did. Did you see Mama?"

He stopped. "No."

"The egg lady."

That he had enough discipline not to turn and look back in shock pleased her. "We'll discuss it later."

And with that, he assisted her up to the carriage's bench, then drove them home.

THAT EVENING, AFTER all the chores were done, they sat on the cottage's porch and discussed the day, beginning with the husband's bedroom and the Lost Cause Ball their employer planned to have.

"Monuments?" Brax asked after she explained the ball's purpose.

She nodded. "As part of a campaign to build similar ones all over the South, she told me."

"Why can't they acknowledge losing the war and allow the country to move on instead of clinging to hopes of reinstituting the past?"

"If I could bottle that answer, I'd be a very wealthy woman."

"Indeed. My grandfather gave a ball every year to help the needy in Boston and now I'm in charge of it." Rather than ranting about the celebrants of the Lost Cause, he asked, "Did you know your mother would be at the market?"

"No. I knew we'd cross paths at some point, just not when or where."

"Do you think Welch could see past her disguise? I certainly didn't."

"I don't know, but she said Welch had been there most of the morning. Since Welch didn't know we'd be at the market, I have to wonder if she was there simply buying items for herself or waiting around to meet someone. And if it's the latter, who is it and are they tied to what we're doing here?"

"Interesting questions," he noted. "Do you think what we're after is in his bedroom?"

"My gut says yes, but I need to search it to be certain. Helen's promised to let me clean in there so we'll see if she actually does. I asked Mama to find me some mice. I want to speed up things here."

"Mice?"

She explained her loosely conceived plan. "I want Helen convinced there are mice in that room. If I can, maybe she'll leave and go stay with her sister for a day or so and we can go in and look around."

He was amused by her cleverness. "That might just work. Was your mother surprised by the request?"

"She raised an eyebrow, so more than likely yes. In the meantime, I'll conduct a hunt of my own—they can be alive or dead. I admit it's pretty farfetched, but farfetched sometimes works."

"If I run across any, I'll let you know."

"That would be helpful."

He was still uncomfortable with all this intrigue even while acknowledging being a bit excited waiting for everything to unfold. "I've been asking myself why would Stipe hang on to something he stole over ten years ago? What does he have in mind for it? Does he intend to sell it?"

"Good questions. My concern is whether he still has it."

Braxton agreed. He could come up with no rational reason for it to still be in Stipe's possession, yet Welch seemed convinced it was.

"Helen apparently holds the purse strings," Raven pointed out. "Men don't usually enjoy being financially beholden to their wives, and it would fetch a good price were it up for sale— maybe more than enough to get out from under her thumb, if that's his intention, but I agree with you, why keep it hidden for over ten years?"

"Here's hoping it's still in his possession."

"Amen."

This was their second evening of ending the day together and he was enjoying the time spent with her. "Is there anything you need me to do for you for tomorrow? I think there should be enough wood for the stove for the next couple of days."

"No, I think I'll be fine. Going to get up early to do the wash, so let me have whatever clothing you want added before you go to bed."

"Even though I chopped enough wood for the stove, you'll probably need more to heat the water. Do you want me to fill the cauldrons, too?" The wash was done in two enormous copper cauldrons that were set atop fires to heat the water.

"No. You're probably right about needing more wood, but I can pump the water when I get up and build the fires."

"Let me handle that. You'll have more than enough to do without having to do everything."

"Thank you for offering, but I've been doing laundry since I was nine, Steele. I can do what's needed in my sleep."

He scanned her and wondered if she was as fierce at that young age as she was presently. At nine years old, his only chores were polishing his shoes, completing his lessons, and making sure his clothing for school or church was set out before bed.

"What are you thinking?" she asked quietly.

"Nothing."

"You don't lie very well."

That amused him. "I suppose you're right. Honestly, I was thinking about how easy my childhood seemed in comparison to yours. Nothing more."

"Your very wealthy childhood?" she replied teasingly.

He nodded, then viewed her seriously. "My only worries at age nine were whether my boots were shined and not getting my stockings dirty at school. My mother was obsessed with appearances and insisted that I remember I represented the race wherever I went, and should act accordingly."

"Which meant?"

"Always being on my best behavior, and being as clean and neat when I returned from school as I'd been when I headed off to school each morning."

"That's a lot to put on the shoulders of a child."

"I didn't realize it then, but looking back now, you're right." A memory rose. "I remember playing stickball after school one day. The field was muddy and I was covered with dirt and grime when I came home. I'll never forget the disappointment in my mother's eyes or the stern lecture I received about the image I presented to those outside the race by being so dirty. She said they were always looking for ways to prove we were less polished than they in every way. I never played stickball after school again." He saw the empathy on Raven's face. "You probably think my life was pretty joyless."

"My opinion doesn't matter, only yours."

He realized she was correct, and he wondered if she knew how wise that made her. "I suppose it was in some ways. I was never encouraged to do the typical boy things like climb trees or kneel in the dust to shoot marbles, or splash in puddles. You and your cousins probably did all those things and more."

"We did. We hunted frogs and dug worms for fishing. Climbed trees, built tree houses and rope swings. We got really, really dirty when we played, and our parents never fussed. But we spent most of our daylight hours working. I grew up without shoes or a pretty dress. My hands were red and covered with blisters all the time from the lye I had to use to wash other people's clothes and mop their floors, but I remember lots of joy and good food and family celebrations. It balanced out the bad parts, I suppose."

"You needed some of my life and I needed some of yours."

"I think you're right."

A part of him wanted to make her life easier so she'd never have to wash the clothes or mop the floors of others ever again. He wanted to gift her with closets filled with shoes and pretty dresses. He wanted to take her sailing. Walk with her through the streets of Madrid and Rome and buy her French pastry from the Parisian shops he'd visited with his grandfather. Again, he wondered what it would be like to have her in his life.

"Did your family do anything that was fun?" she asked.

"We went to lectures, abolitionist marches, and theater performances. My grandfather threw a large gathering for his birthday every year, and most of the city's representative class was invited, but it was always a dignified affair. People wore their Sunday best and discussed things like politics, the state of the race, and business deals."

"No dancing or music?"

"No. I usually made an appearance when the guests arrived, then hid out in the attic and read until it was time to eat."

"You value reading quite a bit."

"I do. It's one of my favorite pastimes, as I said before. My books were my companions." When she looked away and stared out unseeingly, he asked, "What's the matter?"

She didn't respond at first, then said, "Nothing. Just thinking about another way we're unevenly yoked."

"Meaning?"

"If I share this with you and you laugh, I'll never speak to you again. Ever."

Her serious tone matched the fierce flash in her eyes.

He couldn't imagine what this might be tied to, but he nodded in agreement.

"I can't read. I mean—I can, but not very well. I left school when I was very young so I could help Mama feed us."

His heart stopped. He knew some families took their children out of school to assist with planting and harvests; he just hadn't expected to associate that with her because she was so clever and confident. As he took in her chin-raised stance, his heart filled with emotion knowing she'd trusted him enough to share something so personal and private, but he wasn't sure how to respond. The last thing he wanted was to destroy that trust by saying something inadvertently hurtful or belittling. He chose his words carefully. "Have you considered going back to school? Many places have classes in the evenings."

She shook her head. "No, I think I'm too old to learn at my age."

"But you aren't too old. I can teach you if you'd like. We can use times like now, at the end of the workday."

She turned her gaze back to the field surrounding the cottage and didn't respond.

"Please let me help, Raven," he implored softly. "I'd never yell at you or berate you. We could make it fun." Admittedly, he'd never taught anyone to read before, and yet he felt the importance of this for her in his bones. He might not be able to take her to Paris, but this he could do.

"Let me think on it, okay?"

"Of course. And thank you for trusting me enough to share something so personal."

She nodded tightly.

WHEN NIGHT FELL and they went inside, Brax tried to convince her to take the bed, but she was having none of it.

"You slept on the floor last night. I'll take the sofa."

"Raven—"

"No. You carried water, chopped wood, drove to the market, and haven't slept in a bed since we left New Orleans. We had an agreement, remember?"

"We did, but—"

She shook her head. "Take the bed. It's your turn."

"That sofa is past awful to sleep on. I'll feel bad knowing you're out here wrestling with it."

"I'm sure I've slept on worse."

"Then how about we share the bed so we both get some sleep. You're doing wash tomorrow. You shouldn't be exhausted before you even begin, and you will be if you attempt to sleep on that poor excuse for a sofa."

"No. We both know what will happen if we share the bed. Neither of us will get any sleep."

"What if I promise to be on my best behavior?"

"I've seen your best behavior. It's how I ended up walking like a drunken sailor the night on the verandah."

"But you enjoyed yourself."

"That's not the issue here, and stop trying to change the subject."

He folded his arms over his chest. "Is that what I'm doing?"

"Yes. And stop smiling."

"Will I earn a reward if I comply?"

She laughed softly, and he enjoyed knowing she hadn't been able to suppress it.

She said, "I'm going to get my night things out of the room. I'll see you in the morning."

He didn't press any further. "Okay, but if you decide the sofa is a poor choice, just come join me."

As they took in each other in the quiet, he again wondered how he'd be able to return to Boston without her.

She retrieved her items from the room and as she exited, he said softly, "Good night, Raven."

"Sleep well," she replied.

LATER, LYING IN the dark, Raven realized he'd told the truth about the awfulness of the sofa. The cushions beneath her had to be filled with rocks, and the stench of mildew they exuded curled her nose. Both factors made finding sleep a challenge, but her biggest challenge was her pretend husband in the bedroom. How much longer would she be able to keep him at a distance when her body wanted nothing but him? She thought back on their conversation out on the porch. It hadn't been her intent to confess what she had. Her difficulty with reading wasn't something she willingly shared. Yet she had, with him, and still didn't know why. Yes, she'd warned him not to laugh or poke fun at what she intended to reveal, but a part of herself seemed to know threatening him hadn't been necessary. His soft plea to let him help her made her turn away so he wouldn't see the tears stinging her eyes, and just the memory of the tenderness in his voice made them sting again. "Lord!" she whispered, wiping the tears away. Why did he affect her so deeply? In the short time since being introduced, he'd gone from being a man she'd intensely disliked to one she'd entrusted with her innermost secret. Nothing about this made sense, and she didn't even want to think about how she'd relished being half naked on his lap in the moonlight while his kisses and touches reduced her to a legs-spread, orgasming mess. How had this happened? Their differences in upbringing, social status, and views of the world were many, and yet there was a shining kindness hidden beneath his staid, stodgy exterior that overrode them. He'd pumped water for her that morning, chopped the wood she'd needed to light the stove, and gifted her with a bar of rose-scented soap. This evening, he'd offered to help her become better at reading, and tried to convince her to trade places with him so she could sleep in the bed. She'd always pumped her own water and chopped her own wood. There'd never been anyone to take on those chores for her, and she didn't know how to handle someone who believed he should because, outside of family, life had dealt her so little kindness. If she weren't careful, he'd have her eating out of his hand like the women of Boston tripping over themselves to catch his eye. Her attraction to him was undeniable though. Undeniable and unfortunate, because there was no future in it. But did she need a future to enjoy his touches, kisses, and kindness? Truthfully, the answer was no, as long as she kept her heart locked away. Based on what she'd experienced so far, falling in love with him would have her comparing men against him for the rest of her life and she wasn't sure any would measure up.

Chapter Eleven

After the night on the uncomfortable sofa, Raven awakened that next morning with her body sore and feeling as if she hadn't slept at all. She would've loved to crawl into the bedroom and get some true sleep, but Mrs. Stipe was expecting breakfast, so she forced herself to sit up and dropped her head into her hands. From outside she heard Steele and the ringing ax, and although she ached everywhere, she tried not to begrudge him having gotten a good night's sleep.

After washing up quickly with her lovely smelling soap, she dressed and stepped outside. Because the sun was still in bed, Steele was again working by torchlight, and she took a moment to appreciate his strong, lean contours as the flames played over his frame. Seeing her, he stopped, shrugged into his shirt, and walked over to where she stood.

"Morning," he said.

"Morning. Did you sleep well?"

"I did. How about you?"

"I'm never sleeping on that thing again, and I'm grumpy enough to punch you if you say, you told me so."

He grinned. "Then I'll keep that to myself."

"I ache everywhere, and I'll be smelling that mildew until the Second Coming." She shuddered at the memory. "I'm going to start breakfast. Come and eat when you're done here. And thanks for the extra wood."

"You're welcome."

Mrs. Stipe preferred to take her breakfast in bed, so once the scrambled eggs, grits, and biscuits were done, Raven placed everything on a tray and carried it upstairs. She eyed the closed door to the husband's room and the space between the base of it and the floor. More than enough room for a mouse to go in and out, she decided.

She tapped lightly on Mrs. Stipe's closed door. "I have your breakfast, Miss Helen."

"Come on in."

Helen was in bed with a wealth of pillows braced behind her. The worn silk jacket over her nightgown was pink and accented with faded lace. Her wig was on, the heavy makeup already applied, along with the bright red paint on her thin lips. After placing the tray on her lap, Raven asked, "Anything else I can get you?"

"No. This is fine for now. I'll be going to

spend the day with my sister, so tell your man I'll be ready to leave at nine. She lives about thirty minutes away and he's to return for me promptly at four this afternoon."

"Yes, ma'am."

"You're doing the wash today, correct?"

"Yes, ma'am."

"If you'll be washing for you and your man, too, I insist you keep my items separate."

Raven kept her reaction from showing on her face. "As you wish. Do you want yours hung separately as well?"

"Yes."

"Then if you don't need anything else from me, I'll go get started."

"Make sure supper's ready by five."

"I will. Enjoy your day with your sister."

"I won't, but thank you for the thought."

Raven left the room. She'd separate the wash not to honor Helen's bigotry, but because who knew what little beasties might be living in that ratty wig on her head.

BRAX DROPPED HELEN off at her sister's and after being pointedly reminded for the third time when she wanted him to return for her, he headed back to assist Raven with the wash. As he drove through the crowded streets, memories of being in the area during the war rose unbidden, bringing with it the cries of battle, the sounds and smoke of cannon and weapons, and the screams of the injured and dying. He and the men of the Fifty-Fourth were initially assigned manual duties, digging latrines and such. Many in the nation and the Union army harbored doubts about the Black soldiers' ability to prove their worth under fire, however, Brax and his fellows were eager to show what they could do. On July 18, under the command of Massachusetts abolitionist and Harvard graduate Colonel Robert Gould Shaw, the Fifty-Fourth along with five thousand Union soldiers began marching in the darkness towards the rebel-held Fort Wagner on South Carolina's Morris Island. Those in command and their troops were filled with confidence. The Union had been battering Wagner with artillery from its fleet led by Rear Admiral John Dahlgreen, and assumed the battle would be easily won. The Fifty-Fourth led the attack, and when they began the charge, the Southerners opened fire. The screams of the dying and wounded pierced the darkness. In his mind, Brax recalled the chaos, firing back, the ear-shattering explosions of the armaments, and trying to stay alive. The Union had badly underestimated the size of the Confederate forces. Inside the fort were eighteen hundred rebs. More than three times the six hundred men of the Fifty-Fourth. As the rebs' artillery kept up the barrage, the intensity of their return fire made Shaw halt his men and change direction. Brax and the others followed him through a moat and up a slope. At the summit, the rebs were waiting, and in the desperate hand-to-hand combat that followed, Shaw, who'd been injured earlier in the war at the battle of Antietam, became among the first to die. Of the six hundred Black soldiers with him, two hundred and eighty were killed, wounded, or missing and thought to be dead. Brax thought back on the friends lost in the bloodbath: Rogers from Canada, Jean-Pierre, who'd come from Haiti to help with the fight, Prince, an escaped slave from Charleston. Hoping to turn the tide, a second wave of Union troops from New Hampshire, Maine, and Pennsylvania pushed forward after the Fifty-Fourth, but the rebs were determined to hold and they did. In the early morning of July 19, after hours of fighting, the Union forces withdrew.

Brax and the others were devastated by the loss of Shaw. He'd stood up for them when the army paid them less money than its White soldiers, and in the fight to take Fort Wagner, he'd led his men into battle, not sent them ahead as was the conventional method of war. In a mean-spirited show of contempt, the Confederates dumped Shaw's body and the bodies of the dead of the Fifty-Fourth into an unmarked grave and sent a telegram to the Union generals saying, "We have buried Shaw with his niggers." They'd hoped this would make other White officers think twice about leading Black troops. It didn't. The 180,000 Black troops under their White commanders would go on to help the Union win the war. Brax just wished Colonel Shaw had been alive to savor the victory.

In the days and months after mustering out and returning home, Brax had struggled with the question of why he'd lived and so many others in his regiment hadn't. The guilt plagued him. One night at supper he'd discussed his feelings with his father, who told him the question would never be answered, but having returned home whole was a gift Brax should use to honor those who'd died, ensuring their deaths hadn't been in vain. The wise advice brought light into the dark corners of his soul, and in response he picked up the mantle of charity work left behind by his mother and grandmother. Each time he helped a local school pay its teachers, or donated to families needing housing or food, or employed young apprentices to help them learn to make a living, he looked upon it as a tribute to Rogers, Jean-Pierre, Prince, and all the others who'd made the ultimate sacrifice.

He was just about at the Stipe place when he saw a sign on a white wood fence that read: SUZY SEWS. Behind the fence, a small, bright yellow house was set back from the road. Seeing a handful of Black children playing in the yard, he wondered if Suzy was a woman of the race and if the sign referenced a shop inside. Remembering the wonder on Raven's face when he gifted her the soap at the market, he assumed, rightly or wrongly, that being given presents wasn't a regular occurrence in her life. He wondered if Suzy might have some things he could purchase for her. He stopped the carriage and walked to the house.

Inside, he met the short, rotund proprietress, and after looking around the small neat room holding her goods, he found just what he needed. After paying for his purchases, he thanked her, she thanked him, and he returned to the carriage to resume his journey.

He found Raven outside with the wash. In the open field beside the cottage, four sheets were already hung on lines of rope stretched between tall metal poles. Between the poles were two empty poles, which he assumed would hold the rest of the items needing to be hung. She was wearing an old leather apron to protect her clothing, and on her feet a pair of aging brogans had replaced her usual pair of worn black leather slippers. Standing a short distance away, he watched as she used what appeared to be an old broom handle to lift a jumble of steaming towels out of the cauldron of boiling water. Straining from the weight, she eased the load into the one holding the rinse water. As she repeated the process, he walked over. "Can I help you with that?"

She smiled tiredly. "Thanks for the offer but I'm nearly done." She transferred a second mass to the rinse water and slowly stirred the contents with her stick.

He eyed two smaller water-filled barrels. "What are those for?"

"One holds bluing for white things like sheets. The other starch. You've never seen laundry done?"

"Not the full process, no," he admitted. "Ours was always sent out."

"People with means to pay are smart. It's grueling work, especially for a large household. Helen doesn't have many clothes, so I'm counting my blessings. I'm not looking forward to spending the evening ironing the sheets and pillow slips though, but it could be worse. I could be handling the laundry and ironing for a family of six instead of just hers and ours."

Although his knowledge of washday was limited, he knew that the contraption next to the cauldrons, with its rollers and crank atop a tub, was a wringer. "How about I man the crank while you feed the pieces into the wringer?"

"Okay."

Her lack of sleep showed in the small circles below her eyes and the weary slump in her shoulders. The caustic effects of the lye in the hot wash water had reddened her hands. Again, he wished he could make her life easier, particularly in a way more impactful than assisting with a wringer, but a small step was better than none.

"Turn it slowly," she cautioned, feeding a towel into the wringer. "We don't want the rollers to tear it."

Focusing on both the speed and the progress, he kept her words in mind. As the towel made its journey, the excess water drained into the tub beneath. Once the towel came out the other side, she gave the compressed item a few shakes and placed it in the basket with the other things waiting to be hung.

"Can I help with the hanging?"

"Ever hung clothes before?"

"No."

She picked up the basket. "Then I have to say no."

"Why?" How difficult could it be, he wondered inwardly.

"Because if you accidentally drop a piece into the dirt, I'll have to wash it again, then kill you and bury you beneath those trees over there."

"Oh."

"If you want to be useful, dump the water out of the cauldrons and refill them so I can wash our things."

"That I can do."

She carried the basket away and he set about his assigned task.

Two hours later, everything was washed and hung. They took a break to eat lunch, then after emptying the cauldrons for the last time, he helped her scrub them out and set them on the grass to dry. The day was sunny and breezy, and as a result the sheets that had been washed first were all but dry. He checked his pocket watch for the time. It was half past two. He'd have to go get Helen in an hour or so. They were seated on the cabin's porch. Raven was in the rocker, eyes closed. He studied her and asked quietly, "Are you asleep, little corvus?"

"I wish," came her soft reply. Her eyes opened slowly. "Gathering my strength so I can take down what's dry. I may have time to iron her sheets before cooking supper. I'd hoped to search her mother's room while she was away but there's been no time."

She worked entirely too hard, he thought.

As if having read his mind, she smiled tiredly. "Stop looking so concerned, Steele. I'm just feeling the effects of my sleepless night, nothing more. This is how I make my living, remember? I'll be fine. Promise."

In his perfect world, she'd spend the evening leisurely soaking in a tub of bath salts and bubbles instead of ironing sheets and preparing food for someone else. "If I promise to be careful and not let anything fall to the ground, will you allow me to help you?"

She nodded and pushed to her feet. "Sure. Come on."

Pleased that she'd agreed, he assisted with the chore of unpinning the now dry items from the lines, and true to his pledge, made sure nothing ended up in the dirt. They carried the laundry-filled baskets to the building that housed the kitchen and into the room where she'd do the ironing.

She asked, "What time is it?"

He checked his pocket watch. "A quarter past three."

"Ironing will have to wait then. You go fetch Helen and I'll start supper."

"Okay."

"And thank you for the help."

The sincerity in her words moved him. "Just trying to earn my keep."

"You're doing such a good job I may have to keep you."

He knew she was teasing but it still felt good to hear. "You know how much I enjoy being rewarded." Unable to resist, he drew a slow, adoring finger down her cheek. "Later tonight, after your chores, I'll bring in water so you can take a bath. Would that be okay?"

"That would be nice. Thank you."

She pushed up on her toes and kissed him with a slow sweetness that was both arousing and longed for. "Your reward for your kindness today," she whispered.

He eased her closer, relishing her softness and the way her lips fit perfectly against his own. As desire rose and slowly gained strength, he held her tight, savored the hot, teasing invites of her tongue and the feel of her palms roaming languidly over his back. His did the same, re-learning her curves and hollows, the peaks of her nipples, the slope of her hips.

He brushed his lips over her ear. "And after the bath, I'll give you kisses and touches that'll make you come so you'll get a good night's sleep. Would you like that?"

"Only if they're scandalous."

He smiled. "I'll make sure they are."

After a few more moments, they parted reluctantly.

She cupped his bearded jaw. "Go and get Helen."

He took in the heat simmering in her dark eyes, her lips swollen by his kisses, and leaving her was the last thing he wanted. He traced her mouth and leaned in for one last taste of paradise. Only when she was breathless and crooning from the preview of the scandalous touches promised for later did he depart.

After his exit, Raven didn't move. She was encased in a haze of passion that made her want to call him back so they could continue. His touch and kiss were so magical every inch of her was alive and greedy for more. But she couldn't stand there forever. Helen would expect her dinner precisely at five and wouldn't be pleased if it was late. Shaking herself free, Raven forced herself to go and do her job.

While waiting for the stove to heat to the desired temperature, Raven made a pan of biscuits and carved up the last of the hen they'd had the day before. After boiling sweet potatoes in one pot and adding a jar of put-up green beans in another, dinner was on its way.

Steele came in just as she was removing the biscuits from the oven. The way he took her in brought back the memory of the kisses they'd shared earlier, and she sensed he was thinking back, too. Reminding herself that she had a job to do, she refocused on dinner and turned the biscuits out onto a platter. When he snitched a couple and groaned pleasurably after taking a bite, she shot him a smile and began placing the rest of the offerings on Helen's plate. "What kind of mood is she in?"

Still enjoying his biscuit, he replied, "Fussed about her sister the entire way. Not sure why she visits if they don't get along, but not my place to ask."

Raven didn't know, either, and frankly, nor did she care. She dearly wanted to skip having to share supper with her and get the ironing done instead, but her presence was expected. She just hoped she didn't fall asleep at the table.

She placed Helen's plate along with her own on a tray. Accompanied by the man who'd promised her kisses and touches later, she left the kitchen for the short journey to the main house.

Helen was already seated at the dining room table. Raven set her plate down before her and removed the metal cover that had kept it warm.

"Thank you," Helen said, eyeing the meal.

Raven and Steele sat and supper began.

Helen said, "I spoke with my sister's housekeeper about the ball and she's agreed to assist. She plans to hire a caterer to take care of the food and make arrangements for the service staff. I told her only hire people who worked in the house. Field slaves don't know a thing about what's required or what's proper at a function like this. She'll come by and talk to you in a few days."

"I'll look forward to meeting her."

"Did the laundry get done?"

"Yes. I still have the ironing to do."

"Good. I'll need the clean sheets and pillow slips by the time I turn in."

"Yes, ma'am." Raven had been in her employ only a couple of days but had replied with enough "Yes, ma'ams" to last a lifetime.

Supper conversation tended to consist of Helen doing all the talking and Raven and Steele doing the listening. That evening was more of the same.

"I saw in the newspaper that yellow fever is marching through New Orleans again. Hundreds of people are already dead. Texas and Mississippi are talking of not letting trains from there travel through their states. I told my sister yellow fever is caused by all the race mixing they do in that godforsaken city."

Raven knew there were many competing theories as to the cause of the fever, but miscegenation was not one of them. The news of all the deaths was troubling, however. She hoped Vana, Eden, and the others in the city weren't being affected. The sickness had caused enough heartbreak in the Moreau family. She shared a look of concern with Steele. Helen, still waxing about the sins of race mixing, was too self-absorbed to notice.

Grateful when the meal ended, Raven and Steele took the dishes back to the kitchen. As she washed and he dried, he asked, "Is it common for states to stop trains from New Orleans during yellow fever?"

"It's happened occasionally in the past, but hopefully it won't be necessary this time around. I don't want to be stuck here."

"Neither do I."

"You can take a northbound train home once we're done here."

"True, but what will you do?"

She shrugged and placed a platter in the rinse water. "Figure it out, I suppose."

"You're always welcome to come to Boston."

She smiled. "And stay where?"

"With me. I've plenty of space."

Amusement made her shake her head. "I'm

sure your prizewinner would look real kindly
on that arrangement."

"Once Da marries your mother, you'll be
family."

"Uh-huh."

"No?"

"No, Steele. I'm not living any place where
water freezes."

"You might like it."

"No, I know I won't. Let's get these dishes
done, so I can iron her sheets before I drop."

"You've put in a full day."

"I have." But women like herself were expected to work from no light to no light, and be
grateful to have any employment at all. Complaints tied to being overburdened were neither
tolerated nor addressed because you could be
easily replaced by others with children to feed
and debts to pay.

When the last dish was done and put away,
he asked, "How long do you believe it will take
to get the ironing done?"

"Maybe an hour. I also have to put the sheets
on her bed."

"Okay. While you handle that, I'll get started
on heating the water for your bath."

She studied him, her emotions mixed. "You
really don't have to do this."

"Yes, I do," he replied solemnly.

She looked away to hide those same emotions
now welling up inside. As she'd noted last night

while trying to sleep on that awful excuse for a sofa, such small shows of kindness were new to her, and she wasn't sure how to respond. Saying thank you seemed inadequate, but it was all she had. "Thank you," she said. "I feel as though I've said that to you a hundred times today, but your help has meant so much."

"It's been my honor."

A few days ago, she'd wanted him thrown into a bayou, and now . . .

"Go iron," he said quietly. "Your bath will be ready when you're done."

Moved by all he was, she left him to handle her last burden of the day.

WITH THE IRONING done and Helen in her room sleeping on clean and freshly ironed sheets, Raven made the short walk back to the cottage. Night had fallen. The moon was out, and the songs of frogs and insects could be heard. When she reached the cottage, Brax was seated in the dark on the porch. Nearby, the embers of the fire he must have used to heat the water for her bath glowed dully.

His voice broke the silence. "Done?"

"Yes."

"Your bath awaits. The water might be still quite warm, so be careful."

"Did you save some water for yourself?"

"I'll wash up out here at the pump. You go on in. Let me know when you're done."

She was so accustomed to taking care of everyone else, being pampered this way was overwhelming. "Okay."

As soon as she entered the cottage, she smelled roses. Puzzled yet pleased, she walked to the bedroom by the light of the moon streaming through the small windows and into the bedroom where a lone lamp was lit. The sweet scent permeated the air. She had no guesses as to its source until she entered the washroom and ran her hand languidly through the warmth of the waiting tub water. Bringing her fingers to her nose, she realized the aroma was bath salts. But how? She hadn't brought any with her from New Orleans. Was the kindhearted man outside responsible? Not wanting the water to cool further while she contemplated the mystery, she set her questions aside, undressed, and got in. The heat of the scented water was a balm after the long, chore-filled day, and she sighed pleasurably. It felt so good. That he had gone out of his way to offer her this gift put tears in her eyes. Wiping at them, she allowed herself a few moments to bask in the glory before picking up her bar of rose soap from where it waited atop a white towel on a little stool beside the tub. Still teary, she began washing away the day.

When she finished, she pulled the plug on the drain to the pipe that led the water outside and stepped out. Picking up the bath sheet—also new to her—she wrapped herself in it before slowly drying herself. Padding out to the bedroom to get her nightgown, she stopped at the sight of a nightgown lying across the bed. Puzzled again because she'd never seen it before, she picked it up and studied it by the light of the lamp. The garment was soft blue and made of a polished lightweight cotton, perfect for the South's warm nights. It wasn't the fancy, designed-to-catch-a-man's-eye type of nightwear favored by women like her cousin Lacie. It was serviceable, yet still feminine, with small, fluted, capped sleeves trimmed with a delicate line of lace that matched the lace at the neck. Small white buttons trailed down the front. Had he purchased this for her as well? Her own nightgown was old and faded from its many washings, with a side seam mended after being mangled by her mother's ancient wringer. This one appeared brand-new, and she dashed away a fresh show of tears. After the wonderful bath, a new gown was fitting, so rather than let her pride rule and not accept it, she quickly treated her skin with the oil she'd brought from home and put it on.

When she glanced up from her seat on the edge of the mattress, he was standing in the doorway. He was shirtless above his trousers. "Do you like it?" he asked.

"I do. Thank you for the two hundredth time today. And for the bath salts." The room still held the faint scent of roses.

"You're welcome."

He came into the light. His damp skin and hair showed he'd washed off the day as well, and she enjoyed this first, up-close look at his splendidly sculpted form.

"Are you ready for your kisses and touches?"

Her senses flared and heat shimmered between her thighs. "Yes."

He came over and sat beside her on the bed. Reaching out, he gently raised her chin and she saw the fire in his gaze. "Then let's begin . . ."

He started with a slow, lingering invitation of a kiss that was as masterful as it was seductive. His tongue teased hers and she answered with a mastery of her own. Each brush of his lips, each whisper against her ear of what he planned to do to her, and how, stoked the rising fire in her blood. His hands roamed, teasing, caressing, cajoling, and her soft gasps of passionate response rose in the silence. When he eased his mouth from hers, she was already on the edge of orgasm and she hadn't even opened her gown. "Undo your buttons for me . . ."

Caught up in the familiar haze, she did her best to make her fingers work while he watched with glowing eyes.

He slid a fiery-tipped finger slowly down the path of bare skin, then pressed his lips there. "You smell like heaven," he husked out.

Raven had never had a favorite scent before but knew she'd wear roses on her skin for the rest of her life because of him.

When the gown was fully opened, he pushed the halves aside and turned his magic on her unveiled breasts. She'd no idea how she came to be lying on her back with him above her, but it didn't matter because the sensations of his wicked feasting overrode everything else. As he licked and nipped and plied her with his mouth and sizzling hands, her gasps soon became croons and tiny cries. He placed a kiss against her navel and drew a finger over the line of her hair, then trailed it down through the curls. When he brushed a touch against her clit, she groaned aloud and her hips rose for him. "Would you like my kisses here, little corvus?"

He gave her a glancing lick and she slapped her hand over her mouth to stifle her shout.

"I need an answer, Raven."

But in spite of that, he kept touching and teasing the tiny nub of flesh.

"Oh God, Braxton . . ."

He paused.

Unsure of what she'd done to make him stop, she met his eyes.

He smiled. "You do realize this is the first time you've ever used my given name." Holding her eyes, he resumed his play. "Is this all I had to do . . ."

He plied her then with an expertise so deliciously carnal, she whimpered aloud, hips rising.

"What's my name, little corvus?"

"Oh!" She couldn't even recall her own name.

"Wrong." He chuckled and slipped two strong fingers inside her. The erotic rhythm that followed made her approaching orgasm gain speed like a hurricane crossing the Mississippi. Twisting atop the bed, she spread her legs wider.

"More? Okay."

He gave her so much more her orgasm broke like a thunderclap. Crying out his name, she slammed a bed pillow over her face to keep her hoarse screams from being heard by the entire population of South Carolina.

When she finally put body and soul back together, he was lying next to her, propped up on an elbow and smiling. He brushed a finger over her nipple. "I wondered if you knew my name."

She swore that orgasm would be echoing inside her until the next Mardi Gras. "I'm sorry. Have we met?"

Grinning, he leaned over, took her nipple into his mouth, and slowly teased it until she was breathless.

One kiss led to another, and all too soon she was mapping the length of his lean arms, feeling the skin of his hard chest, and doing some heated nipping of her own—the curve of his dark shoulder, the flat discs of his nipples— all the while teasing her hand up and down the hard ridge hidden inside his trousers. His responding kisses and caresses relit her inner flame. Still wearing her unbuttoned gown, she whispered sultrily against his ear, "May I have some cock now, please?"

He ran a finger over her lips. "I love a woman who knows what she wants."

He took a moment to shed his trousers and she fed her eyes on just how gloriously made he was.

"Like what you see?"

"I do." Taking him in hand, she showed him just how much, and it was his turn to groan. As she treated him to her version of the pleasure he'd given her, it took only a few minutes before he raised her head. "I'm not going to last much longer if you keep this up."

She smiled. "Then let me get my sponge."

And once it was inserted he gave her all she'd asked for in a slow, sensual dance that made her purr. Each thrust, each caress of his worshipping hands over her breasts, and each tantalizing kiss sent her higher. The creaking of the bed rose in tandem with the increasing pace and the vocalizing of their passion. He grabbed her hips, raising her to fit himself more roughly and possessively, and worked her faster. Her second orgasm shattered her with another loud cry and his followed on a roar. Lost, clinging to each other as if for life, they rode the storm to its end before slowly dropping back to earth, gasping and breathless.

In the aftermath, he gently rolled her over to keep from crushing her with his weight and she lay atop him, waiting for her breath to regain something akin to normal. She glanced up, and the small smile on his lips matched the one she offered in reply. When he ran a light hand down her sweat-damp back, she lowered her head against his equally dewed chest. He closed his arms around her, and she enjoyed the contentment. "We should probably go to sleep," she said after a while.

"Probably."

She raised up again. His bearded, handsome face gave rise to a now familiar jumble of emotions and feelings that continued to lack explanation or resolution.

As if his thoughts mirrored her own, he said softly, eyes serious, "Let's just let things be for now."

She agreed. "I'll go clean up."

"I'll follow once you're done."

Later, after stripping the bed of the dampened sheet, they doused the lamp and lay spooned together in the silence of the darkness.

He kissed her hair. "The next time we do this, how about we use the porch so we don't waste a clean sheet. I'd enjoy having you undo your buttons for me in the moonlight."

The scenario made her senses flare back to life. "Go to sleep."

"Do I get a reward?"

"Go to sleep, Braxton."

He draped an arm over her, eased her closer,

and whispered, "Okay. Hearing my name on your lips is reward enough. Good night."

Amused by his humor, she closed her eyes and slept.

IN A BOARDINGHOUSE in the center of the city, Detective Ruth Welch was enjoying her brandy nightcap and feeling good about the way her operation was proceeding. Sara Caron, the Pinkerton posing as her sister, Adelaide Clarkston, had just cracked the case she'd come to the city to investigate, a fraudulent railroad stock scheme. One of her sources of information had been a man named Washington Lewis. Having been a swindler himself when younger, he'd used those skills to infiltrate the gang selling the stocks, and the evidence he'd passed on to Sara had resulted in their arrests. During the months-long investigation that led to the charges being filed, Sara learned Lewis was a native of New Orleans and his true name was Tobias Kenny. Thinking of Ruth's case, Sara asked him if he knew the Moreau family. He did. He'd also admitted to having worked with them on a variety of their jobs before moving to Charleston. Sara passed the information on to Ruth, and a meeting was set up. Initially Ruth was to have met the man at the city market the morning after her arrival, but he hadn't been able to get to the city from his home on one of the bordering islands. That had been for the best, as it turned out, because Raven Moreau and Braxton Steele had been at the market that morning. Ruth was certain she'd been spotted, and having Kenny with her might have proved disastrous to her plans going forward, had he been recognized.

She was now set to meet him tomorrow afternoon. If what he provided proved valuable enough, she planned to offer him a portion of the sizable reward put up by San Francisco jeweler Oswald Gant for his assistance. It was her hope that Kenny could shed light on the vast number of crimes she was certain the Moreaux were responsible for, thus arming her with enough vital evidence to use in her quest to turn the ring of thieves in to the authorities, and become as famous as lady Pinkerton Kate Warne.

Should her plan bear fruit, her superiors would have no choice but to appoint her to lead the female division of the company. She was also weighing the possibility of forming her own agency due to the recent tarnishing of the Pinkertons' once great image; an unraveling that began three years ago after a botched attempt to apprehend the notorious outlaws Jesse and Frank James at the home of their mother, Zerelda Samuel. The James brothers had been tipped off and weren't there, but the assault by a combined force of Pinkerton agents and local lawmen resulted in an explosion that blew off Zerelda's right arm and killed their eight-year-old half brother, Archie. The public out-cry condemning the boy's death echoed from coast to coast. Up until then, the agency had enjoyed hero status, successfully hunting down the gangs robbing banks, targeting trains, and terrifying everyday citizens. The James inci-dent changed that. The Pinkertons' increasing role as strikebreakers for large companies had also soured their image in the eyes of America's working class, so maybe starting her own office was something to seriously consider.

First, she had to get her hands on the stolen copy of the Declaration of Independence. Once she did, she could tout herself as having foiled the Moreaux attempts to sell it off, gather the evidence for their other crimes, and bask in the glory brought on by having her name splashed across the front page of every newspaper in the nation. Pleased by the thought, she downed the last of the brandy, doused the lamp, and fell asleep with a smile on her face.

Chapter Twelve

$\mathcal{B}$rax awakened before dawn with the softly snoring Raven curled against his side. The memories of last night's intimate encounter would stay with him for some time. He glanced down at her sleeping form. Everything about her made him want to awaken each morning for the rest of his life with her beside him in just this way. Would it be what she'd want, too, he wondered. If so, how would such a thing work? He now understood why the family had turned to crime and for the most part he'd set aside the moral judgments he'd once held so firmly. Which left how to overcome her firm beliefs that their differing economic statuses made them incompatible because they were unevenly yoked. It was a question he kept coming back to in his private moments, and he sensed she might be struggling with the same question. The answers, however, waited to be explored and resolved.

Hoping not to wake her, he eased carefully

from the bed. Leaning down, he placed a kiss on her cheek and left the bedroom to begin his day.

Outside, once the torches were lit so he could see, he began. He could easily chop enough wood and store it away so he wouldn't have to do it daily, but found he enjoyed the solitude and feeding the muscles that kept his body fit.

"Are you Braxton?"

Startled, he looked up to see a woman walking into the torchlight. He could see that she was Black and wearing a cape against the predawn chill. Her hair was wrapped, but from where she stood he was unable to get a firm look at her features. Unsure how to respond to being addressed by his given name when he was supposed to be posing as Evan Miller, he replied, "Who's asking?"

"Cousin Hazel sent something for Raven."

"Then yes, I'm Braxton. Raven is still asleep."

"Give her this, please." She handed over a small burlap bag closed tight by a drawstring cord. The movement in the bag was so surprising he almost dropped it.

"Be careful. The mice she wanted are inside. There's three of them and they're alive as you can see."

He held the bag at a distance. "I can." The bag was roiling as the little beasts tried to escape.

When he looked up, the woman was gone. Surprised, he searched the darkness but saw no one. Another mysterious Moreau. Carefully holding the bag by the top so he didn't accidentally get bitten, he walked the bag to the door and went inside.

She was up and dressed. "What's that?" she asked.

"Your mice."

Her face brightened. "You caught some?"

"No. A young woman delivered them just now. She said your mother sent her."

"Hand it here."

He gave it over gladly.

She glanced at the moving bag and then at the old clock on the wall. "If I act quickly I can put them in her room while she's washing up. I've learned her routine, and right now, she's in her washroom."

"You need to be careful you aren't bitten."

"I know. I'll take some kitchen shears with me. That way I can hold the bag upside down and when I cut off the top, they'll fall straight to the floor. She'll never know I was there."

He watched her think over her plan.

"It might be better if I turn them out in her bed and cover them with the quilt. The darkness might make the mice think they're safe. And when she comes out of the washroom and gets in bed to wait for breakfast?"

He grinned. "You have a very devious mind, Mrs. Miller."

"Yes, indeed. I'll go and slip these little guests into her room, then go to the kitchen to begin breakfast. When you hear screaming, come running."

He gave her a crisp salute. "Aye! Aye!"

"And thanks for the good night's sleep. I slept like a babe."

He bowed. "Always at your service."

Smiling, he watched her leave holding the bag of protesting mice at arm's length.

RAVEN ENTERED MRS. Stipe's dimly lit, empty room and realized her plan to dump the mice in the bed wouldn't work. The quilt was thrown back and it would certainly be noticed if it was covering the sheet when she returned. Hastily searching her mind for an alternative solution, her choices were to go with her original idea and simply let the mice out of the bag and hope they'd be discovered in a timely manner. Or . . . She spotted the wig on the nightstand. Moving quickly, she picked it up. Holding the bag upside down, she cut the top beneath the drawstring, the mice tumbled out into the wig, and before they could celebrate freedom, she flipped the wig over with them inside. Praying the darkness would calm them, she stuffed the bag and shears in the front pocket of her apron and hastily moved back to the door. She opened it and heard behind her, "Mrs. Miller?"

Raven froze, drew in a calming breath, and turned.

Mrs. Stipe was dressed in her nightgown and staring her way. "What are you doing here?"

Lying for a living came in handy. "I wanted you to know we're almost out of butter, so there won't be enough for both biscuits and your grits. When I got here and realized you were in the washroom, I didn't want to disturb you, so I was on my way back to the kitchen."

"Okay. Thank you for letting me know, but purchase more next time," she scolded.

"Yes, ma'am." Raven hazarded a quick glance at the wig on the nightstand. It was moving. She looked away. "I'll be back with your breakfast directly."

"Fine."

Raven left the room. She was halfway down the staircase when the screaming began.

Running back, she threw open the door. "What's wrong?!"

Mrs. Stipe was on her feet on the bed. "Mice!" she screamed, her skinny legs pumping up and down. "In my wig! Get them! Get them!"

Raven visually searched the room and saw the wig lying on the floor. "Where'd they go?"

"I don't know!" Mrs. Stipe wailed. "Oh my God! Get them!"

Raven spied one as it skittered across the floor.

"There!" Mrs. Stipe cried. She began running back and forth as if the mice were on the bed with her.

"I need the broom!"

"Do something! Hurry!"

Braxton ran in. "What's the matter?"

"Mice!" Mrs. Stipe screamed.

"Bring the broom!" Raven implored.

He took off at a run.

"There's another one!" Mrs. Stipe cried pointing and jumping.

Raven watched it escape through the open door. "How many are there?"

"I don't know! Just get them!"

Her frantic dance made the bed jump up and down. A second later the slats beneath the mattress gave way. The bed crashed and Helen was bounced off the mattress and onto the floor. A mouse ran across her legs. She squealed, kicking and twisting, and fainted dead away.

Brax returned with the broom. He took in Helen. "What happened to her?"

"Fainted."

They shared a look.

He said, "We should probably make sure she isn't hurt."

"I suppose. Let me get a washcloth."

When she returned with a water-cooled cloth, he was helping Helen sit up. Raven wiped the sweaty, reddened face.

"Are they gone?" she asked, eyes frantically scanning the room.

"I think so, but probably still in the house somewhere."

Mrs. Stipe stiffened, pushed them aside, and struggled to her feet. "Help me pack a bag!" she demanded. "Mr. Miller, bring the carriage around. I'm going to my sister's."

She rushed around the room opening the doors to her armoire and throwing clothes over her arm.

"What about breakfast?" Raven asked.

"I'll not spend one more second in this house until those mice are gone!" She snapped at Brax, "Go! Get the carriage."

He left the room.

She placed a large carpetbag on the bed and began filling it with clothing, all the while scanning her bedroom anxiously.

Raven thought her farfetched plan might be working a little too well.

Helen opened a drawer of the nightstand and withdrew a set of keys on a string. She handed it to Raven. "The key to Aubrey's room and the other one. Clean them! I'll send an exterminator once I reach my sister's place. When he thinks it's safe for me to return, I'll come home."

"Yes, ma'am."

A short while later, Mrs. Stipe was helped into the carriage and driven away. Standing on the porch, Raven watched the carriage until it was out of sight, then climbed the stairs to begin her search.

She searched Helen's room first, and then the smelly, dust-filled room once occupied by Helen's mother, and moved on to the husband's room. Four hours later, she'd found nothing—no Declaration of Independence, no hidden panels in the walls, no false-bottom drawers, nothing secreted away in the armoires, the writing desk, hems of the old dresses in the trunks, and no hollowed-out bedposts to hide things in. There was nothing hidden in the books, in the mattresses in the mother's room, or in the few books on the mother's desk. She even swept the ashes out of the hearths in Helen's and her mother's rooms, hoping to find a hidey-hole in the brickwork, but that proved futile as well.

By the time she and Braxton sat down to dinner, she was disappointed and glum. "What if it really isn't here?" she asked him.

He shrugged. "I don't know."

"If Welch presented herself as a reasonable person, I wouldn't worry about sharing my doubts, but nothing about her appears reasonable, which is why we're in this mess in the first place."

"True. You did manage to get Helen out of the house, so give yourself credit for that."

"I suppose." That small success hadn't led to the one needed to send Welch packing though. "I still have the hearth in his room to do. I'll sweep it out after we're done eating but I doubt what we're after is there." Welch's threats to send the families to jail added more weight to her frustration. "Did Helen say what she wanted to do about the broken bed?"

"Yes. She said she'll use the one in her mother's room until she either arranges repairs or purchases a new one."

"Okay. It'll be ready whenever she returns. After I sweep out the husband's hearth, I just want to spend the rest of this evening doing nothing."

"You can also sleep in in the morning."

Her eyes widened. "Oh my goodness. I can, can't I? I can't laze around until noon, but maybe an hour later than usual."

"Up to you."

Raven couldn't remember ever having such an option while employed. "Is it too much to ask that Helen stay with her sister permanently?"

"Probably."

"I'll take what I can get. Let's clean up these dishes and get started on that hearth."

When the kitchen chores were done, they returned to the main house and climbed the stairs to Aubrey Stipe's bedroom.

By the time they were done shoveling, their clothing, shoes, and hands were coated with a layer of fine gray ash once again. "I'll have to mop in here tomorrow and dust everything down to get rid of all this," she said, shaking off the front of her apron. The stone floor of the hearth would need to be mopped as well but the flagstones were visible. Raven picked up a lamp, turned up the wick for more light, and crawled inside.

"What are you doing?"

"Looking for that hidey-hole."

Setting the lamp down beside her, she ran her already grimy hands over the surface of the wall, and rising from her knees, hunch-walked into the space as far as she could. "Sometimes these old houses—" Her words petered out as her hand moved over what felt like a lever.

"Have what?" he asked.

"Levers."

Up North where hearths were used daily during winters, heat from the flames would've fused the metal. This being the South where hearths were used less frequently, the lever turned easily and a portion of the stone wall it was attached to opened. A small cloud of dust filtered out, making her cough, and she backed out of the hearth to clear her lungs.

"Let me get you some water," he said with concern.

Unlike the cottage, the house had indoor plumbing. After going downstairs to the dining room hutch and retrieving a teacup, he filled it with water from Helen's washroom and handed it to the still slightly distressed Raven. She drank it down.

"Better?" he asked.

After a few moments, she nodded and handed

the cup back to him. "Now, let's see what's inside—if anything," she croaked.

Tucked inside was an old metal box. Before pulling it out, she used the lamp to inspect the hole to make sure nothing was attached that might signal the owner it had been removed. Seeing nothing and praying she hadn't missed anything, she slowly withdrew it and backed out.

Studying it, she estimated it to be just over a foot long and possibly three inches high. It was locked with a small padlock that needed a key to open. She lifted the box to gauge the weight. She didn't want to have gone through all this just to find it empty, but reasoned why would anyone hide an empty box? The heft appeared to indicate something inside. She doubted the key it needed was on the ring Helen had given her earlier. Fishing them out of her skirt pocket, she tried them and was proved correct. "Let's clean up in here and take it back to the cabin. I may have a way to open it."

AFTER STOWING THE shovels and disposing of the ashes in the fire pit, Brax joined her inside. She was seated on the sofa fishing around in her faded blue carpetbag. She finally withdrew a small red velvet bag and shot him a triumphant smile. "Found it."

"What's inside?"

"Lock picks."

Not sure what to do with this woman and her

many talents, he watched silently. In spite of his growing feelings for her, moments like this made him wrestle once again with the illegalities the Moreaux embraced. He knew they were originally tied to necessity, but he couldn't just magically erase the values he'd been raised with.

She looked up at him. "Judging again?"

"You're very perceptive."

"And you aren't very good at hiding your thoughts. I'm trying to keep my family and yours from going to prison, Steele. I'm sorry if this bothers you."

In spite of the apology, there wasn't a whit of remorse in her voice. He'd offended her and didn't know what to do with that, either. "It's hard for a leopard to change its spots."

"At least you're honest."

After that frosty retort, she concentrated on fitting the varying picks to the small padlock. On the third try the lock opened. She eased it free and opened the box. He walked over to get a better view.

There were various items resting on a velvet-lined tray. Jewelry, a gold fountain pen, and a small cotton pouch filled with unknown contents. There was a jeweled brooch that he wanted to inspect. He reached for it. She stayed his hand. "Everything needs to be put back exactly the way we found it. Let me memorize the layout first."

Admittedly, that would never have crossed

his mind. He withdrew his hand and waited. She lifted the tray out. Lo and behold, there was a cylinder inside made of thick brown paper. On the outside was curly writing. She handed it to him. "What's it say?"

"Declaration of Independence. Seventeen something. The rest of the date is faded as if the paper may have gotten wet at some point."

Her eyes were bright with the same excitement he also felt. The top was sealed with a tin circle. "We may need a pocketknife to pry this open. I have one."

He found it in his belongings and returned.

"Be careful," she cautioned.

He nodded and gently used the tip of the knife to free the tin circle. When it was done, he shook out the rolled up document inside. Using the same care, he unfurled it and smiled. "This is it."

"Hallelujah!" she yelled, excitedly.

He chuckled and felt like shouting the same. They viewed it for a moment, and sure enough, the signers' signatures were disjointed in the exact way Welch had described. They shared a look of triumph. After placing it back inside the cylinder and resealing it, they set it aside while she went through a stack of papers that were also inside the box. He took the moment to explore the items on the tray. The brooch was crusted with precious jewels: diamonds, rubies, and emeralds. He wondered whom it originally belonged to and why it was there. He placed it back. The small bag held gold coins and by his estimate equaled several hundred dollars.

She held up a thick wad of Confederate one-hundred-dollar bills. "This is the first time I've ever seen a woman on a greyback. Do you know who she is?"

The Confederacy's paper bills known as greybacks were first distributed during the war, as were the first Union-backed greenbacks. He scanned the bill and did indeed recognize the woman. "It's Lucy Holcombe Pickens. She was the wife of the South Carolina governor. I saw many of these during my time here with the Fifty-Fourth."

"Are they worth anything now?"

"Not that I know of. They weren't worth much during the war, either."

She handed him the papers she'd found. "Not sure what these are but I think they're IOUs?"

He read a few of them. "You're right, and if they are still viable, Senator Stipe is up to his philandering eyeballs in debt." He read another one. "I don't believe Miss Helen is going to be pleased to learn he's lost the deed to this place to someone named Sylvester Reed."

"She really will take an ax to him."

He read further. "According to this, the debt is from last winter, and he has until the end of this month to redeem the property. I wonder if he lost it gambling?"

Brax read through some of the other IOUs. "You aren't going to believe this, but he's promised the deed to three other people."

She stared.

"This one has the name of a man named Warlock. This one, a man named Crenshaw, and this is signed by a Phillip Davidson. All are due between now and September."

"Oh yes. She's going to chop him up into tiny little pieces."

"Are you going to share these with Welch?"

"No. My gut tells me the less she knows, the better. I do wish we knew if he still owes money to these men and who they might be."

"Other government officials?"

"Maybe. I'll give Mama the names and see if she can get some answers from the family members here. In the meantime, let's get this box back to its hiding place. We'll keep those four IOUs and our prize. I want to pass the cylinder on to Welch as soon as possible, then we can leave the city. We'll hold on to the IOUs. I'm sure Renay can find a use for them."

The mission was almost over. He was pleased, but not at the reality of heading home without her.

After returning the box to its hiding place, they locked up the house and walked back to the cabin to rid themselves of the ashes. Their work for the day done, they sat outside on the porch to relax. "When do you want to hand the cylinder over to Welch?"

"Tomorrow night before we disappear. The sooner she's out of our hair, the better. I wish we could leave tonight, but that's not possible. It's already dark, and although I know where my cousins live, I've never driven there this late. The countryside is pitch black at night and I don't want to chance getting lost or running into patrolling supremacists hunting for someone to practice their hatred on."

He agreed. She quieted and seemed lost in thought, pulling together loose ends, he guessed, so he went inside to get the newspaper he'd purchased that morning after driving Helen to her sister. Returning, he sat on the porch and scanned it. A prominently placed item caught his attention. "The death count from yellow fever is rising in New Orleans," he told her.

She looked his way. "Not something I wanted to hear. I wish a cure could be found. We've suffered through this every summer for as long as I can remember. I hope the family isn't affected."

"I hope not, either."

"Anything else important in there?"

"Doesn't look like it. Most of it pertains to local news like this piece about the Lost Cause Ball Helen wants your help with."

"She'll have to find someone else. We'll go to the market in the morning and have Mama send someone for us. Leaving tomorrow night will give her time to get our train tickets home, too. I don't want to be here any longer than necessary."

"If your mother isn't at the market, do you think we should drive out to where she and my father are staying to talk about our exit plan?"

"I'd like to avoid taking Helen's carriage and have someone tell her they saw us driving in a certain location. If the location is traced to my cousins, they'll wind up being questioned for whatever reason. Everyone seems to know everyone else here and people talk. And suppose Helen sends word that she's decided to come home tomorrow while we're gone? She'll probably excuse you delaying to come and get her from her sister's because we made a quick trip to the market, but we'll have no excuse for not responding for an hour or more because we've driven to my cousin's place. My cousin goes to the market daily, so we'll pray Mama will be there."

He hadn't considered all the variables. "So many details to manage."

"True."

No wonder she had trouble sleeping.

Her face took on a seriousness that matched her tone. "You're probably anxious to head home and be rid of all this, I imagine."

He thought back to their conversation about cats and spots. "In some ways, I am. Others? Not so sure." Based on their growing connection and the intimacies they'd shared, he sensed she understood his meaning.

She didn't address it, however. "Hopefully, you'll be on your way soon."

He didn't address it, either, and simply nodded in agreement while recalling another conversation they'd had. The one tied to the type of man she wanted in her life, who'd love her like he loved breathing, and accept her the way she was—rough edges and all. He enjoyed being with her and not just in bed. He admired her spirit, her intelligence, her devotion to her family, and in many ways those rough edges. And yet? He didn't know how to complete the thought or if he should. At some point, maybe soon, answers would need to be addressed.

"Since we're celebrating and I don't have to wake up so early in the morning, will you read me some of the *Alice* book you like so much?"

He smiled. "I'd love to."

"And maybe help me read it, too."

"Of course." He admired her bravery and was still touched by the trust she'd placed in him. Dusk had fallen, and the mosquitoes were rising. He slapped one on his hand. "How about we go inside and get away from these mosquitoes?"

"Good idea."

Inside, he retrieved the book and sat next to her on the edge of the bed.

"What's the title again?"

"*Alice's Adventures in Wonderland.* It's a children's book written by an Englishman named Lewis Carroll and published in 1865. Carroll's real name is Charles Lutwidge Dodgson."

"I think I'd call myself Lewis Carroll, too."

That made him smile. "Are you ready for me to begin?"

"Yes."

The first page was an illustration of the King and Queen of Hearts.

"The queen looks very upset." she noted, eyeing the picture. "Who's she so angry with?"

"Everything and everyone, as we'll soon see."

"I didn't know there'd be pictures, but that makes sense if this was written for children."

"Exactly. The book starts with a poem about how and where the story was first imagined. Dodgson and a reverend friend were on an eight-mile rowboat ride with three young girls who were sisters."

"Were they his daughters?"

"No. I believe they were the daughters of another of Dodgson's friends."

"Was he with them?"

"Not according to the background information I've read."

"What kind of father lets his three girls go on a boat ride for eight miles with two grown men? Was their mother there?"

"I believe the men were the only adults."

"The Moreaux would never let Dorrie or any of the little cousins, girls or boys, go anywhere with two men. And one was a reverend? I've known some pastors and priests, and the only holy things about them were the holes in the soles of their shoes."

"The outing could have been totally innocent."

She looked unimpressed. "Until proven guilty."

He waited.

"I'm sorry for fussing. I just find that concerning. Go ahead and read the poem."

"Are you sure?"

She nodded.

He eyed the muted flash in her eyes and had to admit, he'd never questioned the possible impropriety of the boat ride until then. According to the background literature, the group took another boat ride a month later, but he thought it wise not to share that.

"Would you allow your daughters to go boating with grown men without you or another family member there?" she asked.

"No."

"Good."

"Should I read or not?"

"Yes, please. I'm done. Promise."

So he read the poem. When he finished, he looked over to see if more objections were coming. She appeared calm, so he turned the page. "*Chapter One. Down the Rabbit-Hole.*"

At the top of the chapter was an illustration of the rabbit. "That's a nice waistcoat the rabbit's wearing. Ever made a waistcoat for a rabbit?" she asked smiling.

"So far, no."

"What's he holding?"

"A pocket watch."

"A rabbit wearing a waistcoat and owning a pocket watch."

"He's late."

"To what?"

"You'll soon find out."

So he began reading about seven-year-old Alice's initial encounter with the rabbit and following him down a hole. Once inside, she began to fall, describing what she saw and did on the way.

Raven pointed out, "She must have been falling very slowly if she had time to pick up that jar of marmalade, open it, find it empty, and place it back down on another shelf."

"I agree."

As the slow fall continued, Alice wondered if she would reach the center of the earth, and what the longitude and latitude might be, but admitted to not knowing what either word meant.

"I have no idea, either," Raven confessed.

He explained, "They're imaginary lines on the earth to pinpoint a location. You find them on most seafaring maps. Latitude lines go east and west. Longitude conveys north and south."

"Okay, thank you. You probably think I'm terribly illiterate."

"No. I think you're absolutely adorable."

"Are you flattering me to get me to undo my buttons?"

"No, but I'm flattered that you're thinking about it. Have never read to a woman with her buttons undone. There are twelve chapters in this book; surely we could work that into our journey into Wonderland before we're done."

She grinned. "Just read, Steele."

"I see you've forgotten my name again. Shall we take a few minutes to refresh your memory?"

"No. I want to learn what happens to Alice."

"Spoilsport."

"Don't pout. The Boston mamas and their daughters will stop lining up at your door if your face gets stuck like that."

He laughed. What an incredible woman. Feeding his soul on her playful eyes, he returned to the story.

Alice continued her slow fall. She thought she might be near New Zealand by then and worried whether her cat Dinah would be fed while she was away.

He glanced over and asked, "Are you ready to take a turn reading?" He hoped she'd agree.

He was enjoying their time together and she seemed to be as well. He didn't want his request to spoil it or cause it to end. However, he'd promised to help, and the moment felt as good as any to begin.

She gave him a tight nod and he handed the book over. He pointed to where he'd left off. To allay the discomfort he sensed she was having, he said gently, "No one's here but the two of us. I won't shame you in any way."

She looked at the page and then back up at him. "Okay."

He'd left off with Alice getting sleepy as she continued to fall and debating with herself the question of whether cats ate bats.

Her voice small, Raven read, *"She felt that she was*—what's this word?"

"Dozing."

"Ah. *Dozing off, and had just begun to dream that she was—walking—hand in hand with—*"

"Dinah," he coached.

"And saying to herself very—"

He looked at the word by her fingertip. "Earnestly."

She nodded. *". . . earnestly, 'Now Dinah, tell me the—"*

"Truth."

"Did you ever eat a bat?' when—?" She looked to him for help.

"Suddenly."

"Suddenly—" She paused, stumped by the next word.

"Thump."

"Thump! Thump! down she came upon a—" She stopped again and he could see her trying to figure out the word.

"Heap," he offered quietly.

"A heap of sticks and dry—"

". . . leaves."

"And the fall was over. Thank goodness!"

He grinned.

"Alice was not a bit—hurt?" She asked with her eyes if she'd read the word correctly.

"Yes."

"And she—jumped?"

He nodded.

"She jumped up on her feet in a—"

"Moment."

"Moment: she looked up, but it was all dark—overhead?"

"Yes."

"Overhead; before her was another long—" She stopped and met his eyes.

"Passage," he offered.

". . . passage and the White Rabbit was still in—"

"Sight."

"That's how the word *sight* is spelled? Why are the *g* and *h* in it? They aren't pronounced."

"You're right, they aren't. The English language can be very confusing at times."

"I agree. Let me start this part over. *The White Rabbit was still in sight*—what's this word?"

"Hurrying."

"Ah. Okay. *The White Rabbit was still in sight, hurrying down it.*"

She read on, stumbling occasionally, stopping to ask him about unfamiliar words and spellings she found puzzling, as in the word *taught*.

"Another *g* and *h* that have no business there," she said a bit testily.

He smiled and chose not to bring up the similarly pronounced *taut*.

She read a few paragraphs more and handed the book back. "I'll let you finish. As slow as I am, I'll never know what the rabbit is late for, or who the queen is angry with."

"You did well though. I think you just need more practice, is all."

"That's kind of you to say."

"It's true. The more you read, the more comfortable you'll become and the more words you'll learn to pronounce."

He spent a few minutes explaining how to sound out words, how looking for the little word within a larger one could prove helpful, and how the letter *y* often had the sound of the letter *e* in words like *very* and *merry*. "Are you enjoying the story?"

"I am."

That pleased him. He was also pleased by her efforts. He wanted her to be as confident with the written word as she was with life. With all of that in mind, he picked up the story where she'd left off.

At the end of chapter one, he closed the book and asked, "So? What do you think of Alice's adventure so far?"

"Bottles labeled Drink Me that make you shrink. Cakes with the words Eat Me to make you taller. This sounds like a fever dream. Was Carroll an opium smoker?"

He threw back his head with laughter.

"I'm serious."

"I know you are, I just didn't expect you to ask that. However, further along in the story we do meet a caterpillar with a hookah."

"I knew it."

He chuckled. She was indeed adorable.

She asked, "Is this really a book for children?"

"That's supposedly who it's written for, but I believe it's aimed at adults as well."

She hid a yawn behind her hand.

"Time for us to go to bed."

She nodded.

He studied her face and said, "In spite of my fascination with your buttons, I don't want you to think you have to indulge my fascination as payment for my helping you with your reading."

"I didn't think that."

"Okay. I needed to say that, just so we're clear."

"Clear as the sky in June."

"Good."

She reached up and cupped his cheek. "I do want to give you a reward for being so kind and patient. Is that allowed?"

He covered her hand lightly with his. "If you insist."

"I do," she whispered.

The sweetness of the kiss moved through him like the soft notes of a sonata, adding yet more substance to his feelings for her. The pressure of her lips against his increased, making him ease her onto his lap so he could respond with a melody of his own. They were lovers in every way despite the absence of a declaration. She was his. He was hers.

The kiss ended with a series of small reluctant partings that only prolonged things. He nibbled her bottom lip. She teased the corners of his mouth with the tip of her hot little tongue. His hands began roaming and exploring.

"We're supposed to be going to sleep," she said breathlessly.

"Then put your lips away," he replied, brushing his over the satiny skin of her ear. "If you stop. I'll stop."

But they didn't. Buttons were undone. Nipples were bared, licked, and aroused. Her skirt was raised, and he played in the shadow of passion-parted thighs until she cried out, shaken by the orgasm. To increase his reward, she undid his trousers, raised herself on her knees, and slowly lowered herself onto his aroused cock. As she rose and fell with a lazy, sultry rhythm, he filled his hands with her hips, and lost both his breath and his mind until his orgasm crackled like lightning.

When he came back to himself, she was smiling. "Now we can go to bed."

He laughed at how totally outrageous she was. "What am I going to do with you?"

"What you just did suited me just fine." She gave him a quick peck on the lips, then untangled their bodies. She left him to go to the washroom.

He fell back on the bed to recover, and wondered, for the fiftieth time, how on earth he was going to leave her when the time came to return home.

Chapter Thirteen

𝒯he next morning while they were preparing
to go to the market, the exterminator arrived.
In the excitement over finding the box, she'd
forgotten about the mice. His name was Willie
Samson. He was a middle-aged Black man with
a receding hairline and mutton chops. Accompanying him was an adolescent boy, introduced
as his son, Peter.

"Miss Helen said you have mice?" he asked
Raven, who'd answered his knock on the front
door.

"Yes. Come in."

He entered and looked around. "Were they
downstairs or upstairs?"

"Upstairs." Raven felt a bit remorseful about
having Mr. Samson do a job because of something she'd instigated, but the idea that he'd be
paid for his work made her feel better.

"Do you know how many there were?"

"I only saw three."

She escorted them up to Helen's room. The broken bed was still on the floor. Mr. Samson raised an eyebrow. She explained, "It fell when she was jumping up and down on it while the mice were running around."

He suppressed his chuckle. "Okay. I'll look around outside to see if I can find where they may have gotten in. Have you seen any since yesterday?"

"No."

"I'll put out some traps. If they're still in the house, the traps will take care of them."

"Thank you."

She led them back downstairs so he could get the traps from his wagon and left them to their work. She was anxious to get to the market and tell her mother the good news, but knew she couldn't leave before Mr. Samson was done, so she prayed he would be quick. She was eager to return home to New Orleans and if her luck held, her mother would be at the market and she and Brax would be gone from Helen's house by dark. As yellow fever had overrun New Orleans again, she prayed the trains were still going through so she could check on the aunts, Dorrie, and the rest of the family. She tried not to think about how much she'd miss Brax.

He was outdoors handling landscaping duties, so she went upstairs to begin working on preparing the other bedroom for Helen's return, since they were temporarily having to put off the trip for the market. Their plan to leave later made the work in the room unnecessary but helped pass the time while Mr. Samson and his son did their job. She was stripping the bed to put on fresh sheets when Brax appeared in the doorway.

"There's a man downstairs representing Montgomery Ward. Do you want a catalog?"

Her jaw dropped. "Yes!"

"Really?"

"It's Renay. A salesman from Montgomery Ward is one of his disguises."

He looked confused.

Shaking her head, she hurried past him and he followed her down the stairs. Sure enough, beneath the lifelike, but false russet eyebrows, mustache, and goatee was her cousin Renay. She let him inside and gave him a big welcoming hug. He and Brax shook hands.

"How are you?" she asked.

"Doing well. Aunt Hazel sent me to check on you and Brax."

"We've found the prize and are ready to leave." He was posing as a salesman, so that meant she couldn't have him in the house more than a few minutes, so she got to the point. "We want to leave tonight. Can you and Mama arrange it?"

"Of course. Sun sets around eight-thirty. I'll be lurking nearby. Use the matches to signal me and I'll pick you up."

"I also need to hand the package off to Welch. Do you have a pencil and paper?"

He did.

She recited the address and he wrote it down. "Go by the boardinghouse and let her know I'll be stopping by tonight. You don't have to tell her who you are."

"That shouldn't be a problem. Where was the thing hidden?"

She gave him the details and told him about the IOUs.

"Clever," he said, "but no match for a far more clever Moreau. I'll see how Aunt Hazel wants to handle the IOUs." He turned to Brax. "How are you holding up, Brax?"

"Like Raven, I'm ready to go."

Renay said, "I need to finish my rounds in this neighborhood to keep the ruse going. In case anything comes up about my being here . . ." He handed her a Montgomery Ward & Co. catalog. "I'll be back tonight."

"We'll be ready."

He departed.

"Now we don't have to worry about whether Mama will be at the market," she said to Brax. She was relieved. They could spend the balance of the day packing up their things and hoping nothing delayed their leaving.

"We just have to make it to tonight."

"Yes," she said, trying not to worry that something might impact their plan.

"I'll go check on the exterminator," he said.

"I'll go with you, then come back and finish up that room."

"WE PUT OUT some bait around the base of the house," Mr. Samson informed them. "If you'll take me inside, I'll put a few traps on the main floor and upstairs in her room. I'll come back in a couple of days to check on things. If the traps get sprung before then, just put them and the dead mice in the trash bin."

Raven took him inside. He laid his traps and left with a wave and a smile.

With Braxton's help, Raven finished what needed doing to get the room ready for Helen. They then had lunch at the kitchen's table. "I'll miss this place in a way," she told him as they ate their ham sandwiches.

He smiled. "Really?"

"Yes, even though we've been here less than a week, I'm leaving with some nice memories. The bath salts, the undoing of my buttons—"

He snorted a laugh.

"Alice. We can read more on the train ride home," she said. Then as if realizing home meant different locations for them, she said, "I guess not."

"Unless you're going with me to Boston."

She shook her head. "I have to go to New Orleans and check on the family."

Come tomorrow, their time together would

end. She'd see him again at the wedding, but after that, irregularly at best, and more than likely he'd be with the woman he'd chosen to be his wife, one who fit into his Boston world in all the ways she did not.

A loud male voice startled them. "What are you doing in here! Who are you!"

They turned. Raven recognized him immediately from the portrait on the wall in the main house and assumed Brax did, too. Helen's philandering husband, Aubrey Stipe.

Brax stood. "We work for Miss Helen. I'm Evan Miller. This is my wife, Lovey. I recognize you from the portrait on the wall. Pleased to meet you."

The greeting was not returned. Instead, he eyed them suspiciously. Had he found the contents missing from his box? She'd had Brax hide the papers in the privy for safekeeping and was glad she had.

"What happened to Dahlia and Sylvester?"

"Her husband has a sick relative," Brax replied. "They've gone home to Texas. Your wife hired us a few days ago."

"Where is Helen?"

"At her sister's. She'll be back in a couple of days. She wanted to escape the mice."

His confusion was plain.

"The house appears to be infested," Brax continued. "An exterminator was here earlier and laid some traps. Miss Helen asked my wife to clean the upstairs bedrooms because we think the mice came from one of them."

He stiffened. "You cleaned my room?"

"Yes."

"Did you touch anything?"

"Just the dust," Raven replied.

The sudden appearance of another man who was older, taller, and outweighed the short, thin Aubrey by a sizable amount, drew their attention. "What the hell's taking you so long?" he demanded. Like Stipe, he was wearing an expensive-looking suit.

"Just give me a minute," Stipe said, still critically assessing Raven and Brax.

"I've given you enough time. Give me whatever this thing is you boasted about being so valuable, or I file the deed."

Raven now had an inkling as to what this was about. He had to be one of the men named on the IOUs.

Stipe said, "I just needed to know who these two are. The regular help is gone. Didn't want to find out they were squatters. I'll go get it now. Come on back to the house."

Stipe departed but the other man said, "Sorry for the interruption."

Brax offered an appreciative nod in response, and the man left to join Stipe.

Once they were alone, Brax walked to her side. "I think all hell's about to break loose if Stipe promised him what was in the box."

"I agree." And a frisson of fear crawled over her.

As if he'd felt it, Brax told her, "Don't worry, we'll be okay."

She nodded, hoping Stipe's appearance wouldn't delay their departure. Leaving was now more imperative than ever.

They were walking back to the cabin when they heard the older man bellow, "You have until noon tomorrow, Stipe! Not a second more!"

They shared a look and walked on.

Moments later, Stipe appeared on the porch of the cabin and after throwing open the door, yelled at them, "Where is it!"

"Where's what?" Brax asked angrily.

"My property, damn you! I know you have it!"

"We don't know what you're talking about," Brax yelled.

In response, Stipe snatched the few clothes she and Brax owned out of the small closet and threw them to the floor. He then grabbed up their traveling bags, rifled through the items inside, while promising, "If I find anything of mine in here, I'll string you both up before the sun sets!"

The angry Raven and Brax had no choice but to watch as he searched the drawers of the bureau. Finding nothing there to soothe his fury, he strode over to the bed. After tearing off the sheets, he tipped the mattress off the frame, produced a thin-bladed hunting knife, and slit the ticking to search its insides. He slashed the sofa next, followed by its pillows. He marched into the washroom and began tossing the contents of Brax's shaving kit onto the floor before starting in on the small bag holding her toiletries. Raven paid particular attention to where the small glass eye dropper landed. His mayhem trashed the small place but he found nothing. Turning to them, his red face beaded with sweat, he snarled, "I'll be back in an hour! Have my supper ready!"

And he exited.

Raven eyed the mess left behind. Feathers from the bed and pillows were everywhere. The mattress and sofa were candidates for the trash bin. Their clothes were strewn across the floor and their travel bags carelessly tossed aside. The fury on Brax's face broke her heart because as her man, pretend or not, he'd not intervened because doing so might have cost him his life. "Violence and terror are all men like him know," she said quietly. "I'd rather have you alive than dead. Clothing can he replaced. You can't be."

His angry eyes met hers, and whatever his thoughts, they weren't shared. She respected that. In the face of the disrespect, he was allowed to feel what he did privately within himself.

"I vote we leave this mess as is," she told him. "I'll get his supper started and we can focus on getting our belongings ready for when we leave. But first I need to get something."

She walked into the washroom. After visually searching the items on the floor, she picked up the small dropper bottle. Rejoining Brax, she showed it to him. "Stipe's going to take a very long nap."

"What is that?"

"Laudanum."

He smiled.

RAVEN ALWAYS TRAVELED with laudanum because she never knew when she might need to put someone to sleep. It was also a good pain suppressant. Due to its bitter taste, she placed it in the candied yams she piled on Stipe's plate and added just a touch more sugar. She also added a few drops to the collards. Due to their traditionally bitter flavor, she doubted he'd notice they'd been doctored. By her estimation, he'd be on the verge of sleep shortly after finishing the meal. The clock on the wall showed half past three. More than likely, he'd wake up still groggy before it got dark, so she planned to keep giving him drops until it was time for Evan and Lovey Miller to disappear.

He returned to the house within the hour and she brought the plate to where he sat impatiently in the dining room. She was surprised to see the parlor in total disarray but supposed she shouldn't have been. He needed that copy of the Declaration and was apparently searching every inch of the house to find it. Pillows from the sofa and chairs had been tossed aside, the chairs and sofa upended. Some of the carpets were partially rolled up. In the dining room, the hutch holding the china had been moved and was now facing sideways. Its doors were open and the contents stacked beside it. She could only imagine the state of the bedrooms on the second floor. As she looked around, he ordered, "When I'm done here, clean this place up."

"Yes, sir," she lied, and wondered what Helen would think when she came home and found her house turned upside down, and what he planned to say to her when the new owner took possession at noon tomorrow. Raven didn't spend much time on the question, however; it wasn't her problem. "Do you need anything else?"

"No."

"I'll be back to check on you shortly."

"You do that."

Thinking what a nasty awful man he was, Raven left him and returned to the kitchen.

Brax joined her a few minutes later. She couldn't tell if he'd made peace with himself but decided not to worry over it. He was alive. That was all that mattered.

"How's he doing?" he asked.

"I'm going to check shortly." She told him about the mess Stipe's searching had left in the parlor and dining room.

Brax simply shook his head. "Helen's not going to be pleased."

"No, but we'll be long gone by then." She took him in and he held her gaze. What a wonderful man he was: caring, intelligent, proud. She wondered if the country would ever value the men of the race the way their loved ones did. "You've been a great partner, Braxton. Thank you for everything."

"You're welcome."

There was so much more she wanted to say. Revealing that she'd fallen in love with him served no purpose though. He would be going home to Boston and she to New Orleans. "Let's see how Stipe is faring."

When they entered the dining room, they could tell the drug was doing its job by the way he was nodding over his plate. He was trying to fight it off though. Seeing them, anger filled his glassy eyes. In a slurred voice he asked, "What did you give me?"

She smiled falsely. "I've no idea what you mean."

He tried to stand, but his legs gave way and he sank back down on the chair. His eyelids kept closing and he kept forcing them to open. "Going to kill you," he threatened weakly. A few seconds later, the drug took total effect and he fell face forward into the food on his plate.

"Such a messy eater," Raven cracked.

Brax gave her a smile. "We should probably move him so he doesn't drown in collards or get smothered by the yams."

"I suppose." Both fates suited her just fine after the way he'd terrorized them earlier.

In the end, they laid him on the floor. Raven cleaned his face and they left him there to sleep.

Over the course of the next few hours, she and Brax packed their belongings and checked on Stipe. At one point, Raven entered the dining room to find him sitting up, but he was still so groggy she could've been a talking crawdad for all he knew. She knelt down beside him. His puzzled, drug-laced eyes met hers.

"Where am I?" he asked thickly. "Who are you?"

"Cleopatra, don't you remember? Here. Drink this; it will help clear your head."

She placed the glass against his lips and he drank slowly. Some of the liquid dribbled down his chin but he'd gotten enough to send him back into the arms of Morpheus. She stood. "Pleasant nightmares."

Once the sun set and night rolled in, she gave him one last large dose. That done, she and Brax retrieved the items hidden in the privy, picked up their travel bags, and slipped away to meet Renay.

It was a moonless night and so dark, Raven couldn't see if Renay was waiting in a vehicle nearby, so she signaled him by lighting three matches in quick succession. Seconds later, a buggy drove up. Holding the reins was her cousin Marshall, the oldest son of her mother's cousin Maisie, who'd been selling the eggs and hens with Hazel at the market. Beside him sat Renay still wearing his false facial hair and posing as White, in case they were stopped and questioned about their intentions or destination.

"Thanks for driving us, Marshall," Raven said quietly.

"You're welcome. Mama didn't want you all lost in the dark. Where to?"

Renay shared the boardinghouse address she'd given him earlier and the buggy pulled off.

"I let Welch know you'd be delivering her package tonight," Renay said.

Beside Raven in the backseat sat Braxton. He draped an arm over the seat's top edge, and she slid closer and rested her head against his shoulder. It was almost over.

There were a couple of lights on inside the boardinghouse when they drove up, and Raven prayed one of them belonged to Welch. She had no idea what she'd do if the detective wasn't there. She wouldn't put it past Welch to be elsewhere as a way to purposely prolong their servitude. The landlady, an elderly White woman, answered the door. She took one look at Raven and said, "Too late for visiting."

"I'm not here to visit. I have some papers to give to Annabelle Clarkston. She's expecting me."

The woman appeared skeptical, but said, "Wait here."

She returned shortly. "Her room is the second door down the hall. You have five minutes. No more."

Raven offered her thanks, made her way to the designated door, and knocked.

"Who's there?"

"The person you're expecting."

Raven didn't want to give her name in case the landlady or someone else might be listening. The best way to disappear was to leave no trace, clues, or connections behind.

The door opened. Raven handed Welch the tube and turned to leave.

"Wait!" Welch hissed.

Raven stopped.

"I need to make sure this isn't empty. Come inside."

It was the last thing Raven wanted to do, but if this small concession led to never seeing Welch again, she'd make it.

Inside the room, Raven waited and watched while Welch pried the cylinder open and extracted the document. After unfurling it and studying it closely under a lamp, Welch smiled. "This is it."

Raven wanted to verbally flay her for forcing Raven's family to do her bidding, but decided it served no purpose. Instead, she put her contempt into the parting glare she shot Welch's way as she exited.

* * *

THE RIDE TO Maisie's house took an hour. It was out in the country, and the moonless night was so pitch dark, she was glad Marshall had agreed to drive them. Inside the house when they arrived were her mother, Harrison, and her Charleston cousins. Hugs and smiles were shared before the serious talk began.

Braxton stood off to the side with his father and watched and listened as Raven relayed the events of the past few days, the discovery of the hidden cylinder, and their encounter with Aubrey Stipe. She passed the IOUs to Renay, who said, "I know a local Republican newspaper publisher. He may be interested in these."

With that taken care of, Hazel spoke. "I received a wire from Eden yesterday. She and the immediate family are on their way to cousin Dane's in Texas. The number of deaths back home is now close to two thousand and she thought they should leave."

Braxton was stunned, and from the faces of the others in the room, he wasn't alone.

Hazel continued, "As of this morning, Mississippi isn't allowing any trains from or to Louisiana, and some of the other bordering states are considering the same. There are deaths as far north as Memphis. In light of that, I'm going north to Boston with Harrison until the end of August. Raven, I purchased Boston tickets for you, too. Neither of us needs to go home right now. It's too risky. That also applies to you, Renay. Once we're done here, sail to Cuba and stay with my brother, or go to St. Augustine or Savannah and stay with family there, but don't go home to New Orleans. I don't want to bury you. We've all cried at enough funerals because of the fever."

Braxton remembered Raven's recounting of the family members who'd succumbed to the disease in the past. He turned his attention her way. Would she balk at Boston and choose to go to Cuba or one of the other places Hazel mentioned instead? He didn't want her going home, either. If she decided not to come to Boston, he'd be disappointed, but it was better than worrying about burying her. As if she'd heard his thinking, she looked over and held his gaze for a few moments before refocusing on her mother. He wondered what she'd do. He was selfish enough to want her with him even if the time equaled no more than a month. He'd awakened with her beside him the past few days, and he wanted more. Along with more of her smiles, kisses, and the enthralling scent of roses on her skin.

Raven said, "Once Stipe wakes up, he's going to be furious. When he realizes we've left, he'll probably be at the station in the morning looking for us."

Hazel said, "I agree. I packed our nun habits in case we needed them, and I'm glad I did. We can claim to be from the Order back home or the one up in Baltimore. Harrison and Braxton can play the role of Order employees assisting us in travel."

Braxton was impressed. The family always seemed one step ahead, and in this case he was thankful. Stipe would indeed be furious and moving heaven and earth to find them. He'd be looking for a married couple, however. Not two nuns. He spoke up. "Stipe won't recognize you, Da, but he will me, so I should probably shave."

"Good idea," Raven said.

The talking went on for a short while longer, and once everything that needed to be discussed was handled, it was time for bed.

Brax hid a yawn behind his hand. Seeing it, Maisie said kindly, "Brax, there's a tent out back with a cot inside. You're welcome to it."

"That will be fine, thank you. I want to shave first though."

Harrison asked, "You want me to cut your hair?"

Brax nodded.

"Then let's go get started. There's a lamp in the room Hazel and I are using."

Raven wondered what he would look like with a clean-shaven face. His rakish beard and mustache were as much a part of him as his kindness. She looked forward to seeing the altered Braxton.

Maisie's voice interrupted her speculation.

"Raven, you can stretch out here on the sofa. I'll get you some bedding."

Harrison said, "Come, son. Let's see about that shave."

A SHORT WHILE later, Harrison removed the sheet draped over Brax's shoulders. Before taking it outside to shake out the hair covering it, he handed Brax a long-handled mirror borrowed from Maisie so he could see the results. "How's that?" he asked, watching Brax study his new face.

Brax smiled. "I like it, and even if I didn't, the shave is necessary. I'm bald as an apple."

Harrison chuckled. "That you are."

Brax eyed the very close-cropped version of his beard and the bit of hair that remained to accent his chin. The new face would take some getting used to. He was almost unrecognizable to himself and most certainly would be to Stipe. Brax hadn't had a hairless face since his eighteenth birthday. "I wonder what Raven will think of this?" he asked running his hand over his smooth head.

"Will it matter?" his father asked.

"Not really since it had to be done, but I do value her opinion."

"Care about her, do you?"

He met his father's kind eyes. "I do. Very much. Probably in love with her if the truth be told. Not something I planned."

"Moreau women will do that to a man. Have you told her?"

He shook his head. "She doesn't believe we're compatible, socially or economically."

"Sounds like me and her mother a few decades ago, but we're together now, and if the fates are kind, and you truly love Raven, you two will be, too."

Brax smiled. "Promise?"

"Have I ever lied to you?"

"No, Da. Never. And thanks for the shave and haircut."

"You're welcome."

Leaving the room, he walked into the small parlor where the women were seated.

"Oh my!" Raven gasped in response to his new appearance.

"Very handsome," Hazel voiced, smiling. "You look very kingly. All you need is a length of cloth draped over your shoulder and a royal staff in your hand."

"And maybe a leopard or two posed beside you," Raven added, grinning. "Stipe will never recognize you."

"Let's hope you're right." He only had eyes for Raven. He'd grown accustomed to just the two of them being together at the end of the day, but tonight they'd be separated and that was disappointing. He consoled himself knowing she'd be traveling with him to Boston, and it gave him something to look forward to. "Good night, ladies."

"Sleep well, Brax," Raven said quietly.

"You, too."

THE NEXT MORNING, they arrived at the Charleston train station to find a gang of armed men bullying their way through the sparse crowd. Stipe appeared to be their leader. He was stopping couples to study their faces before allowing them to move on. Dressed in her nun's habit and wimple and wearing her mother's false blue spectacles to disguise her eyes, Raven felt guilt rise over being the reason he was targeting and harassing innocent people. She then realized she wasn't at fault. The guilt lay with Detective Welch for setting the events in motion. The scene was tense, however. No one knew who Stipe and his men were after or why, and more importantly, what might happen if the persons were or were not found. As a result, people were keeping their heads and eyes down, and doing their best to stay out of the way. No one wanted to lose their life.

The train finally arrived. Stipe and his people were still angrily snatching women around so he could look into their faces, but he gave the nuns and their poorly dressed escorts only a cursory glance.

The conductor gave the boarding call. This being South Carolina, everyone knew the passengers would be segregated, so the Blacks went to the back and the Whites moved to the front.

The conductor stopped their small party. "Sisters, you're welcome to take seats in the regular car, but you'll have to sit in the last row. Your men will have to ride with the rest of your kind, however."

Hazel said, "Bless you for being so considerate, but we'll ride with our people."

"You sure? I don't want to send women of God to the gambling car."

"We'll be fine. Our faith will take care of us."

He appeared unconvinced but moved on.

On their way to the gambling car, Raven spied Stipe astride a brown horse near the track watching the procession. His face was twisted with anger, his eyes flared with hate. This was the first train of the day and others would be departing for various destinations until dark. She wondered if he planned on searching the passengers boarding each. He only had until noon, however, before the cock crowed at his own personal Gethsemane.

The advantage of the train's early departure meant the gambling car was fairly clean, and the air wasn't fouled as yet by the smoke of pipes and cigars. Seating was limited, however. The gamblers were already crowded around the tables and on the stools ringing the bar. People with families and young children had claimed most of the other tables, but there was a small unoccupied one with two empty chairs available. Brax and Raven let their parents have it. With no place else to sit, they took up a spot in a corner not too far away and sat on the floor.

"We made it," Raven said with relief. The wimple was hot and she was sweating beneath it, but it would have to be endured, at least until they changed trains.

"Stipe didn't look happy," Brax said.

"No. He needs to be worried about what's going to happen at his house when that man shows up at noon to take possession instead of bullying people at the train station."

"I agree."

Stipe aside, Raven was enjoying being with Brax again. She'd missed him last night. She glanced over at her mother and Harrison. They were conversing and seemed content. She had no way of knowing how much private time the two had been able to carve out for themselves while staying with Maisie, but they'd have a lot over the next few days on the long train ride north.

He asked, "Do you want to check on *Alice* while we ride?"

She smiled. "Yes. That will help pass the time. I still don't know what the rabbit is late for and who the queen is so mad at."

He dug into his bag for the book and turned to chapter two. He showed her the illustration.

"Poor Alice," Raven said. "Her neck does

look like a telescope. Drinking that potion and eating that cake, she doesn't know if she's coming or going."

He agreed. "The title for this chapter is?" He waited for her to respond.

She looked at the words. *"The Pool of Tears?"* she asked.

"Correct."

"Oh dear, now what?"

He began, and Raven listened to him describe how Alice kept growing so tall her head hit the ceiling and she could no longer see her feet. After wondering who would put on her shoes and whether her feet would still obey her, she began crying. Her tears flooded the space she was in. She found a fan and shrunk back down to normal size again, Raven glanced up to see a little boy standing in front of them. She touched Brax's arm lightly. He stopped and appeared surprised, too.

"Hello," Raven said.

"Hello. Excuse me. May I listen to the story?"

Raven was even more surprised. She hadn't realized Brax's voice had carried to wherever the boy had been sitting. He looked to be a bit younger than Dorrie. His clothes were old but clean, and like most of the South's poorer children, both Black and White, he was very thin. "Are you with your mama?"

He nodded.

"Go and ask her if it's okay for you to do so.

If she says yes, you're more than welcome to listen."

His small brown face lit up and he speed walked over to a woman seated on the floor a short distance away. Raven smiled at his swift departure. He was using the walk of a little one who'd been told not to run in confined places like church, or in this instance, railroad cars.

He returned with his mother. Her hair was tied up and her clothes had seen better days but there was a smile in her eyes. "Hello, Sister," she said to Raven. "Sir," she said to Braxton. "I'm sorry if he's bothering you."

"He isn't," Raven assured her.

"Not at all," Brax added. "If he has your permission, he's more than welcome to listen."

"What's the story about?"

Raven knew her to be a good mama. Her son was polite and she was looking out for him by quizzing them about what he'd be listening to. Raven opted to let Brax give the explanation, since he knew the story so well.

When he was done with his short summary, he added, "It's a children's book."

"Okay, he can listen as long as he isn't bothering you. I'd like to listen, too, if I can. I like to read but we can't afford books."

The admission tugged at Raven's heart.

Brax said, "Please, join us."

She introduced herself as Ellen and her son

was named Aaron. They sat, got comfortable, and Brax continued with chapter two.

Over the course of the next few hours, their audience grew. Other families took seats nearby or brought their chairs. Hazel and Harrison drifted over, and even a few of the gamblers listened in. When Brax's voice grew tired, he passed the book to Ellen and she had tears in her eyes as she took up the tale. She was a champion reader and her son smiled from ear to ear. When she tired, one of the gamblers, a White man, took up the story. By the time they reached the end of the line to change trains, most of the people in the gambling car were listening, smiling, and discussing Alice's adventures.

As they all said their goodbyes to Brax and Raven the nun, she noticed how sad Aaron appeared. Brax apparently did as well. He asked Ellen, "Do you have an address you can share? I'd like to send you and your son some books."

She eyed him for a long moment as if trying to determine his intent before saying, "You don't have to do that."

"I know," he replied, smiling softly. "But I want to. He's being raised well. I'd be honored to assist you in this small way."

She pressed a hand over her mouth, and her eyes brimmed with tears. Too moved for speech for a moment, she simply nodded. Raven had tears in her eyes, as did her mother, Hazel.

Ellen wrote her address in Brax's journal. "I'm on my way to Boston," he explained to her. "I'll send them by mail as soon as I can. It may take a while but I won't forget. I promise."

"Okay," she whispered. She took her son by the hand and they departed. Aaron turned to give them a wave and they waved back.

Raven looked up into the eyes of the remarkable man standing by her side. "That was so very kind of you, Braxton Steele."

"It's a small thing. One day sometime in the future a little boy like Aaron may grow up to be president."

"We can dream."

"If you don't have dreams they can't come true."

His gesture had so moved her; she didn't tell him but he'd earned the most tremendous, gigantic reward she could think of as soon as they had some unhurried private time alone.

His father patted him on the back. "You're a good man, son."

"I was raised well, too."

Chapter Fourteen

$\mathscr{T}$wo days later, at three in the afternoon, they got off the train in Baltimore. Both Harrison and Brax were well familiar with the city, so they hired a hack to take them to a boardinghouse they used whenever they visited. The owner, a tall statuesque, bronze-skinned woman named Freddie England, smiled upon seeing them enter her establishment. "Well, well. If it isn't the handsomest father and son on the East Coast. How are you, Harry and Brax? Where's your beard? And what in the world are you doing with two nuns? Their souls can't be saved, Sisters. It's too late."

They all laughed, and introductions followed. She was told that Raven and Hazel weren't really nuns, but no one elaborated further.

Freddie said, "I have two rooms open. Here are the keys. You all can decide who sleeps where. Dinner is served starting at five."

They climbed the stairs to the second floor

and found their rooms. Harrison and Hazel claimed one and left Brax and Raven the one next door.

Upon entering, Raven was pleased with theirs. In addition to the comfortable-looking bed with its sea blue quilt that matched the curtains, there was a small sitting area with two cream-colored upholstered chairs flanking the fireplace. "This is nice."

"Freddie runs a fine place. Da and I stay here whenever we're in the city. She has an outstanding kitchen staff, too."

"Good, because I'm tired of the trackside train fare we've been eating since what seems like forever."

She set her bags on the floor and dropped down tiredly into one of the chairs. "This is so much better than the train. I'm not going to know how to handle being able to stretch out in an actual bed."

"I'm sure we'll be able to figure it out."

She chuckled and thought about the last time they'd been alone together. "I've missed us being us."

"I have as well." He walked over and sat on the arm of her chair. She scanned his features. Although they'd known each other for only a short time, their ties to each other felt deep enough to have been forged over years. "Your shave makes you look very regal."

"Regal enough for a kiss?"

She raised herself to get closer and the kiss that followed was deep and welcomed. Hearing a rhythmic squeaking sound, Raven eased back and glanced around curiously. "What is that noise?"

"Our parents."

Realizing his meaning, her jaw dropped and her eyes widened. The noise increased. "Good Lord. They've been in the room, what, five minutes?"

"Probably playing the Nun and the Handyman."

"Stop!" she ordered in a voice filled with hilarity. "You are so scandalous."

"Apparently, they are, too."

Laughter put tears in her eyes. "Where's the washroom? I want to change clothes and go for a walk or something. Being next door to them is going to scar me for the rest of my days."

"Washroom's down the hall."

Thanking him with a quick kiss, she left the room.

After she traded her nun's habit for regular attire, the two set off. It was a warm July day. Not as warm as home or in Charleston, Raven noted, but the sunshine felt good. There was also a water-scented breeze. She assumed it was from the harbor. The smell of it seemed airier and lighter than the deeper tones of the Mississippi. As they walked, she noted the trolleys and the wagon traffic that was far less congested than that of New Orleans, and although the men wore the traditional brown suits all men seemed to wear no matter the location, the women wore fitted, two-piece suits with snug-fitting jackets unlike the loosely constructed ones she was accustomed to seeing at home. All the ladies sported hats. Some fancy. Others plain. There wasn't a tignon in sight.

"I have a friend who owns a dress shop not too far from here," Brax said. "Let's stop by so you can meet her."

The sign above the door read: ROSETTA'S ATTIRE FOR LADIES. In the front window a dress form showcased an olive green two-piece ladies' suit. The fitted jacket was piped in black, and the cuffs were flute-edged. Raven found it very attractive.

"That's a fine-looking ensemble," he said, standing beside her.

"It's lovely."

"Looks to be your size, too."

"Not my purse's size, I'm sure though."

He smiled and let her precede him through the door and inside.

The woman behind the counter, an older dark-skinned woman, looked up when they entered and smiled. Taking in Brax, she paused for a moment. Suddenly, as if recognizing him, her face lit up like a flare. "Oh, Braxton, my love," she said, her voice filled with emotion. She hurried over and greeted him with an embrace. "How are you? I almost didn't recognize you without hair."

"I'm fine, Mrs. Wells. How are you?"

"I am well. And who is this lovely young woman?"

"A friend visiting from New Orleans, Raven Moreau."

"What a beautiful name for a beautiful woman. I'm Rosetta Wells. Welcome to Baltimore. Pleased to meet you."

"Pleased to meet you as well, Mrs. Wells."

"Her mother and my father are to be married," Braxton explained.

Mrs. Wells clapped her hands against her cheeks in shock and surprise. "Harry is getting married?" She turned to Raven. "Is your mother as beautiful as you are?"

Raven grinned. "In my mind, she's the most beautiful woman in the world."

"Oh, those old biddies up in Boston are going to take to their beds knowing Harry's off the market. They've been trying to throw their nets over him for decades."

While the two friends chatted further, Raven drifted away and took in the store's offerings. There was daywear and nightwear. She passed hats, fancy hose, and more dress forms sporting ensembles like the one in the window.

When she saw Mrs. Wells removing the suit from the window and placing it on the counter, she became curious. Mrs. Wells said, "Pretty

Miss Raven, will you come into the back with me and try this on? I want to check the fit."

Raven looked at Brax. He turned his eyes to the ceiling and began whistling as if he wasn't guilty of what she guessed he was up to. But Mrs. Wells had been kind, and if purchasing the suit would add a few dollars to her till, Raven would play along. She'd save fussing at him for when they were alone.

The suit did fit. It was a bit long in the hem though. Mrs. Wells suggested, "Just have Braxton or one of the women at his shop shorten it an inch or so for you, and it will be perfect. How long have you known Braxton?"

"Not very long."

"Well, I've known him for over a decade and he's very special to me."

"He's special to me as well," Raven replied truthfully.

"Good to hear and to know. Go ahead and remove the suit, and we'll tally it up and send it home with you."

Once she changed back into her own clothes, Raven carried the suit to the counter. Apparently Braxton had done some shopping while she'd been in the back, because Mrs. Wells was tallying a small pile of other items and placing them into a canvas bag: hose, two skirts—one brown, one black—blouses, and lovely silk shifts. When she was done, Brax gave Raven a smile and handed over what was owed.

Mrs. Wells and Brax shared a parting embrace. "You take care of yourself," he told her. "I'll look in on you the next time I'm in town."

"I'd like that." She turned to Raven. "It's been a pleasure meeting you."

"Mine, too. Thank you."

They exited, and once outside, Brax looked Raven's way and asked, "Am I in for a fussing?"

"I'm still trying to decide. Tell me how you know Mrs. Wells."

"Her son, William, and I were in the Fifty-Fourth together and we became good friends. He was badly injured during one of our last campaigns and eventually succumbed. On his deathbed he asked that I look after his mother. He was her only child and she has no husband. I promised him I would. Every time I'm here, I stop in to see her. Sometimes I take her to dinner, sometimes we simply sit and talk. She still misses her son very much."

Moved by the story and yet another example of his caring nature, Raven decided not to fuss. As they walked, they came across a book shop. "Let's get the books for Aaron and his mother," he said.

Pleased that he'd be keeping his promise, she accompanied him inside. Aided by the owner, Brax found Aaron a speller, a book that would help him with his arithmetic, and another focusing on mastering penmanship. He also picked out Frederick Douglass's autobiography for Aaron's mother, Ellen, and two copies of *Alice's Adventures in Wonderland*. After paying for the purchases, he arranged with the owner to have the books shipped to the address Ellen had provided. Brax kept one copy of Alice, however.

"Do you need a new copy?" Raven asked.

"No, you do." And he handed it to her.

Filled with emotion, she said, "Thank you. I will treasure this always." And she would because of the role it had played in tying them together.

They arrived back at the boardinghouse just in time for dinner. Joining Hazel and Harrison at one of the tables in the small dining room, Raven chuckled inwardly at their passionate antics and hoped that if and when she married, it would be to a man she'd be still making the bed creak with at their age.

Brax had been right to tout Freddie's kitchen staff; the food offered that evening included stuffed crabs, honeyed carrots, well-seasoned green beans, and soft, warm yeast rolls running with butter. Everything was excellently prepared. It was the first real meal Raven hadn't had to cook herself since leaving New Orleans and it was all so delicious, she wanted to stuff herself until Christmas.

After dinner, the parents retired to their room. Their train to Boston would be leaving first thing in the morning and they wanted to get some rest. Neither Raven nor Braxton believed that for a minute, but wished them a good evening.

Braxton said, "Freddie has a gazebo out back. Would you like some fresh air after that great meal?"

"Anything to keep from hearing our parents through the wall."

He laughed. "Then let's go."

It was a nice evening. He was hoping the gazebo wasn't already occupied. It wasn't, so he and Raven sat together on the bench inside. He placed an arm over the bench's back, and as she leaned against him, her head on his shoulder, he smiled with contentment. Although their time together alone that day had been limited, he'd enjoyed himself. "So did you decide whether I am to be fussed at about my purchases from Mrs. Wells?"

"I have. No fussing warranted."

"I'm relieved."

She gave him a smile. "Lord knows I don't have many things to wear, and you helped put money in her coffers, so there's nothing really to be upset about."

"Good. I like her very much and hope she stays in business as long as she wants to." He wondered if what he felt for Raven was love. Having never been in love before, he had nothing to go by. If wanting to be with someone the way he did with her was any indication, then he guessed he was head over heels. His father had encouraged him to tell her. Brax was afraid it would alter their relationship, and he didn't want that. For now, he'd keep his feelings to himself, especially since he'd no idea where she stood on the matter or how she'd react to his declaration.

"It's nice out here," she said, looking up at him.

"I agree." The gazebo was set in the middle of a wide field. Off in the distance, large trees swayed in the breeze. It was a quiet, peaceful space.

"How long will it take us to get to Boston?"

"On a perfect trip it takes anywhere from twelve to fifteen hours. Baltimore is roughly four hundred miles way."

"Okay. So possibly by this time tomorrow you'll be home."

"Yes."

"I'm looking forward to seeing your city."

"Are you?"

"I am. Home makes us who we are. At least that's what I believe. I'd not be who I am were I not born in New Orleans. I want to see the city that made you—not during the winter though."

He chuckled. "I will enjoy showing it off, then." He thought back on Dorrie and her iceskating dream. Would that really come to be? More importantly would he actually marry the incredible woman by his side? Logic insisted the predictions couldn't possibly be true, but apparently logic knew very little about New Orleans. "The last night we were in New Orleans, your mother said the family was getting out of the business."

She looked surprised. "She did. I wonder if she forgot you were in the room, because you weren't supposed to hear that."

"She may have." He didn't tell her he knew about Fanny's Plan, and asked instead, "Do you have a plan for what you want to do in the future?"

She shrugged. "I don't know. My grandmother left me a small inheritance I can use to buy a place of my own, so I'll concentrate on that first. It won't be big or fancy but it'll be mine, and I might be able to forgo being a domestic, at least long enough until I figure out some other kind of employment. Not that I have skills for anything else."

She went quiet as if thinking before continuing. "Who knows, maybe I'll find a man who'll enjoy my gift for apoplexy and we can make a passel of babies and I'll be a mama for the rest of my days. There's value in that. The race needs all the strong-minded children we can raise. And I'll make sure they can read, too—from the time they're little. I think I'd make an excellent mama."

"I think you'd make an excellent mother, too."

"I had a great example in my own."

He agreed. He didn't agree with the part about her having another man's babies though. He wanted her babies to be theirs—hers and his.

She smiled at him. "And when you and your prizewinner come to New Orleans to see Mama and Harrison, you'll be Uncle Brax and she'll be Aunt Lottie to my children, and I'll be Aunt Raven to yours. For the Moreaux there's no such thing as having too many cousins."

Brax had already decided he'd be having a conversation with Lottie. It might be a difficult one, but he wouldn't be marrying her; not after being with Raven. Because of Raven, he'd learned that passion and spontaneity and laughter far outweighed settling for evenly yoked. He assumed Lottie would be disappointed and he'd apologize profusely for the whispers his decision might cause. Because he hadn't officially asked her mother for her hand, maybe the gossip wouldn't linger and she could move on with her life.

As the evening moved into dusk and the temperature dropped, he felt her shiver a bit. "We should probably go inside."

"I suppose," she said, sounding disappointed. "It's been nice out here with the peace and quiet. Reminds me of our evenings in Charleston." She looked up and met his eyes. "I wanted to put the bed to good use tonight but I've changed my mind."

He stilled. That had been his plan as well. "May I ask why?"

"Call me prudish but I can't possibly be scandalous knowing my mother may and probably will hear us through those paper-thin walls."

He laughed.

"Do you mind waiting until we get to your home?"

He leaned down and kissed her lightly. "I'll wait as long as you want."

"I'm sorry."

"You've nothing to apologize for. I want you to enjoy yourself, not be worried about what our parents are thinking, even though they don't seem to give a fig about what we might think of them."

"I'm hoping to be that carefree at their age."

"Me, too." And he wanted that carefree Raven to be with him.

AT NINE O'CLOCK the next night the train pulled into the Boston station. For appearance's sake, Hazel and Harrison were supposed to stay the first few nights at Brax's large home, but the lovebirds opted to go to Harrison's flat instead.

"We'll move in with you tomorrow," Harrison told his son.

They hailed a hack for themselves and were driven away.

"So much for avoiding scandal," the amused Brax said to Raven. "Let's find a hack for us."

They secured one with a White driver. When he got them under way Raven asked, "Hacks don't segregate here?"

"Some drivers do. Others don't. Boston is well-known for its abolitionist roots but there's bigotry here, too."

The ride didn't take long. After he paid the driver, they climbed the short set of steps to the front door of the tall, flat-faced brick house. Raven eyed the many windows and thought the structure looked more like a business establishment than a home. He used his key in the lock and allowed her to enter ahead of him into one of the largest foyers she'd ever encountered. There was a big chandelier hanging from the tall white ceiling above her head, and she was admiring its size and beauty when he came up behind her.

"Go on in," he said quietly.

The parlor was equally spacious. Not even the turned-down lamps could hide the rich carpet on the floor or the fine furnishings gracing the room. Raven had seen the interiors of some of the houses of the wealthy Black Creoles back home, but not even those could compete with this luxury.

"You live well," she said, taking in the beauty of the lamps, the crown molding, and the gleaming wood of the furniture. On one wall above a large stone fireplace hung a gilt-framed portrait of a stern-looking gray-bearded man dressed in blue seaman's garb. "Is that your grandfather?"

"Yes. Nelson Rowley. Known as The Captain."

"Welcome home!"

Raven turned to see a middle-aged White woman wearing a white robe over her night-clothes entering the room. She was small and birdlike, like Raven's cousin Etta.

"Oh my word! Where's your hair!" she asked.

He laughed. "Hello, Kate. Yes, I'm home. Raven, this is my housekeeper, Kate Dublin. Kate—Raven Moreau."

Kate did a little curtsy. "Pleased to meet you, miss."

"Same here," Raven said hiding her shock at finding he employed a White servant.

Kate said, "And thanks for sending the wire earlier that you'd possibly be home today. I was starting to worry when I didn't hear from you or Mr. Harry."

"He's home, as well, and brought his intended, Raven's mother, Hazel."

Her blue eyes went round. "Mr. Harry's getting married?"

He nodded.

"There's going to be much grieving in the city of Boston once that news gets around. You come home with no hair. Mr. Harry has an intended. Sounds like you had quite an adventure. I can't wait to hear the details."

"I'll share them in the morning."

"Are either of you hungry?" Kate asked, looking between them.

Raven shook her head. She was exhausted from all the travel. She just wanted sleep, and remembering Brax's description of Boston's bland food didn't make her eager to sample it, at least not this minute. She'd wait. Raven noted the housekeeper's eyes kept straying her way as if she were trying to determine if there was more to Raven's role than being the daughter of the woman marrying Harrison. Raven planned to let Brax handle any answers that needed to be shared.

"You can go on to bed, Kate," Brax said to her. "Thanks for waiting up. I'll place Raven in the guest room. We'll see you in the morning. We're both exhausted so we'll probably sleep in. We'll take our breakfast in the dining room."

"Okay. Welcome home again. It's nice meeting you, Miss Moreau."

"Nice meeting you, too."

After her departure, Brax said, "Let's get you settled. I'll give you a tour of the house tomorrow."

"How many days does the tour take?"

Laughing, he picked up their travel bags. "Come on."

He led her up a staircase that could only be described as grand to the home's second floor. A short, narrow hallway lined with paintings of seascapes on both walls led to a much wider horizontally oriented hallway.

"The bedrooms are in this wing," he explained. "For tonight, I'm putting you in one of the guest rooms because we both need sleep. You can move in with me tomorrow if you'd like. And don't worry about Kate knowing; she doesn't gossip."

Raven was pleased to learn that, but when scandal arose the disparagement was usually directed the woman's way. A man's reputation rarely suffered.

He opened one of the gleaming wood doors. "This one will be yours."

Raven entered behind him and stepped into another beautifully appointed room. The four-poster bed was draped in a rich blue color that reminded her of the bolt of silk he'd purchased from Etta. The fireplace was huge and made of polished boulders. The small loveseat positioned near it matched the blue of the bed, and the windows were hidden behind curtains of a soft sky blue.

"The washroom is through that door there. It has indoor plumbing and a tub."

She smiled at the thought of being able to use the rose-scented bath salts he'd purchased for her in Charleston.

"Is there anything else you need?"

"Just a good night kiss."

He opened his arms and she went to him. He

fulfilled the request with a kiss that was unhurried and so passionate it made her want to
change his mind about sleeping apart. When
their lips finally parted she was left in a familiar
haze. He placed a tender kiss on her brow.

"Good night, little corvus."

"Good night," she whispered, and watched
him go.

Chapter Fifteen

The following morning, when Raven awakened, it took her a few minutes to remember where she was. The beautiful bed with its opulent indigo draping and silklike sheets made her wonder if she was still dreaming, or had been magically transformed into royalty because the room and its fittings had to belong to a queen.

Leaving the bed, she walked to windows that ran the length of one wall and peeked through the curtains to look out. It was still dark. Normally, at this time of day, she'd be preparing to start breakfast while mentally listing the chores needing her attention. However, none of that would be required. In Braxton's home, someone else would be doing the preparing and making the lists. As his guest, she could step aside and let the day course without her attention, and she wasn't sure how to do that. It was a wonderful problem to have, of course, but it felt odd knowing she wasn't expected to be of service. So, she decided to do something queenlike and indulge in a bath.

Once done, she dressed in the new clothing Brax had purchased for her and was surprised to find more items in the bag than she'd initially seen. She guessed they'd been added to the trove while she was in the back of the store changing out of the suit before she rejoined him and Mrs. Wells at the counter. There were drawers, garters, and two lovely pairs of ladies' gloves. After putting on her shoes, she did her hair and savored the lingering scent of roses in the room's air and on her skin from her bath salts. It made her think of the bath he'd drawn for her in Charleston and their slow, lust-filled coming together after. She hoped she'd get the chance to be scandalous again with him soon.

She'd just completed making her bed when she heard a soft knock on the door. Walking over, she opened it. Seeing Braxton, she smiled. "Good morning."

"Good morning. Did you sleep well?"

"I did. How about you?"

"I missed falling asleep with you beside me."

"I missed being there." And she had.

"Let's fix that tonight, shall we?"

"I'd like that."

He looked to the room behind her. "I smell roses."

"My bath earlier."

"Ah. The scent makes me want to tumble you

back onto the bed and slowly seek it out on your skin."

"I'd like that as well." Her awakened senses called to him. Even though their last intimate encounter had been only a few days ago, she felt as if it had been months.

"Would you like a quick orgasm before breakfast?" he asked, eyes sparkling with heat and mischief.

"Must it be quick?"

He laughed. "And you accuse me of being scandalous." He leaned down and gave her a soft, blood-warming kiss.

He moved into the room and closed the door softly behind them.

What she saw in his gaze could've set her skirt afire.

"Open your buttons for me. I adore watching you undress."

Holding his smoldering gaze, she slowly worked the small beads free. He bent and brushed warm, worshipping lips over the bared base of her throat. "You smell divine."

He drew her shift down and rubbed a thumb over her tight nipple. The licks that followed made her back up against the door to keep from dissolving to the carpeted floor. He alternated between plying her mouth with kisses and feasting on her breasts.

"Raise your skirt, please," he husked out. "I purchased it just for moments like this."

Her sensations climbed. "Wicked, wicked man."

He placed a kiss on her collarbone and nipped her gently. "You make me want you half dressed every time I see you. Open your legs."

She did so, and he stroked and teased and played through the opening in her new drawers. The entire time, he watched her rising to his wordless seduction, as if viewing her uninhibited responses to his pleasuring fed his own.

"I promised quick." He eased in two talented fingers and bent to possessively claim her damp dark nipple with his mouth. He bit her there with just enough passion to make the orgasm crackle over her like lightning. She buried her scream in his suit-covered shoulder to keep from being heard.

"Like that, did you?" he teased gruffly, fingers continuing to move lustily in and out. Shuddering, she moaned hoarsely. "Wait until tonight," he promised.

When she came back to herself, she dropped her skirt with weak hands and fought to catch her breath. The last peals of the orgasm continued to resonate like a far-off bell. She wasn't sure if she'd ever be able to leave the room.

He gave her a final kiss and whispered, "Welcome to Boston."

Downstairs at the dining room table, Raven studied the unfamiliar dish on her plate. It was made of potatoes and carrots and what she thought might be sausage. She wasn't sure what the other ingredients were. Brax was seated across from her, and when she raised questioning eyes his way, he said, "It's hash."

"Ah," she replied doubtfully.

Kate came out of the kitchen with cups of coffee. Raven picked up her fork and dug in. She didn't want to insult the housekeeper or be disrespectful. For a bayou girl who'd grown up on bacon, eggs, and grits, the hash was plenty terrible, but she kept her distaste from her face.

"How is it, Miss Moreau?" Kate asked.

"It's fine."

Kate asked Braxton, "Is she lying?"

The question caught Raven by surprise and she looked Braxton's way. Over his raised coffee cup, he smiled. "You can tell her the truth, Raven."

Kate waited patiently for the answer.

Raven didn't want to hurt the woman's feelings. "Let's just say this isn't what I'm accustomed to eating for breakfast."

The housekeeper smiled. "Your kindness is appreciated. Honestly, I'm not very good in the kitchen, never have been."

Raven was even more surprised.

Kate explained, "Braxton's grandfather, bless his stingy excuse for a heart, refused to hire a cook, so he made his lovely wife and everyone else who sat at this table eat my terrible food. After that first visit, not many of the people he knew accepted his dinner invitations."

Raven went from surprised to floored.

Brax said, "Raven's an excellent cook, Kate."

"Are you?"

"It's how I make my living. I'm a domestic."

"No," Kate said, sounding astonished. She asked Brax, "Is she pulling my leg?"

He shook his head.

"You cook and clean, too?"

"I do."

"Well, I'll be damned. Oh, sorry. My word."

Raven laughed.

Kate asked, "You know this one is a spoiled prince." She pointed at Braxton. "Silver spoon since the day he was born."

"Hey!" Braxton said, playfully coming to his own defense. "I thought you loved me."

"I do. Doesn't change who you are." She said to Raven, "But he's a good prince. Not an evil bone in his body."

Raven liked Kate.

Kate asked, "So can you teach me a thing or two? My poor husband, Tom, keeps threatening to trade me in for the cook at the pub he usually eats at when he's home. I'd like to fix him a meal that makes him smile instead of grumble. He's out at sea right now."

"I'd love to help you. When I get the chance, I'll take a look at your pantry and cold box and see what you might need."

Kate said to Brax, "Marry this one." And she returned to the kitchen.

Brax said, "First Dorrie and now Kate. There seems to be a common theme here."

Raven rolled her eyes. "What are we going to do today, Prince?"

"I'd like to give you a tour of the area and then take you by my shop."

"I'd enjoy that, but can we eat elsewhere for dinner?"

"Yes. I usually do. Food's not as good as your New Orleans fare but it beats Kate's."

"You don't mind me helping her?"

"Will I get gumbo?"

"Only if you're a very good and scandalous prince."

He smiled. "The challenge is accepted."

AFTER LEAVING THE house, they set out on foot for his tour of the area near his home. "We call this part of town Beacon Hill," he told her. "The race has lived in this neighborhood since the country's earliest days. In fact, this house here was owned by George Middleton, the leader of a Black militia group known as the Bucks during the Revolutionary War."

Raven found that surprising. "I don't believe I've ever heard anyone speak about members of the race fighting in that war."

Walking beside her, Brax said, "Many of the colonies back then had Black units. Washington refused to let Black men enlist at first but eventually changed his mind."

He showed her Philips School, which became one of the first integrated schools in the city in 1855. They then stopped at the home of abolitionist and barber John J. Smith and his wife, Georgiana. Also on the tour was the home of Lewis and Harriet Hayden. Their boardinghouse was famous for providing shelter to runaway slaves.

They continued over to Smith Street to the African Meeting House, considered the oldest Black church structure in the country. "I went to school here for a few years," he told her. "And this is also where I signed my recruitment papers when I joined the Fifty-Fourth."

"The building must mean a lot to you."

"It does. It started as a Baptist church, then became AME. The New England Anti-Slavery Society was formed here by Black abolitionists and William Lloyd Garrison, publisher of the famous *Liberator* newspaper. The meeting house was the center of the free community here. So much history took place within its walls. It's one of our most treasured places."

Raven was moved by his telling of the building's purpose and the reverence in his voice. "Where to next?"

"My shop, to let my employees know I've returned, and I want you to meet them."

"Lead the way."

His shop wasn't very far from where they'd toured. It was positioned next to a barbershop and a diner. The words STEELE'S HABERDASHERY were painted on the window in an elaborate gold script she found very impressive. Upon entering, they were greeted by the excited squeals of his two seamstresses, who embraced him like a long-lost relative. He introduced them as sisters Hattie and Alberta "Bertie" Clemons. They appeared to be about Hazel's age and smiled Raven's way upon learning her name. Raven couldn't determine who was the elder. She made a mental note to ask Brax later. Both sisters wore spectacles, were brown-skinned and stout, but Bertie was the taller of the two.

Hattie took in Brax's shaved appearance and asked, "What in the name of Fred Douglass did you do to yourself?"

"Thought I'd try something different."

Bertie said, "I like it."

Her sister didn't look impressed and said so. "I don't. Grow it back."

Raven found the exchange amusing.

Hattie asked, "Is this the woman you bought the blue silk for?"

Raven's eyes widened. She stared up at Braxton.

"Hat!" Bertie said admonishingly. "I think it was supposed to be a surprise."

"Well, it isn't anymore. Come with me, young lady. I need to measure you to make sure my gorgeous creation fits."

And before Raven could respond, Hattie

took her by the hand and led her away. In the small fitting room, Hattie brought out her tapes and made Raven turn this way and that and noted the findings on a piece of paper. Raven, overwhelmed by the idea that he'd purchased the silk for her, did what she was told by the short, bossy Miss Hattie. "You remind me of my aunts," Raven said to her.

"Are they forces of nature?"

Raven snickered. "Yes, ma'am."

"Good. Somebody has to run the world because the folks claiming to be in charge are doing a terrible job. Stand still so I can get your waist."

Once all the measuring was done, Raven was released. When she and Hattie returned to the front of the store, Brax was speaking with two well-dressed women—one young, one older. Both had ebony skin and were extremely pretty. Their resemblance to each other led Raven to believe they might be mother and daughter. Behind her Hattie said under her breath, "This will be interesting."

The curious Raven turned around, hoping Hattie would explain, but the seamstress didn't add more.

Braxton introduced Raven to the women. "Raven Moreau, this is Lottie Franklin and her mother, Mrs. Pearl Franklin."

His prizewinner. Now she thought she understood Hattie. "Pleased to meet you, ladies."

The mother trilled, "What a novel accent. Where's home?"

"New Orleans."

Lottie said, "Nice to meet you, Raven."

She seemed sincere so Raven responded in kind. "Same here."

Pearl, wearing a gray suit that probably fit her better a few years back, scanned Raven's skirt and blouse and asked, "Are you a new seamstress here?"

"No. My mother is marrying Braxton's father. Braxton wanted to show me his establishment."

"WHAT!"

Raven guessed Pearl would be counted among the mourners. "Yes, they fell in love before I was born."

The sisters expressed their surprise as well. Hattie asked Brax, "Why didn't you tell us earlier?"

"Because when I arrived, you were too busy spilling secrets, and I wasn't able to get a word in edgewise."

Hattie hung her head in mock shame.

"Is he your father?" Pearl asked Raven.

What a rude woman. "Not that it's any of your business, but no."

Pearl drew back.

Braxton was viewing Pearl with furious eyes.

Hattie said, "Raven. I hear there are lots of cottonmouths in Louisiana."

Raven decided she loved Hattie Clemons.

"You're right, Miss Hattie. In fact, we have one on the family crest."

"Your family has a crest?" Pearl asked.

"Doesn't yours?"

A ghost of a smile crossed Lottie's lips, and it told Raven much about who she was and the relationship the young woman had with her mother, Pearl. Raven said to her, "Braxton speaks very highly of you, Lottie. I'm glad to finally meet you."

Lottie turned to Brax, who was still viewing Pearl with simmering eyes. "That's good to hear."

He nodded her way.

Pearl said, "Yes, the community is hoping they'll marry soon. His mother and I were lifelong friends."

"He shared that with me as well," Raven said.

Pearl looked her up and down again. "I have an appointment to make. Alberta, make sure that waistcoat for my son is ready for him to wear to the Captain's Ball. I'll stop by next week to see if it's done."

"Certainly, Mrs. Franklin."

Pearl said to Braxton, "Welcome home, Braxton. Please let me know when you and your father are free for dinner. I'd very much like to meet his intended. Let's go, Lottie."

"Just a moment, Mama. Raven, my friends and I will be at the African House tomorrow afternoon. I'd love for you to come and meet everyone."

Raven looked to Brax. "It's up to you," he replied. "I'll be here working. Being with Lottie will keep you from being bored."

"I promised Kate I'd help her do some shopping," she said to Lottie. "If we get done, I'd like to meet your friends. What time?"

"Two o'clock."

"Okay."

Mrs. Franklin said impatiently, "We're going to be late, Charlotte."

"I'm ready now."

Pearl sailed out with her daughter on her heels.

Once she was gone, Raven said, "If Pearl thinks Mama will put up with her rude, condescending behavior, she's going to end up with her eyebrows snatched off."

Hattie said, "Bertie and I would pay to see that."

"Definitely."

AFTER PROMISING TO return to the shop soon so that Hattie could put the final touches on the gown, Raven said goodbye to the Clemons sisters.

"Are you hungry?" Brax asked her once they were outside.

"So, you purchased that silk for me?"

"Should I have not?" Brax asked. He was still simmering from Pearl Franklin's rude conduct and if he never had to see her again, he'd be fine.

How someone as sweet-natured as Lottie could be the daughter of such a nasty shrew had been asked numerous times by many.

"I'm trying to decide."

"You once told me you never had pretty dresses."

"That didn't mean I wanted you to buy me any."

"And that's why I bought the silk. I get the impression that you rarely ask for anything for yourself, Raven, and I want to shower you with gifts because of that. You deserve nice things."

They were standing outside his shop and the Clemons sisters were in the doorway watching and listening as if he and Raven were on stage. "We have an audience."

Bertie said, "Don't mind us. Continue. You were saying she deserved nice things. And he's right, Raven."

Brax shook his head and steered Raven into the diner next door. "Let's let Shirley feed us and we can discuss this while we eat."

"Who's Shirley?"

"Charley Shirley, the owner."

Once inside, Brax picked out a table near the back. The few other tables up-front in the small place were occupied. "That you, Brax? Where's your hair?"

The question was posed by the owner. Brax sighed. He was getting tired of the question. "Thought I'd try something different."

"It's different, all right. So much so it took me a few blinks to recognize you. Who's this lovely lady?"

Brax made the introductions. "Raven Moreau. Charley Shirley, the owner."

"Pleased to meet you, Mr. Shirley."

"Same here. Thanks for brightening up my place."

"You're welcome."

"Raven's mother is marrying Da," Brax told him.

"She must have poor eyesight."

Raven cackled.

"I'm serious. Have your mama get her eyes seen by a good doctor. Something's wrong with them if she thinks that old piece of shoe leather is worth marrying."

Smiling, Brax asked, "What's on the menu? What are you poisoning your customers with today, Shirley?"

The gray-haired Charley said to Raven, "See? Neither one of the Steele men is worth a Confederate coin." He rattled off what he had to offer.

Raven said, "I'll take a ham sandwich, please."

"And you, Mr. Hairless?"

Brax cut him a look. "The same."

"Okay. Will bring them to you directly."

When he walked away, she said, "Now about the gown. You've given me bath salts and clothing. What's next?"

To himself he thought: *My name, my love, a*

big house, and that passel of babies. "I don't know. What else would you like?"

She smiled and sighed. "Never mind. Thank you for the gown. Not that I have any place to wear it."

"Sure, you do. My grandfather's Captain's Ball is coming up in about two weeks."

"I don't go to balls, Brax. I'm the woman who cleans up after all the drunken guests go home."

"Not this time. Someone else will clean up. You get to wear your gown and dazzle every man in the room."

She studied him silently. "What am I going to do with you?"

"I'll let you know tonight. I think maybe we'll begin by reading a chapter of *Alice* with you sitting on my lap. How's that?"

She laughed and he loved the sound.

THAT EVENING, WITHIN the quiet confines of his bedroom, he loved the other sounds she made: her sighs when he kissed her, her moans when he slowly feasted on her breast and then between her spread-wide thighs, her passion-toned hiss when he entered her, and especially the sounds she made when the orgasms he gave her made her cry out his name. They never did finish that chapter of *Alice*, but neither of them cared.

Chapter Sixteen

$\mathcal{B}$rax arrived at his shop the following morning and was surprised to see Lottie sitting on the bench in front of Shirley's place. "Morning, Lottie. He doesn't open until ten."

"I know. I'm waiting to speak to you."

He found that curious. "Okay. Come in."

He put his key in the lock and entered. The Clemons sisters hadn't arrived yet, so he led her into his small office. "Have a seat."

As she complied, he sat down at his desk. "What can I do for you?"

She didn't reply right away. He got the sense that she was searching for the right way to begin whatever she'd come to talk to him about, so he waited.

"I don't think we should marry."

Because of his feelings for Raven, he was relieved but nevertheless surprised. "May I ask why?"

"I saw the way you looked at Raven when she

first came out of the back with Miss Hattie. You love her, don't you?"

"I admit to having strong feelings for her, yes."

"I saw it in your eyes. You've never looked at me like that, Braxton."

He didn't know how to respond.

"I'm not faulting you. It's—it's just I realize I want the man I marry to view me the way you viewed her. I watched you watch her the entire time Mama and I were here, and I envied her."

"Until I met her, I didn't think love was needed, Lottie. I'm sorry if I've hurt you."

"Oh no. I'm not hurt. Please don't think that. It made me see what I might be missing by settling for what you and I were going to have. You're an extremely wonderful man, Braxton, and a stellar friend, but I know now that I want more."

"And there's nothing wrong with that, Lottie."

"Mama's going to think so."

"You won't be marrying her."

She smiled. "Raven certainly put her in her place yesterday. Your Raven's very brave, isn't she?"

"Yes, she is."

"After we left here yesterday, Mama ranted on and on about her. I'd like to be that brave someday."

"You're probably braver than you know."

"That's very kind of you to say, but I have a ways to go before I think of myself in those terms." She got to her feet. "Thank you, Braxton. I don't want to take up any more of your time. You've always been a good person to talk to and I needed to tell you what was on my mind. I hope we will remain friends."

"Of course."

"And if you and Raven do marry, I'd like to be a friend to her, too, if she'd agree."

"I believe she'd like that."

"Good. I'll see you soon, and thanks again."

"You're welcome."

She exited and left him alone to ponder the amazing ways things in life worked out.

THAT NIGHT AS they lay in Brax's bed after another evening of lovemaking, he told her about Lottie's visit. He left out the part about what made Lottie decide she didn't want to marry. Instead, he said she wanted a love match.

"Good for her," Raven said. "Mama and your father stopped by earlier. They're heading to Philadelphia in the morning to see some old friends. They may or may not be back in time for the ball."

Brax shook his head in amusement. "They're having entirely too much fun."

"Agreed."

"Did you and Kate go to the market?"

"Yes. There will be real food in this house in the morning. She's agreed to let me cook breakfast."

"You're a guest, Raven."

"Do you want gumbo later for dinner or not?"

"Remaining silent here."

She laughed. "Smart man."

He asked, "How'd the meeting go with Lottie's friends?"

"Not well. The head friend, I forget her name, was trying to treat me like Pearl Franklin did. She went around the room asking each woman what they considered their most accomplished undertaking was. One told us about the poetry she'd written. Another touted all the books she'd read. One mentioned having met Frederick Douglass. The in-charge one then looked at me and asked in her best Pearl Franklin voice if I had one."

He began to laugh. "I can only imagine your response."

"I told her I'd learned to gut and skin a rabbit at the age of twelve. Lottie laughed so hard the tea she'd been sipping came out of her nose. The others just stared with their mouths open. The one in charge was so distressed by my country girl response, she adjourned the meeting and everyone left. I told Lottie she might need to find better friends. Once she stopped laughing, she agreed."

"You're so incorrigible."

"And proud to be."

OVER THE NEXT three weeks, Raven and Brax spent as much time together as they could. His time was limited due to his role as the host of his grandfather's ball, his work at the shop, and the many organizations he supported and volunteered his time with. With Raven's help, Kate became a better cook and her husband no longer grumbled or threatened to trade her in when he came home from the sea. Raven and Lottie became fast friends. They shopped and talked, and Raven taught her how to make a perfect roux for gumbo, and answered all the questions the younger woman had about the physical aspects of marriage that her mother refused to discuss because proper women didn't need to know such things.

But Raven most enjoyed her time with Brax, especially the day they took his sailboat out to one of the many islands off the coast and had a picnic. While there he told her how his grandfather and other abolitionist seamen helped escaped slaves. "The slaves in places like Maryland and Virginia would board ships headed north either aided by crewmen or by secreting themselves aboard, and jump ship at night near these islands. My grandfather and his friends took turns patrolling the area, and if they found anyone out here, they'd bring them to Boston and take them to a place where they could be helped. The fugitives would either move on into Canada or integrate themselves in the Beacon Hill community."

"Something else I never knew."

"It was a maritime escape route. Many fugitives found freedom that way."

A few days later, a newspaper article featured something they both found interesting. Brax read aloud to Raven: *"Local South Carolina legislator Aubrey Stipe found dead inside his home. Mr. Stipe was hacked to death with an ax wielded by his wife, Helen. She has been sent to a facility for hysterical women and will not be tried, according to police. No other details available at this time."*

Raven shook her head and asked, "Would you like bread pudding or a cake for dessert tomorrow?"

"Bread pudding."

THE NIGHT OF the ball, Kate helped Raven with her gown, and when she was done, Raven stood before the mirror and viewed herself in Miss Hattie's gorgeous indigo silk creation. She loved the square bodice, the capped sleeves, the draped train on the back, and the delicate pleating on each side. It was the most beautiful garment Raven had ever worn in her life.

Kate said, "Braxton is going to be so enthralled when he sees you, he may never leave the house."

"Thank you for your help."

"You're welcome, and if any of those witches try and disparage you, just curse them under your breath for me and walk away."

She and Kate had become fast friends, too,

and Raven couldn't thank her enough for her kindness. "I will."

With her hair up and her matching gloves and the gold hoops Brax had surprised her with for her ears, she felt like a queen indeed.

She all but floated down the staircase where he, dressed in a formal black suit and tails, stood waiting for her at the base.

Taking her in, he whispered, "My God, Raven. Look at you." He appeared mesmerized.

"You look pretty grand yourself, Mr. Steele."

He kept staring.

From the top of the staircase, Kate said, "Brax, you're going to be late."

He shook himself free, offered his arm, and escorted her out to his carriage.

The ball was held at the African Meeting House. The ladies' auxiliary headed by Lottie had done the decorating, and the interior was filled with flowers. As Raven and Brax were announced, applause greeted their arrival and eyes popped all over the room at the sight of Raven in her gown. Not everyone was pleased, however. As she and Brax made their way around the room, she noticed some of the women she knew to be friends with Pearl Franklin subtly turn their backs. Raven had not been to many formal events but she'd worked some, and knew a cut when she saw it. Brax didn't seem to have noticed and she was glad of that. She didn't want the witches to spoil his mood. But the cutting continued. Lottie noticed it, too, and came over to lend moral support as did a few of Lottie's good friends. The treatment was maddening, embarrassing, and yes, hurtful. Raven told herself she didn't care, because when she returned to New Orleans, she wouldn't spend a minute thinking about them, but Brax lived here, worked here, and socialized here. She didn't want how they felt about her to affect him or his standing in the community he loved so much.

After dinner, needing some air, Raven stepped outside into the darkness. Her mother and Harrison would be returning to New Orleans the next day now that the yellow fever deaths seemed to be on the decline. They'd not come to the ball, however. Harrison said they wanted to spend their last night in town with his friend Charley Shirley and others. Raven wished she had joined them. She and Brax were scheduled to travel back to New Orleans in a week for the wedding. But after what she'd encountered inside, she thought she might return home sooner.

Other ball goers had stepped outside by the time Raven made up her mind about returning. Yes, going home early would be best for all concerned. In the meantime, she decided to enjoy the cool breeze just a few minutes more before going back inside. She was standing in a spot that couldn't be seen from the door, and because of the darkness she was rendered nearly invisible. And that's when she heard Pearl Franklin's voice. "I can't believe he's parading that whore around as if she's quality. My daughter broke things off with him because of his association with her."

The other woman chimed in, "I hear Harrison's been parading around the mother. You've heard of two peas in a pod. The Steele men have two whores in a pod." Raven didn't recognize the voice.

They laughed.

Pearl said, "I hope Braxton isn't planning on marrying her. If he does, I will do my best to make sure she's given the short shrift she deserves. Can you imagine having her at your dinner table with decent folks?"

"No. Never. And that horrid accent."

Pearl added, "I agree. He's obviously so besotted he doesn't care about his reputation. His grandfather and my dear friend Jane, his mother, are probably spinning in their graves."

Raven had had enough. Furious at them and heartbroken to hear them disparage Brax that way, she peeled herself out of the darkness and approached them. Seeing her, they both jumped like fish on a line. "Yes, I heard every word. I hope you don't sing hymns on Sunday with those nasty, hateful mouths. Enjoy the rest of your evening."

Raven plastered a fake smile on her face and

made it to the end of the ball. When she and Brax went home, she didn't tell him what happened. Instead, she let his kisses soften her hurt as she slowly removed her gown. Let the worshipping path of his hands soothe her anger and the feel of his nude body flush against her own salve her desire to demand the witches meet her to duel at dawn. By the time Brax was done making her orgasm above him, below him, and on every flat surface in his bedroom, she couldn't even remember Pearl Franklin's name.

A QUIET KNOCK on the door made Raven look up from her packing. "Come in."

It was Brax. He'd spent the day working at his shop and the early part of the evening dispensing some of the funds raised by last night's ball to some of the charitable organizations the affair supported. She watched his eyes brush her carpetbag before he asked, "What are you doing?"

She put her nightgowns into the bag. "I'm going back to New Orleans in the morning to help Mama with the wedding."

"I thought we were going to go together next week."

"I have to go now."

"Why?"

"Because I don't belong with you, Brax." She now wished she'd taken the coward's way out and disappeared earlier while he was away and spared herself the heartache, but he deserved to know she was leaving. She owed him at least that, and so much more. "You should be with someone who's more evenly yoked." She gave him a smile at the reminder of their frequent conversations. "Someone more like Lottie."

"But you know that isn't what I want."

"You say that now, but in the years ahead, suppose you realize being with me was a bad idea. What if someone or something from my past shows up? The last thing I want is for my life to splash on you in a way that diminishes your standing here. You're a pinnacle of the community. People respect you. They look up to you. I'm just a bayou girl from New Orleans. I don't own fancy slippers, wear fancy gowns, or know how to conduct myself like a lady. The last thing I want is to embarrass you in any way." She refused to share what she'd overheard last night at the ball.

"Raven—"

She shook her head and tried not to show the tears falling inside. "It's better this way. We've had a good time, Brax. You've taught me so much." If she ever wanted another man, he'd set the bar incredibly high.

There was pain in the dark eyes holding hers. "Please stay. The other issues don't matter to me. You're the woman I want in my life. Stay. Marry me."

She looked away and closed her eyes to keep her brimming tears from sliding down her cheeks. "I can't," she whispered, emotion clogging her throat. "I won't say you deserve someone better because I know my own value. You deserve someone different. A woman comfortable swimming in your pool."

"I'd never be ashamed of you, little corvus."

His nickname twisted in her heart like a knife. "I'd like to think I'd never do anything to bring you shame, Braxton Steele. And I can ensure that if I'm in New Orleans and you're here."

"Darling, please stay and let me spend the rest of my life loving you."

The powerful words almost brought her to her knees. "I love you, too, so please don't make this harder than it is. Okay?" Her tears, refusing to obey, slid free. She dashed them away. "My love for you is why I'm going home. I don't want you ridiculed for being with me."

"By whom? Did someone say something hurtful to you? Was it at the ball?"

"It doesn't matter. I shouldn't be in your life, and I love you enough to realize that. As I said, you should be with someone different."

They studied each other in the silence. He opened his arms to her and she ran to him and held him as tightly as his strong arms held her.

He whispered, "You're killing me, woman."

"I know and I'm sorry." And she was, but she couldn't stay.

He gently raised her chin and she viewed

him through watery eyes. "I'll never forget you, Braxton Steele."

Leaning down, he kissed her. It was bittersweet, filled with loss and love, and then became an intense, desperate goodbye to what they'd never have again. She fed on it, and let it fill her because it would be the last time. When it ended, she rested against him, her cheek against his heart, and she let herself hold him and be held for a few moments longer before stepping away. She wiped at her tears. "I'm going to flood this place like Alice."

He offered a small smile.

"I should finish packing."

"Okay."

He viewed her as if needing to commit her to his memory, and she did the same.

He finally turned, exited the room, and she was alone.

SEATED IN HIS bedroom illuminated by the flickering glow of the turned-down lamp, he attempted to make sense of what just happened. He'd prepared himself for her return to New Orleans for the wedding but assumed he'd somehow convince her to return with him to Boston. Apparently, that was not to be, and he wanted to throw open a window and scream out his pain into the night. Who hurt her to the point she felt she needed to leave him when all he needed was her? The question would probably never be answered, adding rage to his anguish. Next week, he'd be traveling back to New Orleans for the wedding. How was he supposed to respond to seeing her again? He'd never force his attentions on her, but could he be around her and not want her smile, her sassiness, her love? That she'd professed her love for him had made his heart sing and offered hope that a solution could be found. The man who loved her like he loved breathing didn't want them to end this way. He'd talk to her again in the morning.

WHEN HE CAME down for breakfast, Raven wasn't at the table. He walked into the kitchen to find Kate removing a pan of biscuits from the oven. "Good morning."

"Good morning, Braxton."

"Has Raven not come down yet?"

She paused, and he saw sadness in her eyes. "She said to tell you goodbye and that she'd see you at the wedding."

"She's left already?"

She nodded. "A hack took her to the train a bit past dawn."

Disappointment deflated him.

"I'm so sorry," Kate said softly. "She seemed very unhappy."

He wondered if he could drive to the station and catch her before she boarded, but he had no idea what time the train would be leaving. With his luck it was pulling out now, or had departed an hour ago. "Thank you, Kate."

"Do you want your breakfast at the table, or on a tray to take up to your room?"

"The table will do."

"I'll bring it directly."

"Thank you."

He took a seat in the dining room and viewed the rising sun through the window. For the first time in weeks there'd be no Raven in his day. Or in the days to come.

RAVEN WAS DRIVING the buggy and Hazel was seated beside her on the bench. They were on their way to look at a cabin being sold by a family friend named Viola Bing. It wasn't located very far from Hazel's home, and if it turned out to be as nice as claimed, Raven planned to use part of her small Fanny inheritance to purchase it. After arriving back in New Orleans three days ago, she'd hoped her longings for Brax would lessen, but they hadn't. She'd awakened each morning missing his presence beside her in bed, his voice, and his companionship. Not even the excitement of the wedding plans kept her from wondering what he might be doing, how he was spending his time, and if Kate had thrown out her spices and was feeding him bland food again. She longed for him dearly and her heart longed for him even more.

"How long are you going to mope, sweet-heart?"

Raven glanced her way. "I'm not moping."

"So the sad face is for . . . ?"

Raven sighed. Her mother was always so in-sightful. "I just miss him, that's all."

"And you will for the rest of your life if you don't do something about it."

"Mama. He needs somebody equally yoked."

"Do you think you're not good enough for him?"

"No. I just think he needs someone different."

"Because you can't set a fancy table?"

Raven set her eyes on the horse leading them down the road so she didn't respond in a way that would draw her mama's ire. "It's not just about fancy tables."

"Then what?"

"It's difficult to explain."

"Indulge an old woman, and try."

"I just don't want my shortcomings in things like fancy tables to reflect badly on him."

"That's our turn up ahead," her mother pointed out.

When they reached it, Raven reined the horse and buggy off the main road and onto a smaller one.

Her mother continued, "You've been a cha-meleon your entire life. Are you saying you can't be one for that sweetheart of a man?"

"Meaning?"

"Meaning, you are smart enough to have posed as any number of people. You've done jobs that took courage and guile. Has Brax ever not let you be yourself?"

"No. He's taken me, rough edges and all."

"Does he attend or give social events every weekend?"

"I don't know, but I don't believe so. At least he didn't while we were there."

"So you'd be spending most of your time with him and a small portion with the people in his circle."

"Yes, I suppose."

"Then if you want him, you'll learn the things you need to learn, pretend like it's a job when you must rub elbows with his circle, and then come home with him and be yourself the rest of the time. Seems very simple from here. There's Viola. This must be the cabin."

For a moment, Raven let her mother's advice sink in. She'd never thought about the problem in that way. And now that she had, her mother was right. It really was simple.

"Having an epiphany, are you?"

Raven chuckled. "I love you so much."

"You'd better. Now, let's go see about buying you a home."

The interior was small. There was only one bedroom but she needed only one. In many ways the size and layout reminded her of the cabin she and Brax had shared in Charleston.

There was even a porch for a rocker and the flowerpots she wanted to have. When Viola quoted an easily affordable price, a happy Raven handed over the money and Viola handed her a key.

LATER, AFTER DINNER, still happy about her new house, and a possible solution to her Brax dilemma, her mood plummeted when Detective Welch arrived along with two uniformed policemen.

"We have an arrest warrant for Raven Moreau," one of the policemen announced.

"On what charge?" her mother asked angrily.

"Theft and embezzlement."

Welch explained, "Thanks to my investigating, I now possess all the evidence needed to lock you up for years to come."

The furious Raven didn't respond. She was handcuffed in front of her stunned mother and aunts and led away. She had faith that her mother would move every star in the sky if necessary to get her freed and that Welch would go to hell for this betrayal. Before Raven was put into the police wagon, Welch boasted, "You're going to make me the most famous lady detective in the nation. See you in court." That said, she walked to a waiting hack, stepped inside, and was driven away.

The police wagon's windowless interior stank of urine. One of the two metal benches that served as seating was occupied by a group of five men whose bloodied, angry faces bore the signs of a brawl. On the opposite bench sat three rouged up, scantily dressed women and a drunk who greeted her arrival by calling out in a slurred voice, "Welcome to the party, pretty lady," then promptly passed out on the dirty floor. The cuffed Raven stepped around him and chose an empty spot near the women. One of them gently took hold of her elbow to guide her down. Raven thanked her.

"You're welcome, honey. What did they grab you for?"

"Supposedly, embezzlement."

The three looked impressed. One, wearing a red wig as long as a horse's tail, said, "They got us for being Good Samaritans."

The one seated beside her, wearing a battered gold tignon over her hair, cackled. "Yes, we offered aid and comfort to men in need."

Their amusement was infectious and Raven smiled.

She and the other women were brought before a magistrate at the courthouse. Welch was seated in the back of the room but Raven ignored her. The Good Samaritans were ordered to pay fines and released. When it was Raven's turn, the prosecutor representing the city's interest argued against granting Raven anything close to that. He wanted her jailed until the circuit judge arrived. "She's being accused of running a swindling ring that's preyed on people all over the country for years. A jeweler in San Francisco is her latest victim, and he's going to be sending a statement to the court with the details."

Welch stood and announced, "She'll flee the city if she's granted bail."

The magistrate, an older man with gray hair, looked her way. "And you are?"

"Pinkerton detective Ruth Welch. I'm the person responsible for her capture."

"I see. Are you also her lawyer?"

Welch laughed. "Of course not."

"Then please remain silent. I only want to hear from lawyers."

Welch's face reddened and she sat. Raven kept her smug smile hidden.

In the end, the prosecutor and Welch were granted what they'd requested. Raven was remanded to jail until the circuit judge arrived to hear the case.

IN BOSTON, BRAX was at his shop when a young man arrived with a wire from the telegraph office. Brax tipped the messenger and opened the sealed paper. It was from his father. *Raven arrested*. His blood turned to ice.

Two hours later, he was on a train going south.

THE FOLLOWING AFTERNOON, Ruth Welch had lunch in her room at the boardinghouse where she was staying and wondered smugly if Raven Moreau had enjoyed her first night in jail. According to the magistrate, the circuit judge was due in the city in two days. Ruth had hoped his arrival wouldn't be for weeks so as to deflate some of the Moreau woman's uppitiness, but Ruth would settle for knowing she was imprisoned. The sworn statement from San Francisco jeweler Oscar Gant had arrived earlier. They'd been corresponding over the past two weeks about the case. He hadn't seen the face of the fake princess who'd robbed him, but Welch's strong belief that Raven Moreau was indeed the culprit convinced him to lie to the court and say he had. She planned to present his statement at the hearing along with the testimony from Tobias Kenny.

The Declaration of Independence she'd been instrumental in recovering had been returned to its owner, and solving the case had earned her high praise from her superior. Now this case was falling into place as well, and she was pleased. Tobias Kenny was also in New Orleans. She'd met with him last evening, and he'd had news that added further ammunition to her evidence. He'd spoken with a disgruntled Moreau family member willing to testify about the gang's network and past jobs. The person had fallen out of favor with them after being accused of not turning over his take from a swindle a few years back and been shunned.

According to Tobias, the family considered the man dead to them, and no longer allowed him to participate in family business operations, or social gatherings of any kind. He supposedly had information on their fences in the States, Canada, and overseas. Welch couldn't wait to speak with him.

She got to her feet to return her tray of lunch dishes back to the kitchen when a knock on her door broke the silence. "Who's there?"

"Tobias."

Hoping the meeting hadn't been called off, she went to the door and opened it. He stepped in and said anxiously, "You need to move to a different location."

"Why?"

"The Moreaux know where you are. Word is, they plan to kidnap you tonight to keep you from testifying."

"That's outrageous." Admittedly, the news filled her with a good amount of fear.

"I know, ma'am. I've found a place for you that will be safer. I've a hack outside. You should pack up so I can get you out of here."

"Of course." She hastily gathered her things and stuffed them into her travel bags. She placed the files she'd need for the court case into her valise, and ten minutes later, she'd left the room, paid the landlady, and been hastily escorted to the waiting hack.

Tobias said, "You get in. I'll ride with the driver."

Nodding and breathless, she yanked open the door and stepped in. There was a woman dressed in black seated in the corner. Ruth hesitated, puzzled.

"Hello, Wilma," the woman said in a French-accented voice. "Remember me?"

Eyes wide with alarm, Welch panicked and quickly tried to back out, but Tobias, standing behind pushed her forward, sending her tumbling inside. The door slammed shut and the coach began moving.

From her spot on the floor where she'd landed, Welch stared up into the beautiful ebony-skinned face of the LeVeq family matriarch, Julianna LeVeq-Vincent and was told, "You should never have returned to New Orleans, my dear. Six years ago, you almost cost one of my beloved daughters-in-law her life, and my pirate's blood has been thirsting for revenge ever since."

Dread made Welch's voice crack. "Where are you taking me?"

"To a place so far away you'll never trouble anyone's family again."

Ruth threw herself against the door hoping to escape, but it held. "The Pinkerton Agency knows I'm here," she swore hotly. "They'll begin searching when I disappear."

"It won't matter, because you won't be found."

Julianna showed a smile and added, "Isn't being betrayed fun?"

TEN YEARS AGO, when Tobias Kenny betrayed her, Raven was sent to a prison in Detroit. Unlike the White women convicts who were sent to an all-women's facility where they were taught things like sewing, how to set tables, and cooking in order to maybe become law-abiding wives and homemakers upon release, Raven and the other women of color were incarcerated with the men. The prison had the decency to house them separately, however, but in an airless, attic-like space. The food there, little more than broth with potatoes floating in it, was withheld if you complained about it or anything else, and the women spent their nights fighting with whatever they could get their hands on to keep the male convicts from breaking in. It had been the most terrifying and awful experience of her life. She'd been given a three-month sentence, and when she finally returned to New Orleans emaciated and with a headful of lice, she swore she'd never go to prison again. And yet, after being arrested three days ago, and now being escorted into the courtroom wearing a faded blue dress that more resembled a cotton sack, and shackles hobbling her bare feet, there was a good chance she'd be returning. Seeing her mama, the family, and Braxton of all people in the seats buoyed her. Him, she wanted to run to, be held by, and promise to love for the rest of her life—if she could escape incarceration.

A young White Republican friend of Renay's named Mitchell Morgan was to be her lawyer, and he offered an encouraging smile as she was escorted to the table where he sat at the front of the room. She didn't see Welch but assumed she'd arrive to gloat and present her evidence shortly.

The judge, Daniel Bradshaw, entered, and the small snatches of conversation that she could hear earlier from the small crowd faded into silence. He was White and younger than judges usually were, but in Louisiana the mix of blood made people age differently, so his youthful appearance could possibly be deceiving.

The lawyers introduced themselves and then came her turn.

The judge said to her, "State your name for the record, miss."

"Raven Moreau."

She was asked to spell her last name and she did.

The prosecutor, Gavin Swain, stood and began presenting his case. While speaking he kept glancing back at the people in the seats.

The judge said, "Present your evidence."

Once again, he panned the people behind him. "Well, the evidence is in the hands of a Pinkerton detective."

"And where is he?"

"He's a she, sir, and I don't know."

"You don't know where she is?"

"No."

Raven's lawyer stood. "We can't conduct a hearing without evidence."

"I know that. Sit."

The prosecutor said, "But based upon what the detective shared with me, the Moreau woman is guilty."

The judge replied, "I know that in many parts of this country, the law is being subjected to many things tied to people who look like the defendant, but in my court, I don't convict anyone based on hearsay, Mr. Swain. Here we are ruled by the law. I'm going to give you two hours to produce the detective with her evidence or this case will be thrown out. We are now in recess."

An angry and agitated-looking Swain hurried out of the room.

Raven turned to where her mother was seated. Hazel sent her a wink and a smile. Surprised because she had no idea what that might mean, Raven turned back around. Where was Welch?

The matron arrived to take Raven back to the waiting room until court was reconvened. As she shuffled out, she sent the concerned-looking Braxton a small smile. He gave her a nod.

Time passed at an agonizing snail's pace. Sequestered as she was, she had no idea whether Welch had arrived or not, but the longer she sat, the more hope she felt. Logically, had the detective been found, the judge would've had Raven brought back into the courtroom, and so far that hadn't happened. She suddenly remembered Dorrie's words telling Raven not to worry. They won't find her, Dorrie added. Was this what Dorrie had been referring to?

Raven was finally called back in. She quickly searched the room for Welch's face, and not seeing it made her want to cry tears of joy. Instead, she calmly took her seat and waited for the judge to speak.

"Due to Mr. Swain's inability to provide any evidence that would prove Miss Moreau guilty of the charges lodged against her, I hereby rule this proceeding adjourned. Miss Moreau, you are released and free to go."

A shout went up in the seats and a smiling Raven thanked Mr. Morgan, her lawyer.

"I wish all my cases turned out this way," he replied. "Give my best to Renay. Now, go get some loving from your family."

Chapter Seventeen

𝒯he very first thing Raven did once arriving home was to take a bath and wash her hair to rid herself of the prison grime and to soothe her soul. Many of the cousins were still on the road, but those in New Orleans like Renay, Lacie, and Emile came by to give her hugs. Brax vowed to never let Raven out of his sight again, and chomped at the bit to have some time alone with her, but due to the number of Moreau relatives he decided that might not happen until Christmas.

Julianna LeVeq-Vincent dropped by that evening and everyone trooped up to the library to hear what she had to say. "Wilma Gray, also known as Ruth Welch, is presently on a ship heading to a friend of the House of LeVeq living in Arabia. He's a sultan. She will be owned by him as a servant until her death and never be able to leave the country to put another family at risk ever again. I want to thank you for helping me exact a revenge that has festered inside me for years. Raven. My son Archer has offered you the use of a suite at his hotel in the Quarter to recover from the jail as his thank you. It was his wife that the Pinkerton betrayed."

Raven looked up at Brax seated on the arm of his chair, and he smiled. She replied to Julianna, "Please give your son my deepest thanks. I'll be at his hotel as soon as we're done here."

Julianna thanked them again and departed.

Hazel spoke up next. "We also owe Tobias Kenny our thanks."

Raven stiffened. "What on earth for?"

"He arranged for Welch to be handed over to Julianna."

Raven was stunned.

Hazel explained, "Remember the day you came to the market and saw Welch there? And we wondered if she was there to meet someone?"

"Yes."

"She was. He met her there a day later and I had Renay follow him home."

Renay said, "So I did. He offered to play both sides of the coin for the family because he felt he owed us for what he did to you, Raven."

Hazel said, "Julianna and I came up with a plan, and he executed it splendidly."

Raven said, "I'm glad he helped and that he's remorseful."

But what she didn't say was that despite his help, she still hoped to never see him again.

* * *

LATER THAT NIGHT in the sumptuous suite at Archer LeVeq's Hotel Christophe, the exhausted and sated Raven lay beside Brax in the bed.

"I know why you left me, Raven."

She sat up, and the sheet slipped away to reveal her nudity. "You do?"

"Lottie told me. She'd stepped outside the ball that night to look for you, and heard every cruel word her mother said. And when I told her you'd left Boston, Lottie relayed what occurred."

Raven still felt the sting of Pearl's words.

He continued, "I understand that your love for me made you want to protect me, because that's who you are Raven. And because of my love for you, I spoke with Pearl and put the fear of God in her. You see, I own the deed to her home. If she so much as looks at you sideways, she'll be out on the street."

"But what about Lottie; she lives in the house, too."

He shook his head. "Not anymore. Pearl has a sister in Boston who adores Lottie, and Lottie adores her in return. Lottie's now living with the aunt, and will do so until she finds a man who loves her as much as I love you. Her quote."

"I guess I should ask you to marry me then?"

He smiled.

"Marry me, Braxton Steele. Give me your

name, your love and a passel of babies who'll grow up to read and maybe one day also grow up to accidentally hear us making the bed creak through the walls."

He laughed uproariously and pulled her naked body atop his own. The kiss they shared lasted almost a lifetime. "I will marry you."

"Good. One last thing. I want Dorrie to live with us. Mama and your father are going to visit my uncle in Cuba for a while, so I told her I'd raise Dorrie while she's gone."

"Do you think Dorrie would let us raise her until she's ready to attend a college?"

Tears stung Raven's eyes at his wonderful offer.

"She's a very special girl," Brax added. "And she needs to be showered with love, and gifts, and joy just like you. Plus, there's no sense in teaching her to ice skate if we're just going to send her back to New Orleans." He paused. "I suppose I should have asked: Where are we living?"

"Boston. I just bought a cottage here before I went to jail. Lacie will rent it out for me. That way I'll have some income. I know you'll say I won't need it, but I do, for my own peace of mind."

"Then Boston it will be and I won't say more."

He kissed her again and whispered, "Thank you for loving me."

"Thank you for loving me."

* * *

TWO SATURDAYS LATER, the Moreaux celebrated a double wedding. Raven was married in her beautiful blue gown and Dorrie wore the dress she'd asked for—complete with roses around the middle. Brax had Bertie make it the day Raven left to return to New Orleans. A preacher spoke the words, Hazel cried, and Harrison wore his best suit. There was food, music, dancing, and cake. And two very lively wedding nights in two suites at the Hotel Christophe, courtesy of the still grateful House of LeVeq.

Epilogue

❦

A very pregnant Raven stood in the February cold watching Brax and Dorrie ice skate. Brax no longer had to stand in front of Dorrie and hold her hands and pull her along. She was proficient enough to skate beside him now and could also slowly skate backwards. Raven smiled watching the two glide by. She thought she might want to try to learn next winter, as long as she wasn't carrying another child.

A few weeks later, on March 1, Braxton Moreau Steele came into the world yelling his little head off. Once the midwife gave him permission, Brax entered their bedroom, and with eyes filled with love looked down at his beautiful but weary wife lying in bed with their sleeping son.

He leaned down, gave her a soft kiss, and tenderly caressed his son's small head. "Thank you for my son."

"You're welcome," she said tiredly. "And thank you for my beautiful son."

"You're welcome. Is it okay for Dorrie to visit with you for a moment? She wants to see you and the baby."

"Of course."

He left to get her and when they returned, Dorrie took in the baby and said, "He's very little."

Raven smiled. "He'll be big before you know it."

Dorrie replied, "And when he does, he and I will teach Hazel and Lacie how to ice skate."

Raven shared a confused look with Brax before asking Dorrie, "Mama Hazel and Cousin Lacie?"

"No. Baby Hazel and Baby Lacie. They're going to be born on the same day."

Raven's eyes widened. Brax stared at Dorrie then began to laugh.

Eighteen months later, Raven gave birth to twin girls, Hazel Jane Steele and Lacie Avery Steele, proving once again that Dorrie was never wrong.

Author's Note

Dear Reader,

To Catch a Raven is the final book in the Women Who Dare trilogy. It's been a great series and from your e-mails and tweets, you've let me know that you've enjoyed reading it just as much as I have writing it. Raven's family is distantly related to the grifting pirate family of Cuban Pilar Banderas that we met in *Destiny's Captive*. I had no idea the Lovely Julianna from the House of LeVeq would make an appearance. What a surprise. If you're a reader unfamiliar with Pinkerton Welch's past role as Wilma Gray, please pick up a copy of my Avon historical romance, *Winds of the Storm*.

Here's a short look at some of the historical nuggets tied to *To Catch a Raven*. The premise of the story grew out of an article I came across about a rare 1778 parchment copy of the Declaration of Independence found in 2018 among the papers of Charles Lennox, the Third Duke of Richmond. Lennox was known as the Radical Duke for his support of the American rebels during the Revolutionary War. Testing of the document proved not only its likely date of publication, but that there was a high content of iron in the holes found in it. Researchers think it may have been originally hung by nails. Further testing also proved the parchment was made of sheepskin. This copy is also highly valued for the way it's signed, which this author borrowed for the copy stolen by Aubrey Stipe. For more info on it and another rare copy found in England recently, please Google: *Rare Copy of Declaration of Independence found in the UK.*

Many have seen *Glory*, the 1989 film about the Black soldiers of the Massachusetts 54th and their part in the Battle of Fort Wagner. Actors Denzel Washington and Morgan Freeman played fictional roles, but in real life two of the more famous members were the sons of Frederick Douglass. Another real person was regiment member William H. Carney. Born into slavery in 1840, he became the first Black man to be given the US Medal of Honor for his bravery during the Fort Wagner fight. Although the battle took place on July 18, 1863, he wasn't awarded the medal until May 23, 1900. He died in a Boston hospital eight years later.

Lucy Holcombe Pickens was the only woman depicted on Confederate currency. She was known as the Queen of the Confederacy and was also the First Lady of South Carolina. She led a very interesting life. Google her for more info.

The Mississippi Plan, noted by Mr. Golightly, was a campaign of terror, violence, and death that began in Mississippi in 1875 to keep Black people from voting, attending school, and holding political office. The Plan eventually spread across the South and became entrenched.

Before the true cause of yellow fever was finally tied to mosquitoes, the numbers of deaths it caused varied in New Orleans. In some years, the numbers were low. In 1831, only two people died. Five deaths occurred in 1826 and 1836. But in other years, the numbers were heartbreakingly high. 1853 saw 7,849 deaths. 1858—4,845. In 1878, the year Raven's story takes place, 4,046 people succumbed. Health officials initially tied the disease to miasma and mistakenly believed Black people were immune to yellow fever.

I hope this short take on some of the history piques your interest to seek out more information on the subjects highlighted.

As noted above, this is the last book in the Women Who Dare trilogy. Thank you so much for your support, love, and patience. I've been at this writing thing going on twenty-nine years now and many of you have been with me every step of the way. There'd be no Beverly Jenkins without you dear readers. What's next? Stay tuned.

Happy Reading,
B

JULIA QUINN SELECTS

Looking for your next favorite romance? The #1 *New York Times* bestselling author of *Bridgerton* recommends these new books coming from Joanna Shupe, Julie Anne Long, Charis Michaels, and Beverly Jenkins.

THE BRIDE GOES ROGUE
"Joanna Shupe is the queen of historical bad boys!"
— Julia Quinn

MAY 2022

In Joanna Shupe's latest Gilded Age romance, find out what happens when the wrong bride turns out to be the right woman for a hard-hearted tycoon.

YOU WERE MADE TO BE MINE
"I am in awe of her talent."
—Julia Quinn

JUNE 2022

A rakish spy finds more than he bargained for in his pursuit of an earl's enchanting runaway fiancée in this charming romance by Julie Anne Long.

A DUCHESS BY MIDNIGHT
"Charis Michaels will make you believe in fairy tales."
— Julia Quinn

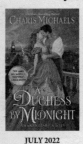

JULY 2022

Charis Michaels enchants us with a romance between Cinderella's stepsister and the man who can't help falling in love with her.

TO CATCH A RAVEN
"A living legend."
— Julia Quinn

AUGUST 2022

A fearless grifter goes undercover to reclaim the stolen Declaration of Independence in this compelling new romance by Beverly Jenkins.

Discover great authors, exclusive offers, and more at hc.com